I0685003

VAMPIRE JACQUES THE LAST TEMPLAR

—ɯ—

Book 1

Rebirth of the knights Templar Trilogy

Charlie 2-Shirt

ISBN 13: 9780692377697
ISBN 10: 0692377697

DEDICATION

To my family and the small town of Wolf Point, Montana, where I grew up. Every morning was a bright new day, every day an exciting adventure, every night a slumber of winsome dreams.

About the author

Though he doesn't have any Sioux or Assiniboine blood running through his veins, Charlie 2-Shirt grew up on the Fort Peck, Sioux and Assiniboine Indian Reservation in Montana. While fishing one summer day, a Native American friend declared he was sick and tired of the two shirts, one blue and one pink that Charlie kept wearing to school, and if he kept wearing those shirts, his new name was going to be "Charlie 2-Shirt."

So, Charlie is very proud to adopt, in homage to a great guy and friend, the pen name Charlie 2-Shirt.

CONTENTS

PROLOGUE

Formed in AD 1118, the original Order of the Knights Templar consisted of nine knights whose mandate was to protect Christian pilgrims en
route to the Holy Land. The Templar vows included chastity, poverty, and
obedience. Their symbol of poverty was two knights riding on one horse,
as the order could not afford a horse for each man.

From its humble beginnings in poverty, the order quickly grew to one
of wealth, influence, and power and had the backing of European mon-
archies and the pope. Eventually, due to the order's immense wealth and
power, the monarchs of Europe began to fear the Knights Templar. During
this time, it was believed that many of them had turned from Christianity
and were practicing black magic and worshiping idols.

The last and most powerful of the Templar Grand Masters was Jacques
de Molay of France (AD 1244–1314). During an interrogation by royal
agents under the command of King Philip IV—also known as Philip the
Fair, due to his long blond hair and blue eyes—de Molay, after being tortured, confessed to having rejected Christ and to defiling the cross. When
he was forced to repeat this statement in public the following day, the damage was devastating for the Knights Templar.

To regain his authority, Pope Clement V ordered the arrest of all Knights
Templar throughout Christendom, on the charge of heresy. Beginning in
the early morning of Friday, October 13, 1307, nearly all of the thousands
of Knights Templar in France were arrested and their assets seized. On
November 22, the pope issued a bull, *Pastoralis Praeeminentiae*, instructing
all Christian monarchs in Europe to arrest the remaining Templars and to
appropriate their property for the Church. Most of the Templars were killed,

wiping out an order that had existed for nearly two hundred years. Those who weren't killed were savagely tortured until they confessed to desecrating the cross, engaging in homosexual acts, practicing black magic, and worshiping idols. Two of these idols were Baphomet and Mithras. Baphomet was thought to either represent the devil or to be an incarnation of the god of the witches. The god, Mithras, was a dark, mystical being who had as one of his families the Ventrue, individuals who perceived themselves as being the most powerful of the vampiric clans.

On August 20, 1308, the pope granted the mercy of absolution to Jacques de Molay and Geoffroi de Charny, as well as to the few hundred other Knights Templar who remained in Europe and who had sworn on the Lord's Holy Gospel and humbly denounced heresy. De Molay, de Charny, and the other Templars were now reinstated to the unity and sacraments of the Church and to the communion of the faithful. Over time, however, the accused Templars, of which only six hundred remained, denied their previous confessions and began to verbally defend their order against King Philip. They proclaimed to Church officials that their statements had been made under the pain of torture and the threat of death. On May 12, 1310, King Philip, to intimidate the remaining Templars, ordered fifty-four of the knights to be burned at the stake in a field outside of Paris. The Templars went to their deaths with their heads held high, displaying the mental and moral strength that was characteristic of their order.

During this time, Jacques de Molay and Geoffroi de Charny were held in King Philip's cold, dark dungeon, sleeping on wet straw and subsisting on bread and water. Of the two, only de Molay knew the hiding place of the Templar treasure and the Ark of the Covenant. What he didn't know was that de Charny had made a deal with King Philip. If de Charny could get de Molay to tell him the hiding place of the Templar treasure, the king would release de Charny from prison. His reward would be a king's ransom. If he failed, the king promised him the most gruesome death imaginable. To encourage de Charny's participation in his scheme, King Philip allowed him, on rare occasions, to be released from the dungeon and taken by royal carriage to the king's summer palace. At the palace, female servants bathed him and cut and combed his hair and beard. He was dressed in a rich, red tunic and matching surcoat that he wore over a white linen shirt along with red hose and pointed shoes—the fashion of the day. And it was a handsome hall in which he dined, with dark-oak walls, greenish-red stone tiles on the floor and fireplace, a portable altar with a small cross, and four oak tables that sat on trestles.

Other than the one servant who waited on him, Geoffroi de Charny always dined alone, as his visits were a royal secret. He enjoyed red wine, bread spread with honey, vegetable soup with almonds, pasta, and, as a very rare treat, venison. Only the lords and nobles were allowed to hunt deer, boars, hares, and rabbits. The feudal system dictated that the land belonged to the royal family and these animals were on their property.

De Charny always ate his fill, gorging himself, as he knew his days were numbered. Even if de Molay had told him where the Templar treasure and the Ark of the Covenant were hidden, he never would have told King Philip, as he was a Templar to the end. Each time he dined in the hall, he lifted his cup and quietly recited the Templar oath: "Our white garments decorated with the Blood Red Cross remind each of us that we must be capable of making sacrifices. Do not strive for worldly wealth—perhaps tomorrow we might have to give account of ourselves. We shall not know, until it is too late, for excuses are not acceptable to the Greatest Being, Almighty God."[1]

Needing the Templar's hidden treasure to solve his financial problems, King Philip IV, along with Pope Clement V, sentenced de Molay to death for not revealing its location. On the evening of March 18, 1314, de Molay was burned to death—or was he? Legend has it that while the flames engulfed him, he cried out for revenge, cursing the pope and King Philip IV, and stating that he would meet both before the tribunal of God within a year.

"Pope Clement, hear me! Before this year is out, you will answer for your crimes before God almighty. And you, King Philip, no punishment is too heinous for the great evil you have inflicted upon the Temple. I curse you! Curse you to the thirteenth generation of your blood! You shall be cursed!" [2]

Approximately one month later, on April 20, Pope Clement V died from a mysterious illness. On November 29 of that same year, King Philip died in a freak hunting accident. De Molay also cursed the king's descendants, and indeed, between 1314 and 1328, King Philip's three sons died. As none had been able to provide a male heir to the Capet throne, the three-hundred-year-old House of Capet collapsed. These Capetian deaths led many to believe the dynasty had been cursed—thus the phrase "the accursed kings."

De Molay took with him to his death the directions to the hiding place of the Templar treasure and the Ark of the Covenant. Neither has ever been found. After his execution, a group of monks went to pick up his body and bury him. The remains had mysteriously disappeared, seemingly whisked away by the wind.

Not long after the elimination of the Knights Templar and the fall of the House of Capet, the black plague struck Europe with a force greater than that of any invading army. In 1337, in what became known as the Dance of Death, strange black swellings approximately the size of an egg or an apple began to appear in people's armpits and groins. The swellings oozed blood and pus and were followed by spreading boils and black blotches on the skin that were caused by internal bleeding. The sick suffered severe pain and died quickly. As the disease progressed, other symptoms appeared, such as continuous fever and the spitting up of blood. So lethal was the disease that some people went to bed feeling well, but they died before morning.

During a four-year period, Europe lost approximately 45 to 50 percent of its population, while France lost 75 to 80 percent. Amid this macabre dance, morals sank to new lows. Disease was understood as punishment for sins, and so the plague was proof of humanity's incorrigible corruption. Values such as honesty, integrity, and compassion were inefficacious. God, it seemed, had abandoned the people. Demons walked the earth.

The malignity of the pestilence appeared more terrible because its victims knew of no cure. Individuals, believing their pets were carriers of the disease, slaughtered their own cats and dogs. The practice of black magic spread while people experimented with perfumes and potions in hopes of finding a miraculous cure. As many people believed their bodies were possessed, bleeding was widely practiced, and witches, mystics, and magicians were sought out for cures. There weren't enough graveyards or caskets for the populace to bury their dead, so decayed; rotting bodies were stacked in the streets. When the streets were filled, the people sank the corpses in rivers.

It was within this context that France and England gathered their young men, armored their knights, strung their longbows, and shouted their battle cries, and the Hundred Years' War began. Widespread famine stalked the land, so much so that there were reports of cannibalism as well as infants and children being abandoned. The elderly starved themselves to death so their children could work the fields and survive. Malnutrition, disease, hunger, moral decadence, and the perceived failure of the Church, coupled with war, made Europe ripe for tragedy, for evil, for the Ventrue, for the vampire.

1

THE VENTRUE

France, AD 1314

The livery stable is located in the countryside off a dirt road going nowhere. The clank-clanking of the blacksmith's hammer reverberates in the dank night air. A young man, spread-eagle, is strapped naked on a butcher block alongside a fire pit. His hungry body is so weakened from fear that he makes no effort to struggle against his heavy, worn, leather restraints. A leather gag, pulled tightly across his mouth, muffles his groans. The heat of the fire dances off the withered skin that hangs from his ribs. His crime: stealing food. His wife and two young children are starving. He did everything he could, gathering edibles from the forest—roots, berries, plants, grasses, nuts, and bark—but it wasn't enough. So he stole several handfuls of seed grain from his lord's horse stables.

Claude de Lavoe, the supreme commander and marshal of the Knights Templar, is a thick, heavily muscled, imposing man. A blacksmith's blackened, scarred, leather apron is cinched around his fleshy belly. He picks up a small, razor-sharp knife, pulls the leather gag off his prisoner, and makes several precise cuts around the tops of the cheeks, across the forehead, and on the back of the young man's neck. It's then that he begins his flaying ritual, peeling off the facial skin first, exposing the raw flesh. The young man begs, his eyes burning red with tears. His sharp, wild cries pierce the air as he flails against the bonds.

The lad's uncontrolled screams of agony arouse Claude's carnal desire. He closes his eyes and runs his wet tongue across his lips, savoring the moment. Attracted by the smell of fresh blood, flies circle and then land on the exposed tissue. Females immediately begin to lay their eggs; the larvae will hatch in a couple of days.

Claude's plan is to slowly work his way down the young man's body to his ankles, cutting and peeling expertly, exposing the internal organs and the blood vessels. He only stops to wipe the blade across his tongue, licking it clean, tasting the warm sweetness of blood while staring into the young man's terror-stricken eyes. At first they burn and then lose sensation as the young man succumbs to shock. The sweat from Claude's face drips onto his victim as he peels the skin along the length of the man's side to his hip, pushing the envelope of the malevolent to the gruesome and macabre. The young man is dead before Claude reaches his waist.

Shaking his head, Claude puts down his knife. Once again the victim has died too quickly, and he feels cheated. The very demon that provides him his victims—France's great famine, driving the population to the desperate acts for which he exacts retribution—has also weakened his victims so they can withstand very little punishment. This one died with barely a struggle. The worst pain was knowing his wife and children would starve to death, believing themselves abandoned. But that kind of torment brings no satisfaction to Claude. Yet again he's been denied the erotic high that a slow, calculated skinning provides. He calmly strolls to the fire pit and lays down the spit-cleaned knife. His sandaled foot pumps the bellows, flaming the hot coals. The steel anvil echoes from the sound of his heavy hammer banging the red-hot iron poker. Sweat soaks the trimmed black beard that shadows his face. He rolls the poker over in his large calloused hand, pounding away, shaping the end to a sharp point.

A carriage pulled by four sweat-drenched horses, nostrils flaring, rolls up. Five men haul Geoffroi de Charny from the carriage. His arms are tied behind his back, and his mouth is stuffed with dirty sheep's wool. The men push, kick, and drag Geoffroi across the dirt yard, through a heavy oak door, and into the livery stable. They slam him facedown onto the heavily worn, rough-cut oak table, his quivering legs dangling.

The carriage driver, André, wraps the leather reins around the wooden brake handle, drops down from his seat, and hurries into the woods.

One of the captors yanks Geoffroi's red hose down to his ankles. His stubby legs bang against the bottom of the table, struggling to reach the hardened dirt floor. Through his sweat-burning eyes, he can make out the blacksmith skillfully honing the metal rod, and he immediately recognizes Claude. Everything that can smell foul issues uncontrollably from his body—breath, sweat, urine. Blackened shit cakes the insides of his legs. The spit-soaked wool chokes his screams of terror. He has heard that Claude had betrayed the Templars, but he refused to believe it. He has known him ever since Claude was ten years old. Geoffroi took him to the Templars when he didn't have a home, a place to go. He watched him grow up, helped raise him, helped groom him, promoted him to his position of supreme commander of the Knights Templar—and now this. Emotionally and physically exhausted, Geoffroi lays his head on the hard table. His eyes fill with tears as he tries to fathom the incomprehensible pain Claude will inflict on him.

"Each day," Geoffroi asserts loudly enough that his captors can hear, "we must help our brethren for whom we are responsible, for one day God will say, 'Where is thy brother?' Accept no reward; always be a pillar of the Templar, for the order holds for us the opportunity to flee the sins of the world, to live charitably, to be penitent, and above all, to be the servant of Almighty God."[3] He chokes up. His most beloved Templar oath will be the last words he ever speaks. He gathers his courage, feeling a great sense of pride, thankful that Jacques de Molay, his friend, may very well be the last Templar when this evil is over.

Claude de Lavoe brushes his long black hair away from his face, holds up the burning iron, and through a craftsman's eyes, checks his work. *Perfect*, he thinks, inhaling deeply, savoring the moment. He so relishes these opportunities. He lives for them: the divine power of taking away life, the infliction of unlimited pain, the complete control, the unfathomably arousing highs, the physical and emotional rape of his victims. He knows Geoffroi will never give up the location of the Templar treasure and the Ark of the Covenant, even if he does know where the treasures are hidden. King Philip IV has no plans of keeping his promises to Geoffroi anyway. Even if he does reveal the location of the Templar treasure and the Ark of the Covenant, Geoffroi is finished.

Claude turns and ever so slowly forces the blazing-hot iron up Geoffroi's anus. It takes the strength of all of the captors to hold down his crazed, thrashing body. Claude turns the poker like a drill bit, burning through the tender flesh. It gives way before him, and he pushes it deeper and deeper into Geoffroi's body. The eyes of the Knight Templar burn with terror, as if they might blow from their sockets. Finally, Geoffroi's eyes close as Claude shoves the poker until the man's body collapses into eternal silence.

"Take him and the young man out back," Claude orders the men as he jams the poker back into the hot coals. "Bury them, and be quick. Riders will be coming soon." He turns back to the pit and pumps the bellows again, raising the fire back to life.

—⁂—

Limp from exhaustion, four of the five captors stumble back to the carriage.

"Remind me never to bend over when Claude's around," Pierre-Louis, one of the captors, blurts.

André strides confidently up to the others. Except for his long, wavy, gorgeous, brown hair, he's a homely man—short, and with a bulbous nose and heavy jowls. His tiny butt makes his belly appear large.

The darkness is accentuated by the tall, thick growth of sweet chestnut trees. A full, red moon, frowning murkily, shines the only light on the countryside.

"Where've you been?" Pierre-Louis angrily shoves his friend. "Coulda used your help." He attempts to straighten his raggedy, brown, oversize shirt and appear as someone with authority, but the attempt is futile. His mangy, black hair hangs in matted strands like strings of licorice, making his head appear enormous over his thin body and big rear end. "We had the most terrible time holding him down. We dump him and the other guy in a hole out back behind the livery. All we could do. That guy, Geoffroi—who was he? So heavy. Push dirt, branches over the hole so nobody the wiser. Never find 'im."

"Had to take a crap…bad," André responds. "That pasta Geoffroi was eatin' at the king's house…too much of that spicy stuff. Tore my belly up."

"You was eatin' the king's pasta!" Pierre-Louis never will understand his friend. France could be burning, and André wouldn't notice. "We was waitin' in the carriage, holding Geoffroi, while you was eatin' the king's pasta? We coulda been caught. Heads chopped off…guillotine, maybe worse."

"I drank mouthfuls of almond milk and red wine." André stands proudly while patting one of the horses' rumps. "Ain't ate for five days—'cept ol' breads is all. Dog-hungry I was. Belly button to me backbone it was."

"Dog-hungry!" Pierre-Louis shouts. His face contorts with anger while he waves his arms madly. "You the biggest stupid in history! Me so hungry my farts have no 'p-u' anymore! Still blast away but no stink! We kill you now. Marcel will cut your balls off. Then we leave."

The breeze picks up, moving the smaller branches on the sweet chestnut trees. André, inhaling the invigorating night air, places his hand on his longtime friend's shoulder. "I got you bread, meat from the king's own oven, two jugs of the king's own wine. The meat...the best I ever ate. You gotta try." He grins widely, revealing a mouthful of blackened teeth. "Used weeds to wipe my ass. Musta had seeds on it. Stuffin' me up a little when I walk."

"The king's own wine?" Pierre-Louis glances at the others while shrugging. "You must think I'm big stupid like you. You had no time to get all that food, wine."

The others nod in agreement.

"The food, the wine—all in the carriage," André brags. "When we at king's house, I go into kitchen and put everything in king's own blanket. You boys so busy tusslin' with Geoffroi, you no see me. When we leave king's house, I put next to me up by coachman's bench seat where I drive the horses. I put it all inside the carriage when you were in the livery with Claude." He grins, holding his chest high and displaying his soot-colored teeth while sticking his tongue out. Then he grabs his crotch and shakes it.

"Need to see to believe." Pierre-Louis opens the squeaking carriage door and glances inside. "This time you lucky...keep little bitty balls. We go now before somebody comes."

A dejected André crawls up and into the coachman's bench seat and picks up the worn leather reins. Pierre-Louis never likes anything he says or does. One of the other captors quickly joins him.

"Riders are coming!" Pierre-Louis calls out frantically, as he bangs the side of the carriage with his fist. "Claude tell us earlier. I so angry with André, I forget. We need to go. Now! Now! Claude kill us all."

André unexpectedly hands the reins to the other man sitting next to him. "Drive to deserted farm down the road," he says. "I go find out who's

coming…who meet with Claude. We did bad, bad things tonight. Go now!"
He slides off the seat and drops quietly to the ground. Pierre-Louis, who's
now inside the carriage, won't even know he's gone.

Four horsemen, wearing capes with hoods pulled tight, ride up to the
livery. Two quickly dismount and post guard. Another, Baron de la Force,
dismounts and guardedly walks inside. The last one, carrying a cloth-
covered bundle under his arm, follows him closely. Claude obviously is
expecting them, as greetings aren't exchanged. The livery is lit by a few
candles, their flickering flames reflecting shadows of horror and dread
across the thick-planked, soundproof walls. The fire pit is smoldering.

Baron de la Force, in his position with King Philip IV, has heard all the
rumors, the stories, but glancing around the room of torment at the tools
for torture, he realizes the true extent of Claude's evil work. There's a knee
splitter, a breast ripper that Claude can use either hot or cold, a tongue
tearer, a thumbscrew, a head crusher. The baron's eyes rest on the brazen
bull. He's heard of them but never has seen one before. Claude must have
brought it back from the Crusades. It's a bronze statue that looks like a real
bull and has a door on the side. A naked prisoner is locked inside, and a fire
is then built around the bull, heating the metal red-hot. The victim's insane
thrashing from the heat makes the metal bull shake, giving it a semblance
of life. As the prisoner slowly roasts to death, special tubes inside the head
of the metal beast make the victim's agonizing screams sound like the bellowing of a raging bull.

When Claude's eyes meet the baron's, they're as cold as frozen tundra.
Violence and rage are visible in his scarred hands and battering-ram arms.
The baron had a difficult time believing King Philip, who said that Claude,
the supreme commander of the Knights Templar, Jacques de Molay's best
friend, would betray them all. But he has already seen enough. Claude will
betray anyone for a reward—*anyone*. The baron determines he will quickly
conduct the king's business and then leave, get away from this evil place. He
can smell it, the stink of death, the poisonous rot, the venomous decay. It
has a distinct odor; he's lived with it on the battlefields. Now he knows why
the man standing in front of him is known as Claude the Butcher. Claude
de Lavoe had better pray that de Molay will give up the hiding place of the

Templar treasure. If he does, then de Molay will only die, but it won't be a brutal death. King Philip will be merciful.

After the death of his wife, King Philip attempted to join the Knights Templar. The Knights, however, turned down his request, setting in motion his hatred for the order and his pledge that he would make de Molay pay with his life for having rejected him. Philip is possibly the most powerful king in Christendom. No one—not even Pope Clement V—turns down his requests. If de Molay doesn't give up the location of the Templar treasure, both he and Claude will die in the most horrific way. King Philip does not tolerate insubordination.

Deciding he will not to talk to the swine, Baron de La Force steps aside and motions to the knight standing behind him to step forward.

"Did Geoffroi de Charny tell you anything of importance?" the knight asks.

Claude, his eyes yellow like the flames, stares at the knight. He shakes his head contemptuously and mutters, "No."

"Let's hope for your sake," the knight responds coldly, "that Jacques de Molay will be more cooperative in giving us the location of the Templar treasure."

The knight uncovers a cape and long brown wig. "Wear this and no harm will come to you," he says, handing the items to Claude. "None with their allegiance to you will be arrested either. Beginning tomorrow morning, all the Knights Templar in France will be rounded up—condemned as heretics. His Majesty, King Philip, will reward you for your allegiance to the throne."

The baron, with the knight shadowing him, briskly pivots and marches out the door.

André, hiding in the tall weeds behind the back door, has heard everything. Claude has betrayed his best friend, Jacques de Molay, and all the Knights Templar. Betrayed him and Pierre-Louis too. He holds his face between his hands, eyes closed, slowly rubbing his cheeks, woeful that he and his friends followed Claude's orders to take Geoffroi captive.

2

THE TEMPLAR TREASURE

France, 1314 AD

The French coastline during spring is characterized by rain. Running next to the coastline, yellowish sand dunes scattered with green grass and herbs rest against white-chalk cliffs and several large, outlying lakes. Gusts of winds slap the rocky inlets and jagged faces of the granite cliffs, rustling up waves. Pockets of stone, weatherworn into the rocky crags, are dotted with white birds. The white sails of ten heavily laden French ships disappear over the horizon. Sheltered by tall cliffs, seven others are anchored in the secluded bay. A large number of Knights Templar are loading the cargo holds. Their hunched-over bodies look like busy ants moving crumbs of food to storage. They've labored unceasingly for weeks.

The massive, grayish-white skeleton of an ancient coral reef shimmers through the low tide. Using ropes and pulleys, other Knights Templar are lowering wooden platforms through the mouth of the reef and into the fingerlike passageway that leads into a vast underground sanctum.

Jacques de Molay is a tall, ruggedly handsome man, in the way of a Renaissance sculpture, with chiseled shoulders and arms. He stands six feet four and wears a white Templar cloak with a red cross on his chest and back. His long, wild, dark-brown hair hangs past his waist. His deep-blue eyes are startling and direct. He's accompanied by his mistress, Margaret, the baroness of Passavant; several Knights Templar; and Jude, the Templar general. Margaret, from northeastern France, is a tall, slender beauty of French nobility, with rich, ruby-red, shoulder-length hair; exquisitely soft, captivating, brown eyes; and a fine nose. Normally Jacques wouldn't have allowed her to accompany them into this dark, dangerous place, but he wants her to see something—a treasure of untold fortune, a family secret of countless generations revealed. Few have ever seen it, and none may ever again. Jacques wishes things were different, but with King Philip IV rounding up and killing all the Templars, he knows his time with Margaret is limited. She is the only woman he's ever loved. Today she's dressed as a man, with her hair pulled up and hidden under her cap, so no one will notice her. As Jacques's Templar vows of chastity forbid him from associating with women, their relationship has been conducted in secret, hidden from everyone except their closest friends. Claude once was one of those friends and confidants, but Jacques knows he has betrayed him and the Templar order. He also knows he may never see Margaret again. Now, Jacques is leading them into the dark chambers of the underworld. Only he knows the way. His uncle, Master de Lezines, taught him the directions years ago. He follows the signs that are carved onto rocks and visible only when the light from one of their torches strikes them at a certain angle. He carries a small, red, leather-bound, ivory chest in one hand, while a large, rolled-up paper scroll hangs at his side.

The passageway they've been following seems to continue without end, deep into the bowels of the earth. They descend large stone steps and travel into yet another subterranean tunnel and through massive, stone-slab doors that open smoothly with the push of a hand. Rotted, broken wagons and decayed human skeletons—the bones of slaves picked clean years ago—lie all around them.

The ocean waves crash above them. Salt water seeps down the chiseled stones and drips down the walls. Serpents, attracted by the dampness and the stench of salt water, retreat from the light and into the shadows of the cave.

Jacques, his knights, and Margaret continue into the depths—places of darkness unexplained, with eerie sounds of the unseen—until they reach a long corridor lined with stone pillars. Paintings of birds, animals, and unusual creatures are fading on the walls.

Jacques stands in front of a gold fresco of a bearded Knight Templar holding a shield, armed for battle. Like many others it's molded into one of the stone pillars, making it impossible to know the location of the keystone. Jacques takes off his gold necklace. Two matching pieces form the Templar emblem: two knights riding one horse. One knight and the warhorse, both made of gold, are decorated with emeralds and diamonds. The other knight, of silver, is embellished with rubies and pearls. After locking the two pieces together, Jacques inserts them into a slot in the front of the fresco knight's broad-brimmed kettle hat. He turns the keystone until the movement of heavy weights begins to change positions. Gratingly slow, the gold fresco turns, opening an enormous door constructed of a single slab of stone, with no cracks or joints, that blends into the rock wall several feet behind them. Master de Lezines called it the "hidden door." It seals the passageway to the sanctuary where the Templar treasure is hidden. One could pass within a few inches and never notice it. Jacques removes his emblem, and the group enters the sanctum. The slabs in the stone floor have been mortised and grooved to fit tightly.

The room is filled with gold, silver, chests brimming with priceless gems from all parts of the known world, bejeweled armor in solid gold and silver, and holy relics—plunder from the Crusades, Egypt, the Great Pyramids, Khufu's tomb, the Guardians of Egypt, the Valley of the Kings, Ramesses II and III, and other powerful nobles of the New Kingdom of Egypt.

Four pharaohs of solid gold sit on matching thrones, each wearing double gold crowns inlaid with precious jewels, representing the cardinal direction each faces. North is cold, with blue sapphires representing trouble and defeat; south is warm, with white diamonds symbolizing peace and happiness; west, the direction of the moon, wears black pearls, representing the souls of the dead; east, the direction of the sun, has red rubies, symbolizing fire. This last is the greatest deity of all.

Paintings by all the great masters hang on the walls. One depicts a knight dressed in gold and another in silver, charging each other in a joust. Emerald prisms, dabbed with diamonds and pearls and inlaid on gold slabs, display the visible universe. Large, golden, garden baskets hang from the ceiling on braided gold-and-silver vines in each corner of the room and at an equal distance down each wall. The baskets are filled with diamonds, rubies, sapphires, emeralds, and amethysts.

Margaret and the Knights Templar are astounded. They admire the incalculable splendor, the work that Jacques's family and their fellow soldiers in God have done for two hundred years to accumulate and protect this rare, untold magnificence. Never did they imagine such unworldly beauty.

Several wooden platforms are on the floor. "This is the last room," Jacques tells his men. "King Philip and his knights are looking for us. Only work during the day. If you move the treasure to the ships at night and someone sees your torches, all will be lost. The king and his army will attack, killing everyone and taking the treasure. No one leaves this area; no one is safe. To do so will mean certain death. You'll sleep on the ships. Time is of the essence."

Light inside the sanctuary is nonexistent except on perfectly clear days when beams from the sun, shining through an aperture in the reef above, are caught in a prism of jade and focused on the jeweled gardens. It's low tide, and the rays are dancing up and down, bouncing from garden to garden, creating an animated rainbow ribbon of colors that pulsates around the room in a dazzling display of Egyptian artistry.

Margaret is speechless. She and the Knights Templar are so engrossed in the electrifying beauty that they aren't paying attention to Jacques and the Templar general, Jude, whose nickname is "The Tall." Jude is a handsome man with a long, golden mane of hair and a beard to match. His yellow-green eyes are spellbinding.

Jacques hands Jude three large parchments. "These are the maps of the Norsemen," he says. "Navigate the trade winds of the Viking longships. Follow the route I've laid out for you. When the ships are loaded, set sail in the morning when the wind and tide are right. Make sure you have plenty of provisions. If you get lost or find yourself off course, remember to set fleas on a flat surface to point the way. They always hop or crawl north."

Jacques takes one of the maps from Jude and unrolls it against one of the chamber walls. He points to a large river on the parchment. "This is the Pechora River," he says. Then he moves his hand. "This is the Murman Sea. It lies between the northern coast of Russia and Norway. For some reason its waters are warmer and remain ice-free most of the year. This is where you will build your new life. The people who live there are called the Forest Dwellers. Treat them as friends…and they will be." He points at the Kara

Sea and the Arctic Ocean. "I don't know the names of these bodies of water, but they're frozen over most months of the year. No one can live in these regions." He shows Jude the place where Master de Lezines told him that a Viking king had constructed an impenetrable castle fortress in the Ural Mountains, with the help of Odin, the Norse god. "It's easy to defend yourself there from any invaders," he tells Jude. "Protect the Templar treasure and the Ark of the Covenant at all costs." Using a sharp rock, Jacques marks the castle's location on the map, rolls it up, and hands it to Jude.

"As soon as you arrive," he continues, "you must prepare the castle for the unforgiving Russian winter. Have a group of your knights do nothing except chop down trees and gather kindling and firewood from the forest. Send hunting parties out to kill game. Stock up on winter provisions. The skies can be clear, the air calm, but you'll never see the sun. The cold will turn spit into ice before it hits the ground. Your hands and beard will be trimmed with frost. The vicious Russian wind will only make it worse. Never venture out in it. You won't be able to see your hands in front of your face. You'll get lost and freeze to death just a few feet from safety."

"I have been told," Jude says, looking exceedingly troubled, "that we have a Judas among us."

Jacques shakes his head indignantly.

"Is it…?" Although Jude leaves the name unspoken, Jacques still refuses to utter the name of that most foul Knight Templar. "Do you want me to take your pendant?" Jude offers in order to protect the symbol of the great fraternity.

"No, nothing about me must change," Jacques replies. "King Philip must believe the Templar treasure is close. If he captures me, takes the pendant, and opens the keystone to the hidden door, all they must find is an empty room."

"What about Margaret?" Jude whispers, as she stands a short distance away. Her attention is focused on the animated ribbon of lights. "She should leave with us."

"She will never betray me," Jacques responds firmly.

"Time has a way of changing things," Jude answers.

"She stays here with me. I haven't told her a Judas walks among us. Whatever time we have left together must be happy."

The jeweled-light display ends.

Jacques walks over and grabs Margaret's hand. "Come. I want to show you something." She follows him to a floor-to-ceiling fence of solid-gold rails. Jacques points to a box inside the enclosure. It takes a few moments before she begins to understand what she's looking at.

"Is that what I think it is?" she says, gasping. "Does anyone know? How long has it been here? It's impossible…I thought it was lost forever." She finds it hard to stand up. Thunderstruck, she grabs Jacques's arm tightly. "It's the most beautiful thing I've ever seen."

Margaret reaches up and places her hand on the back of Jacques's neck, softly caressing his multicolored birthmark. It seems to generate its own heat—not hot but warm, arousing. Jacques's mother called it the "Rider of the Sun," a great flying horse with powerful, outstretched wings—one of dark and melded violet, the other a reddish starlight, both dancing with rays from the unassailable, lava-hot, white sun the animal soars past. Its rider is a fierce, handsome man of deep, haunting resolve, a Knight Templar, a soldier of God. His long, thick, wavy, brown hair is peppered with sparkles of starlight; his face shimmers with the reflection of gold dust. The silver pinpoints of twinkling stars, the infinite darkness of space, galaxies with an infinite number of stars—all are his constant companions.

"Have them make a chest of acacia wood, two and a half cubits long, a cubit and a half wide, and a cubit and a half high," Jacques recites with authority. He's a soldier of God, a Templar to the end. He lifts Margaret's hand with his, toward heaven, and articulates loudly so everyone can hear. "Overlay it with pure gold, both inside and out, and make a gold molding around it. Cast four gold rings, and fasten them to its four feet, with two rings on one side and two rings on the other. Then make poles of acacia wood and overlay them with gold. Insert the poles into the rings on the sides of the chest to carry it. The poles are to remain in the rings of this ark; they are not to be removed. Make an atonement cover of pure gold, two and half cubits long and a cubit and a half wide. And make two cherubim out of hammered gold at the ends of the cover. Make one cherub on one end and the second cherub on the other. Make the cherubim of one piece with the cover, at the two ends. The cherubim are to have their wings spread upward, overshadowing the cover with them. The cherubim are to face each other, looking toward the cover. Place the cover on top of the ark, and put in the ark the testimony, which I will give you. There, above the cover between the two cherubim that are over the ark of the testimony, I will meet with you and give you all my commands for the Israelites. Amen."

"Amen!" one of the knights shouts. "Amen!" shouts another. "Amen! Amen!" they all shout, giving Jacques the Templar salute with their heels together, eyes front, their right hands closing into fists. They strike their chests just above their hearts and snap their right arms straight. "Amen!"

"What about you, Master Jacques?" one of the younger Knights Templar asks. "Are you going with us?"

"I will stay here in France. King Philip must never know the treasure has been moved. If I go, he'll follow. You'll leave through the mouth of the reef! Ride up on the platforms!" Jacques refocuses his attention on Jude. "Out of everyone," he says proudly, "I chose you to lead this insufferable journey across oceans and the nearly impassable Ural Mountains. I chose you to master the dreadful Russian winters and rebuild the order of the Knights Templar. Accomplish the unthinkable. Hide the Templar treasure and the Ark of the Covenant in a place deep and dark, with no flicker of sunlight and no breath of fresh air—a place in the castle only the spirits frequent. Make the Castle of Odin, the wisest of the Norse gods, your home, your fortress. I will join you later." Jacques extends his arm and places his right hand on Jude's shoulder. "The patriarch of your family, more than one hundred fifty years ago, was one of the greatest knights in the French army during the disastrous Second Crusade. Our armies were crushed. King Louis VII knighted him for bravery and gave him the name Jude the Great. In Persian it means 'eternally great.' And so…here you are again, Jude the Great."

Jacques hands him a parchment scroll. "These are the old Egyptian diagrams you'll need to build the maze. In many ways it's identical to the one Jude the Great built beneath the de Molay castle a hundred fifty years ago. There are some additions in the plans of the old master, Lord Guarin de Molay, that were never made part of that maze. You'll be pleased with them. You've been in the maze almost as much as I have." They begin to walk. "I still remember how frightening it was and how we used to scare each other. You and I, Clarete, and Thomas, daring each other to go in. Those will always be some of my most cherished memories. Start as soon as you land."

"I'm assuming Bisu goes with me," Jude says, "to protect the maze in the Odin castle." He brushes his long blond hair from his face. "For us to survive, we need powerful spirits like Bisu."

"As you know, Bisu, the dwarf god, lives at the de Molay castle. He protects the maze. For a century and a half, he's been loyal to the de Molay family. That must not change. He will stay with me until I join you." Jacques opens the chest of Horus, the Egyptian God of light and sky. A yellowish-sapphire, ultraviolet, pulsating light radiates out, enveloping it. "For hundreds of years, the Egyptians bred the worms of the Nile River. They created a creature that, when mixed with blood, burns as hot as the sun." He reaches into the chest, takes out a couple of the glowworms, and lets them crawl across the back of his hand.

Margaret, visibly repulsed by the worms, covers her mouth with her hand and steps behind Jacques.

"They feel as you feel. Love as you love. Hate as you hate," Jacques says. "They were brought back during the Crusades." He closes the chest.

Margaret wraps her arms tightly around his waist. "I don't think I like them," she mutters.

Smiling, Jacques gently places his hand on top of hers. "You, Jude the Great, will be the keeper of the worms," he says. "Fill a hole in the ground with animal blood and raw chunks of flesh. Feed the worms; nourish them. Let them thrive. Mix the blood and worms together. It is the potion of life. Drink it. You will become one with them. Only the keeper of the worms can cover his body with theirs. You must be covered completely to acquire their power. The sun's bright light can't glimpse your skin. Let them crawl into every opening: your mouth, your ears, your nose. Leave no space on your body untouched. When the time is right, you'll know. When their flesh has melted and blended with yours, you'll find the strongest, the fastest, the brightest, the most determined, and the most trustworthy men for your new Templar army. The worms will kill insects, rats, mice—anything that moves—and transfer that energy to you and your Templar knights. They will preserve you for eternity. Saboteurs, betrayers, all enemies who come in contact with you will be blinded from the light and burned as if by the fires of Satan himself. The heat will destroy their bodies—turn their skin to ash and burn their hair so that none will know whether a man or woman once inhabited the flesh. Blood will pour from the mouths and noses of your victims, and they'll plead for death to relieve them from the terrible pain. Even with the great executioner riding at their side, with the power of death, Satan's armies won't be able to defeat you."

He grasps Margaret's hand more firmly. "From this day forward, all of you are the guardians of the Templar treasure." Jacques ushers Margaret toward the hidden door. "There is little time left," he tells his men. "A couple of days maybe. You must hurry. The ships will lift anchor soon. No one must ever know the treasure was here." He tips his head back toward Jude and the other Knights Templar then drops to one knee, giving them a good-bye gesture of respect. He and Margaret step into the passageway.

The room with the Templar treasure darkens.

"The sun has moved," Jacques says, the hidden door closing behind them. He can't help wondering whether he'll ever see Jude and the other Knights Templar again. He abruptly takes Margaret into his arms, holding her tightly, inhaling the freshness of her soft skin, running his tongue slowly up the side of her neck—feeling, wanting to remember every curve of her. She slides her knee between his legs and slowly moves it against his thigh.

"Jacques," she whispers, "I love you so much. I'm so worried. I've heard so much…and…and you're moving the Templar treasure and the Ark of the Covenant. Are you sure all this is necessary?" She looks at him with her earthly, rich-brown eyes that always make him feel so special, so loved.

"King Philip must never find the treasure," he answers flatly while taking her hand and leading her down the passageway. "Come. We need to leave this place. Go to the de Molay castle. Wait for me. I'll come for you when it's safe."

"But why can't I stay with you?"

"It's too dangerous right now. King Philip and his men are looking for me. You can't be seen with me. No more!" He waves his hand to silence her.

Margaret's frustration wrinkles her face. There will be no changing his mind.

The sun is beginning to set behind a ridge of black-shaded hills when Jacques and Margaret reach the surface. Its bright-yellow blush reflects across a small, crystal-blue lake a short distance away. Their horses, tied to a tree, paw the ground impatiently when they see them; they're tired of waiting. Margaret's horse is a medium, smooth-gaited, gray palfrey—a horse of stature and nobility. She calls him Étienne, which means "crown." All the women she associates with ride sidesaddle, but she only rides aside when others are around. When riding with Jacques or alone, she always rides astride like a man—it's far more exciting, and she believes Étienne enjoys it more. She finds it invigorating to lean forward, her hands feeling the animal's powerful shoulder muscles as he runs flat out.

Jacques places his arms around Margaret and kisses her passionately, pulling her firm ass toward him. It's times like this, when he longs to make love to her, that are the most difficult. He longs to possess her, yet her flesh is a distant dream, and this moment may be the once unimaginable good-bye. He pulls her closer, pressing his body against hers. The sweet scent of her hair unleashes a torrent of memories: spreading a blanket across the cool grass after a day of riding horses, grabbing hungrily for each other, feeling the rush of Margaret's breath against his neck. Her breasts pressing against his body weaken him more than a blow from the most powerful knight. One day, if providence allows and they get married, he'll make love to her. It will be worth the wait, but for now it must be farewell.

"You must trust me," he says assuredly, holding her close. "When it's safe, I'll come for you."

Tears run down Margaret's face. Something terrible is going to happen; she can feel it, see it in Jacques's eyes. She hopes whatever happens won't destroy their feelings for each other. She couldn't live without his love.

Knowing he may never see her again, Jacques watches Margaret ride off. Gathering his strength, he mounts his black, very rare, expensive destrier, a well-bred, highly refined war-horse. He loves Thibault; they've been close friends for several years, taking long jaunts across the French countryside. He leans over and lays his head on the stallion's neck, feeling his strength and warmth. "Ah, yes, my friend, I named you well. You're bold, and I will miss you. We all try to plan the end of our life. How often it fails." He gently pats Thibault's shoulder and nudges him into their last gallop together, using the inland forest and trees for cover. His hope is to work his way eastward to Prussia, as he knows several Teutonic Knights there who are sympathetic to the Templar cause. When it's safe, he and a group of these knights will return to France to pick up Margaret and Bisu. From there they'll all board a sailing ship to Russia.

Riding to the de Molay castle, Margaret is lost in thought. She knows something is horribly wrong—the way Jacques held her, kissed her, as if they'll never see each other again—when suddenly a pack of wolves tears out of the dense pine forest. Fortunately for Margaret, Étienne sees the wolves first and spins away. Margaret, catching her balance, leans forward over Étienne's shoulders and hollers at the horse to run faster. They race off in the direction of Jacques. In the stables she heard other riders talk about hungry wolves taking down horses and riders. She knows their lives are in danger, but they have a good lead. Then two other snarling wolves race out of the forest after them. These are closer than the others and could catch them. Margaret pushes Étienne until the horse is running flat out. She imagines a horrible death from the jaws of the beasts. Her heart races from fear, and perspiration drips down her back. Using all of her strength, she tries to push the horse to run faster while yelling as loud as she can for Jacques' help.

Jacques hears screams as he rides over the top of a hill, but they seem so distant that he assumes it's a hawk or a golden eagle, a bird of prey soaring through the sky, waiting to catch the movement of a squirrel or a rabbit. Below him is a small band of French soldiers, a highly mobile light-cavalry unit out on patrol. Their weapon of choice is the deadly crossbow with a range of three to four hundred yards, which would pierce the chest-plate armor on a knight, killing him. One knight with a crossbow is equal to ten foot soldiers. They see Jacques at almost the same time he sees them, and they quickly break formation, spreading out.

At first Jacques is surprised to see the cavalry so far out here. King Philip IV must be turning over every stone to find him. Thibault can outrun their horses—he's not worried about that. He surveys the countryside, the forest, the weatherworn cliffs where eagles are the masters. Mentally he chooses a trail through a box canyon that he's familiar with. That's where he'll lose the light cavalry, but there it is again, that cry. Now he realizes it's Margaret. What could be wrong? What will he do about the cavalry? He turns Thibault around and gallops off in Margaret's direction, hoping he can get there in time. The soldiers will most likely catch him, but what happens to him is no longer important.

The wolves have overtaken Margaret. Étienne, breathing heavily, is tired and losing his stride. The lead wolf rushes up. Its powerful jaws rip at one of horse's haunches, slashing the leg. A second wolf attacks another of Étienne's legs, but the horse manages to kick it in the head, crushing its skull. Suddenly a weakened Étienne steps into a hole and stumbles, throwing Margaret off. She hits the ground hard, banging her head. The wind is knocked from her body, and her leg is severely twisted.

Étienne, instead of running away, holds his ground, kicking and charging the wolves with his sharp hooves, protecting Margaret. His aggressiveness causes the pack to hesitate. Their amber eyes follow Étienne's every movement. The largest wolf, the leader of the pack, circles the horse and positions itself a short distance from Margaret, who's lying on the ground, her dirt-soiled body scratched and bruised. Knowing her life is in peril, she struggles onto her stomach, pulling her one good leg under her body, attempting to gather her senses. She sees the blurry form of the wolf but is having trouble focusing. Then Jacques appears out of a cloudy haze. He's on Thibault. The mighty stallion's powerful shoulder muscles ripple as he runs.

Jacques, his sword strapped across his back, is concentrating on the menace that's ahead. Leaning forward, he wraps his arm around Thibault's muscular neck and, with great agility and skill, slides his body down the side of the powerful horse until his leg touches the ground. He then vaults through the air, landing in a crouched fighting position over Margaret. Brushing his long hair back, he draws his Templar sword. The sharp edges of the long blade run most of the sword's length, tapering to a fine point. It's capable of slicing through the toughest leather and penetrating a knight's chain mail.

Thibault, sensing Étienne is injured and needs his help, joins him. The two of them, rearing up on hind legs, take on the snarling pack, landing deadly blows with their powerful hooves.

Jacques holds his position over Margaret. He has seen big, vicious wolves leap so high that they appear to be flying as they take a person down by the back of the neck. Unexpectedly, the heinous wolf, teeth glaring, goes in low, ripping a chunk of flesh out of the back of Jacques's thigh. Jacques stumbles and manages to hack the wolf across the back with a swing of his sword, but the wound isn't life-threatening. Another wolf breaks away from the pack and grabs a shrieking Margaret by her yellow riding boot. Growling savagely, shaking its ravenous head, the beast drags her by her injured leg across the ground. She's so frightened that she's chokes on her own cries. She digs her fingers into the dirt, grabbing handfuls of grass and grasping for the sky, desperately attempting to hold on to anything while frantically kicking at the vicious beast with her good leg.

Jacques sees another pack of wolves break out of the pine trees. They're drawn to Margaret's panicked cries and the smell of blood. Limping, Jacques closes the distance between himself and the crazed animal that's attacking Margaret. He drives his sword through the wolf, killing him. But there are just too many for him to fight. He knows he and Margaret are going to die when—*whoosh, whoosh, whoosh*—suddenly the sound of arrows rips through the air. And then it's over. The light cavalry, some distance away, has shot the wolves with their mighty crossbows, killing them all.

Jacques goes to Margaret immediately. Kneeling next to her, he checks her wounds and attempts to console her without revealing the intimacy of their relationship to the approaching cavalry. He praises God for his mercy, thanking him for bringing King Philip's knights at this most opportune moment.

The entire countryside is on alert, and rewards have been offered for Jacques's capture. It doesn't take long for King Philip's knights to arrest the fugitive. His death already has been planned, so there are no delays.

Margaret wrestles with the shock of seeing the cavalry take Jacques away. She's shaken from the battle, and her wounds burn. It takes several minutes for her to gather her composure and muster the strength to remount her horse. Her heart cries tears of longing as Jacques is led away on Thibault. How can she say good-bye to her one great true love? How can she shake so much sorrow from her heart? *Bury this grief,* she tells herself, knowing Jacques no longer will be in her life. King Philip's men won't even let her get close to him. She cries, thinking she won't see him again until heaven's gates swing open for her. He'll be there waiting.

Even with the light cavalry providing escort, her ride to her family's manor is grueling. Nothing seems real. How does she take the first step from this abyss of anger and hurt? How does she begin this journey and make it on her own? Where will it lead?

3
THE KILLING OF JACQUES DE MOLAY

Nobles dressed in all their pomp and pride have been filling the grand-stand for more than an hour. The women look especially regal in their richly colored, embroidered gowns—some with puffed, patterned sleeves trimmed with fabulous furs, and others without sleeves. Bright pinks, greens, burgundies, blues, and reds adorn their bodies. They wear matching linen caps with lappets that hang over their shoulders. The spectators have the pleasure of witnessing the execution of a very important man, so they're wearing their best.

Most of the men are drunk, standing in haphazard order, laughing, joking, and bragging about their conquests and valor. Their arms are out-stretched, and they're pushing and shoving, forcing their mugs in front of one another, challenging to see who gets the next refill. Gold chains hang from their necks. Diamond and pearl ornaments adorn their silk and linen shirts, which are artistically decorated with hand-stitched symbols of order, rank, and family status.

Eight monks from the French region of Vosne-Romanée, wearing gray tunics with scapulars tied around their waists with cloth belts, are manning a large wooden vat of ale. Their long, baggy sleeves are soaked to the elbows with beer as they fill the mugs as quickly as possible. Most of the nobles are slobs, spilling ale down the fronts of their food-stained clothes, drool hanging from their faces. Beards drip with froth. Arguments erupt among the nobles, swords drawn. The monks, always alert, move in quickly and break up the fights.

A squire is thrown into the vat of beer, to the resounding laughter of the others. His master holds his head under the ale as he kicks and thrashes and fights to catch a breath of air. The nobles are in hysterics, enjoying the carnival-like atmosphere. They haven't had this much fun since the last killings, fifteen days ago—three prisoners, enemies of the crown. Their crime? Sympathizing with the Knights Templar. The means of execution? Death by boiling in large cauldrons of red wine. The nobles had great fun with this, laughing and shouting, "What a waste of good wine! Use water! Let's drink the wine!" The naked victims, each in a separate cauldron, were immersed in the wine before it was heated. The nobles took bets on which captive would die first. The boiling caused severe scalding before it burned the skin off the men, exposing their raw flesh and bursting their blood vessels as they were cooked to death. Their screams for a merciful end to their lives fell upon deaf ears.

Each time a squire is tossed into the vat of beer, the monks manage to either rescue him or pull the pitiable, dead body out and roll it off to the side. Nothing interrupts the fête.

A few of the nobles will flop off into the night, passing out in the stands, having gorged on food and spirits, their urine-stained britches soaked through more than once.

Most of the women already are sitting in the stands, waiting for the execution of Jacques de Molay to begin. Jacques once was one of the most powerful and feared men in Europe, but now he's nothing more than a common criminal. A large iron cage, its steel rails blackened from years of flames, sits on a pile of charred wood. A debtor criminal hangs from chains, his arms and legs shackled. His body is blackened, the flesh charred and skin peeling. Agony is seared into his disfigured face. A guard heaves opens the heavy door, unshackles the debtor, and lets the lifeless form fall outside the cage. Chunks of blistered tissue are scraped off the corpse as French soldiers drag it across the ground and roll it into a freshly dug grave. Later the birds will peck away, finishing off the flesh.

Flanked by two royal guards, Jacques de Molay, his hair matted, dirty, and untrimmed, stands nearby. Over a dark, woolen, monastic-style tunic, he wears a lightweight mantle of white, symbolizing purity, with a red silk cross, symbolizing martyrdom, sewn onto the left breast. Around his neck hangs his two-piece, jeweled pendant with the seal of the Knights Templar.

Jacques finds it difficult to stand. Fleeing enters his mind, but all it would provide is great merriment for the nobles along with death by a knight's crossbow. Worse, if he were mortally wounded, they'd probably let the birds eat at him for a while—peck out his eyes, his lips, the insides of his ears—and then they'd burn him anyway. Why add to their enjoyment? He won't suffer the loss of his dignity. Jacques's lower lip quivers slightly; otherwise, he gives no indication of fear as he imagines the excruciating pain to come. One of the knights unshackles Jacques's leg-irons and hand-cuffs while two others shove him into the cage. He stumbles but manages to catch himself. It's late in the day, early evening. The first burning took longer than expected.

The nobles are taking bets as to how long Jacques will live. Will he die screaming like a coward or in silence like a Knight Templar? Guards pile wood around the cage, kicking it up as close as possible. A couple of the guards poke sharpened sticks into Jacques's side, and his blood reddens the wool cloth of his white, Templar tunic. Jacques stands, gazing out into the evening sky. The French sunset has an unusual, enchanting beauty tonight. The darkened, distant hills dabbed with trees, overhung by huge billowy clouds, are face-like, with blackened highlights, orange-and-yellow hypnotic features, and bluish streams of haze staring from starlit eyes.

Glancing over the unruly crowd, he's surprised and bewildered when he spots Margaret. He didn't expect to see her at his execution. She's accom-panied by Claude de Lavoe, the supreme commander and marshal of the Knights Templar and once Jacques's right arm. Now Jacques knows he's nothing more than a Judas, and his anger flares. Claude is dressed strangely, in a long, brown robe and brown wig, and Jacques realizes he's worried about being recognized. He also knows that all the other Knights Templar have been captured and killed and that the rumors are true: Claude has betrayed them all.

Claude has gone through so much with the Templar order, including the battle at Rehad. Although he joined the order at sixteen, his size and demeanor led everyone to believe he was much older. With Geoffroi de

Charny's guidance and support, at twenty-one he had become the youngest supreme commander of the Knights Templar.

Now, seven years later, Claude watches the execution of Jacques de Molay, once a trusted friend. But Claude's hidden feelings for Margaret have made him a sworn enemy. He believes Jacques will break at any moment—fall to his knees and ask King Philip for forgiveness, give up the location of the Templar treasure and the Ark of the Covenant in exchange for his life. Claude looks intently at Margaret. Tears of anguish fill her large brown eyes and wash her cheeks. Secretly he always has loved her, but he never has had a chance with her with Jacques around. He's also a ruthless opportunist, and with Margaret, the Baroness of Passavant, as his wife, he would become a baron—a position that offers great wealth, respect, authority, and control. Jacques's death is definitely worth it.

Well, Claude thinks, *things are about to change.* A quiet smile breaks his stern face. Jacques won't be around much longer. King Philip will kill him, even if he begs for forgiveness and gives up the hiding place of the Templar treasure and the ark. And then Claude will have Margaret. He attempts to put his arm around her, offer her support, but she's inconsolable. *Oh, well,* he thinks. *There will be plenty of time for that after Jacques is gone.* He wishes he were closer to the flames so he could get a better earful of his old friend's screams for mercy. He relishes the scent of burning flesh.

Staring at her, Jacques wishes he had spent more time with Margaret. Once again, her beauty leaves him breathless. Today she's wearing a loose, dark-blue gown with light-blue trim and a high collar. She always has been there for him—always has waited faithfully for him to come back when he's gone off into battle and always has been his loyal confidant. The Templar vows of celibacy do not allow him or any of the Templar order to marry. His vows forbid him from even looking at a woman, much less becoming romantically involved with one or kissing one. Claude is one of the few people who know of his love for Margaret. Jacques has suspected that Claude has feelings for Margaret because of the way he looks at her—the stolen glances or occasional long stares. Only their enduring friendship and mutual respect have kept Claude in his place when it came to Margaret. The possibility that Claude might possess her leaves Jacques burning with jealousy. Struggling to maintain his composure, he opens up his hands, lifts his head toward heaven, and asks God, *Why? What did the Knights Templar and I do to deserve the destruction of the order? Our torture? Our deaths? Why?* He asks this again and again.

As darkness begins to settle over the sky, Jacques can't help wondering what's taking so long. If they wait much longer, the nobles might pass out from drinking and miss out on all their fun. Will God save him? With everything that's happened, he doesn't know, but he doubts it. He's always been on God's side, a faithful follower. He deeply inhales the cool French air. He doesn't want to die. He inhales deeply again. He couldn't have done anything differently. He couldn't stop King Philip IV and Pope Clement V, two of the most powerful men in the world. He lifts his head high and stands military-proud, staring directly into the stands. There isn't anything they can do that will make him lose his poise. Margaret and all the others must know—he fears neither demons nor men. He's a Knight Templar, a soldier of God to the death, and proud of it.

The inquisitor, William of Paris, loudly reads the charges from a scroll. "Jacques de Molay, King Philip IV of France and his Holy Eminence, Pope Clement V, have convicted you of heresy. You are to die, consumed by the flames of God, driving out the evil that possesses your body and soul. Satan, your master, welcomes you to the depths of hell." William hurriedly motions to four of King Philip's knights to light the fire. The knights, standing at each corner of the cage, torches in hand, set the wood on fire.

André and Pierre-Louis stand next to the vat where the monks are serving beer. André bends over and pulls up his torn pant leg, pretending to inspect a bruise on his scrawny calf. "See?" he whispers. "What I tell you is true. Claude wears the robe and silly-looking wig. All our friends dead. Now they kill Master Jacques. Maybe we next."

"Don't ever let him hear you," Pierre-Louis cautions, stepping close to his pal. "He skin you."

"Come to me home, the château," André whispers while rubbing his belly. "I cook up some leg of lamb." He smacks his lips together. "Mmm-wha!"

"You always so full of the crap," Pierre-Louis pops back, worrying about being arrested. "Never the serious. I've been to your home many times. Château de la Dump. So many holes in roof, rain more inside than out. We need to find place to hide."

"The leg of lamb," André repeats convincingly, "from King Philip's own home. It empty. Nobody go there, so I go there. Got jug of king's best wine."

"The king's summer palace," Pierre-Louis responds, nervously surveying the crowd. Sometimes he doesn't know whether his friend is yanking his leg or not. The royal guard should still be watching the palace, but maybe André got lucky. Maybe there was a changing of the guard when he went there. King Philip would never leave his summer palace empty.

André grabs his friend's arm. "Let's get away from this place."

Pierre-Louis has never known a time of such fear for himself, his friends, his family, and the French people. André only has him, no one else.

The two of them move quietly away, melting into the unnoticed.

Jacques watches as the flames slowly consume the logs, first the outside ones, and then the fire crawls over the others, rolling closer to the cage. The smoke surrounding him burns his nostrils, fills his lungs, making him cough. The heat from the flames warms his legs as the dry wood burns quickly. Jacques strains to see Margaret, but the thick smoke hides her from his view.

The vociferous sounds of nobles reveling in the carnage, rattles the fading day. Grabbing the bars of the cage as the heat from the fire leaps between the metal, Jacques shouts, "I, Jacques de Molay, the last of the Templar Grand Masters, curse King Philip IV and Pope Clement V for their greed! Within one year, your ashes will join those of the Knights Templar you unjustly tortured and condemned, while their souls will remain protected by the armor of God."

Jacques tries desperately to find Margaret in the unruly crowd, to capture her enchanting beauty one last time, but it's useless. The flames leap higher, and the smoke creates a strange grayish hue around the cage. "Margaret! Margaret, my love, my beauty!" he cries, craving that she'll hear him. "Remember me! Remember Jacques de Molay! Walk with me in your dreams. In sleep, listen for the sound of my whisper."

He cringes and tries to pull away from the flames, moving to the center of the cage, where the floor burns beneath his feet. He nods his head. Will

God save him? Will he miraculously change this course of events? Jacques knows the answer is no. He doesn't want to accept his impending death, yet God has spoken; he has chosen King Philip and Pope Clement over him and the Knights Templar. How else could they be destroyed so completely? So easily? It had to be God's work. He shakes his head, vowing to escape at all costs, even if it means defying God. Dropping to his knees, bowing his head, and raising his arms to the night sky, he cries, "Mithras! Mithras! God of darkness, the child born from the stone. The Great White Wolf. I call on you, Mithras. Grant me, only me, all your powers! Dress me in your image. Replace all my good with evil, and I will be your obedient servant. Save me from the flames, and I will give you my soul."

Fear and anxiety fill Claude when he realizes Jacques isn't going to plead for mercy. He won't ask King Philip and Pope Clement to forgive him for being a heretic of the cross. Jacques won't give up the hiding place of the Templar treasure; he has chosen to die as a Knight Templar.

Claude grabs Margaret's hand and steps back into the crowd, urgently pulling her along. She resists, but she's no match for his strength. Claude knows that as soon as Jacques is dead, King Philip's knights will come looking for them. They need to escape—go to the de Molay castle and prepare for battle. Any Knights Templar who have survived will make their last stand there. It's the most heavily fortified castle in all of Europe.

Mithras, slaps his hands together, and the smoke from the fire feeds on itself, getting heavier, thicker, darker, engulfing the cage. The nobles become even more belligerent—between the boozing and the vanishing daylight, they're having a frustratingly difficult time picking out Jacques's form through the deep, unnatural, blackish haze. They catch a glimpse, and then he disappears.

Mithras, blows a cooling breath on the metal cage and Jacques, shielding him from the burning fires. With two claps of his hands, the dark god plants his seed of vampiric quintessence inside Jacques's body in exchange for his soul.

Jacques's body erupts like a volcano into massive seizures as he crashes onto the cage floor, kicking, shivering, pissing himself into unconsciousness. His legs and arms become rigid as his muscles tremble and then contract violently, flexing back and forth. His pupils dilate, saliva runs down the sides of his face, and he defecates as he gnaws at the air. His skin stretches and tears as the bones break and shape-shift, contracting in size. He sprouts fingers like bat wings, hairy legs, razor-sharp teeth, small ears, large eyes, and a black, furry body—the requisite to drink blood every day or die.

The sun sets. Eventually, as shadows creep across the countryside, the smoke clears from the cage. The women are speechless with fright. "Where is he?" they ask one another. "Where did he go? What's happening?"

The men are drunk and arguing among themselves over Jacques's disappearance. One of King Philip's knights opens the door to the cage and steps back so everyone can see that it's empty. The nobles are at a loss for words. There is no trace of the man's body.

The monks who have been working the beer vat fall to their knees, hold up their crosses, and pray, attempting to ward off any evil demons that might have risen from the depths of hell to possess Jacques de Molay's spirit. It's as if he never existed at all, as if his corpse has been whisked away on the smoke-laden breeze.

Unnoticed, a large vampire bat flies into the smoky night.

4

BATTLE AT THE TEMPLAR CASTLE

Sunlight slides over the French countryside, casting shadows across the ravaged battlefield. King Philip IV appears magnificent in his command and dress. His light-blond hair curls out and lies down the full length of his back. He's festooned in full battle gear. A royal-blue field of crushed sapphires strewn with golden lilies adorns the front and back of his plate armor, while a white silk cape, banded to his shoulders, floats in the breeze. A tall comb of blue-and-gold feathers roosts on top of his gold-trimmed, fully enclosed, silver helmet. Its narrow brim is lined in sparkling rubies and sapphires. The charcoal war-horse he sits astride is covered from head to tail in a matching silk, elaborately decorated, ground-skirting blanket and a matching face mask and plume.

The king surveys the rolling valley. The de Molay castle, with its majestic towers and cylindrical keep, is perched on the rocky knoll like a massive bird of prey, claws extended. It stands proudly and defiantly, dominating the region like an angry, disobedient falcon.

From the size of the killing field and the tired, dirty remnants of his army, it's obvious the king's men have been battling the small squadron of castle defenders for days. Wounded and dying knights scream in the fading light, their armor crimsoned with blood. Many struggle through the fallen pine trees and tangled underbrush to reach the grass-covered banks of an enchanting, blue-water, trout stream not far from the battlefield. The peaceful current washes around moss-covered rocks, undercutting the banks, forming tranquil pools of crystal-clear water that reflect brightly colored wildflowers, birds, insects, fallen trees, and a roe deer and its fawn lapping their fill. King Philip's men quench their thirst and wash their wounds and open sores, struggling to soothe their flesh in the refreshing water. Some, mortally wounded, stagger into the stream and fall, floating away, their bodies popping up and down like bobbers. The ones milling about on the banks don't do anything to save their fellow men-at-arms. If they were to live, their debilitating wounds and injuries would condemn them to a disease-infested life of begging and scrounging for crumbs of food. Everybody's garbage would become their cuisine. It is better to die in a watery grave, adorned by nature's pastels and the last thoughts of loved ones, hoping for a final blessing from God the Master.

Before, with the castle's Templar defenders, assaulting it would have been a fanatical, suicide mission. However, with the elimination of nearly all of the Knights Templar, this day may prove to be successful beyond King Philip's dreams. By dark the Templar treasure—more wealth than all of Europe's kingdoms combined—will be his, he believes. It will make him more powerful than any other living man, including the pope. Philip must conquer England, and then Europe will be his for the slaughter, but first he must deal with Claude de Lavoe and the last of the Knights Templar. He plans to kill as many as possible and then brutally torture any left alive until they are dead. Vengeance will be his for having been denied membership to their order. Vengeance will be his for Claude's failure to discover the hiding place of the Templar treasure. He considers himself the greatest king in the world. He has eliminated all the Jews from France and annihilated the order of the Knights Templar, appropriating all their known properties and treasure. He was in debt to both groups, but all that has changed now. No one will dare refuse him anything. The reward he has offered his knights for the head of Claude de Lavoe is great, and the reward to bring Claude in alive is much greater. The king cautiously nudges his mount forward across the battlefield.

One man, Claude de Lavoe, in maddened defiance, stands like an indestructible giant upon a tall, imposing, embattlement wall in plain sight of King Philip. He bellows orders to his small group of defenders. From the ravages of the battle, his white wool cappa with its red cross over the left breast hangs in threads, leaving exposed a highly polished, silver, chain-mail shirt. Its reflection is blinding in the fading sunlight. Directly over his head flies the white-and-black banner of the Knights Templar, the *beauséant*. It's held in place by two poles, one on top and one at the bottom, so a breeze isn't required for the knights or their enemies to see it. As long as the beauséant flies, the Knights Templar must fight on. And as long as the Knights Templar fight on, the beauséant must fly.

Claude, raising his sword, shouts encouragement to his men. "Beau séant!" ("Be noble!") "Beau séant!" ("Be great!") "Beau séant!" ("Be noble!") "Beau séant!" ("Be great!")

Just as the sun disappears behind the centuries-old hemlock trees dotting the hillsides, several of King Philip's knights, using a long, heavy, wooden, battering ram mounted to a wagon, crash through the enormous, oak doors that protect the castle entrance. Once inside, the sheer numbers of the attacking army overwhelm the remaining defenders. The Knights Templar are extremely well trained and disciplined, and for every one killed, several enemies die. However, it's not long before the invaders take control and send knights down every passage and hallway, ransacking rooms, butchering everything that moves. In the shadowy distance, two of King Philip's knights spot a young, muscular squire who's a shield bearer in the Order of the Knights Templar. His body is pressed flat against the fieldstone wall as he attempts to be inconspicuous, slowly easing his way along.

"Halt!" they shout. "In the name of King Philip, stand where you are!"

Thomas breaks into a run, his long, blond hair flapping against his shoulders. He knows escape is the only way to survive. There are more than two hundred rooms in the castle. He has lived within these walls his entire young life and still hasn't been in all of them. It would take days for the knights to search the entire castle. All he needs is a few minutes.

During the long French winter—cold, sunless days and colder nights— he stayed warm and in shape, and he conquered his boredom by going for runs through the endless, chilly hallways. Moving easily, his soft leather slippers quietly landing on the stone floor, he felt invigorated when running. He knows his way through the castle by heart. They will never catch him.

The French knights give chase, but it's hopeless. Under their armor they wear padded clothing to protect themselves from blows. Over the padding they wear long-sleeved chain-mail shirts, along with chain-mail hand coverings, leggings, hoods, and shoes. Over this they wear full-length, wool, battlefield surcoats. They wear some seventy pounds in all. After a few laboring steps, exhaustion prevails.

Thomas pushes open the door to Margaret's bedroom, making no attempt to hide his uneasiness. "My lady, we must leave," he blurts. He moves quickly to the large poster bed where she lies. "Please! We must leave!"

"Leave me," Margaret cries, her face and eyes swollen from weeping. "I want to be left alone." She whimpers, rolling over so her back is to him.

"The castle has fallen." Thomas's urgency grows. Leaning over the bed, he grabs her shoulder and shakes it lightly. Under other circumstances he would never have considered touching her—placing an uninvited hand on a noble would have cost him his life. He doesn't notice the revealing black nightgown that hugs her body. "King Philip's knights are slaughtering every-one in the castle. Please, please, my lady! We don't have much time! King Philip won't leave without the Templar treasure."

Margaret turns and aggressively faces him. "The treasure and the ark will never be found! King Philip—this senseless killing of so many!" She waves her hands in frustration while closing her brown eyes so as not to reveal the lie beneath her lids—the fact that she knows of the journey taken by the treasure and ark. "All for naught!" She begins to weep again.

Thomas grabs Margaret by the arms and pulls her across the bed. The covers roll up under the weight of her body. She doesn't resist his efforts. The sleepless nights, hunger, tears, dark depression—her grief at losing Jacques has taken its toll.

"Jacques de Molay is dead, but you are not, my lady. He pulls Margaret off the bed and hauls her to her feet.

She attempts to stand but loses her balance. "I'm sorry," she moans. "I fell off my horse. I don't think I can walk." Thomas wraps his arm around her waist as she tries to hobble down the passageway, but he quickly decides against it. He bends over and hoists her over his shoulder.

"I'm sorry," she cries. "Please let me try to walk again."

"No," he responds, steadying himself, balancing her weight. "It'll just slow us down." He feels the warmth of her body against his, her breasts pressed against his back, the pounding of her heart, her bare legs against his bare arms—his years of strict discipline have helped him control his feral feelings. His training began when he was a child and consisted of many years of study and practice, practice, practice—the desired goal: perfection. He developed into a master of self-discipline, and he acquired the skills of combat and chivalry necessary to become a Knight Templar. He became a page at age seven and received Templar coats in the colors of black, white, and red, as well as the livery-of-the-lord uniform in the colors of red and white. His education consisted of religion, riding, hunting, and games of skill such as chess and backgammon. He trained to excel in swimming and athletic trials and to withstand extremes in cold, heat, exhaustion, and hunger, and to master weaponry—especially the lance. The Templar Code of Chivalry includes social skills, courtly etiquette, jousting, music, and dancing. At twenty-two years of age, Thomas obtained the most envied of squire positions, the Squire of the Body. Such squires are considered the closest to their lord and are trusted to accompany the Knights Templar in battle.

"My lord de Lavoe would die if anything happened to you," Thomas states reassuringly. He tries not to imagine what Claude would do to him if something did happen to Margaret. From nobles, usually drunk, he has heard stories of Claude's brutality, and on occasion some have talked freely in front of him—Thomas is often invisible. They're so used to his waiting on their table, performing his duties in the kitchen, arranging for the upkeep of their clothing, carrying messages, and guarding them when they sleep that he could be standing next to one of them and not be noticed.

At least, he attempts to reassure himself, Margaret isn't that heavy. Stepping into the hallway, he stares up and down both lengths. The wall torches, unattended, are burning out, casting flickering, haunting images. It's a long way to the old boat that's hidden deep under the castle, two levels down.

Holding Margaret firmly, he takes his first step—they just need to make it to the underground maze in the de Molay castle before King Philip's knights catch up with them. Jacques took him and Clarete through its suffocating blackness years ago. There wasn't even a sliver of sunlight. The maze is a rectangle with thirty-one interior walls—*right corner in, left corner out*. He hopes he can remember Jacques's instructions. It's their only chance for escape.

Thomas is strong and moves easily through the passageway despite the failing wall torches. However, Margaret is heavier than he initially suspected. His thoughts take him back to his younger years. Reflecting on happier times helps him block out the inevitable. He recalls playing hide-and-seek games in these castle halls with Jacques, Jude, and a girl when he was six. The girl, Clarete, was twelve, Jacques and Jude were both fifteen. Master de Lezines was Jacques' uncle.

The maze was designed more than one hundred fifty years prior by the Templar General Jude the Great and Egyptian craftsmen when the castle was being built. The craftsmen were captured in the Second Crusade and brought back to France. Thomas, his breathing labored, remembers the words chiseled into two of the keep's massive wall stones: THE YEAR 1169, KING BALDWIN IV OF JERUSALEM, VICTORIOUS OVER SALADIN, RULER OF EGYPT.

Clarete, he remembers, could be so entertaining—must have been those dark eyes and hair so long that she could pull it around to the front of her chest and tie it below her breasts. One time she tried to teach him and Jacques how to eat by holding food with one hand instead of two, which everyone knows is impossible. They were the best of friends. Thinking of Clarete now saddens Thomas. He remembers how they used to tease her when she dyed her eyebrows and eyelashes using different-colored, crushed berries or soot from the fireplace. A reddish tone was her favorite color.

She said, "It makes me more memorable."

They never told anyone because the Church considered it a sin.

The thought of Clarete glowing in the sunlight gives him strength. He remembers her flashing smile. "Someday a great man is going to mix a magic potion and splash it all over my face, hands, and body, making me the most beautiful and admired woman in all the world. Like a master's painting, I'll live forever." She was so funny.

"Nobody lives forever," Thomas had told her.

She would flip her head back, tossing her long brown hair, and declare, "You'll see."

He wishes he had done something to protect Clarete from King Philip's guards. But he took the coward's way out thirty guilt-ridden days ago and watched them drag her away.

Margaret's weight bears down on him, and his legs tire. *Must keep going*, he repeats to himself. *Almost there. Must keep going.*

Jacques swore Jude, Thomas, and Clarete to secrecy—a childhood blood pact among four companions, each sworn to their death. They were to tell no one that Jacques had taken them through the maze. Now, with Jacques and probably Jude dead, the oath has died. Maybe he should tell Claude, Thomas thinks. He believes the Templar treasure is hidden somewhere in the maze. Claude would know what to do with it, how to prevent it from falling into King Philip's hands.

Thomas's legs feel like water; pain crushes his back. Maybe he won't make it to the maze. He imagines failure—but he can't fail.

After Master de Lezines died years ago, no one went down to the maze. It became a lost and forgotten secret. Thomas hopes, after all these years, the old boat is still intact.

Breathing heavily, he stops to rest. He shifts Margaret on his shoulder, attempting to achieve better balance. He gasps and sets her down. "Walk. You must walk. King Philip's knights are right behind us. The maze isn't far! Put your arm around my shoulder. If we hurry we can make it!"

Torches appear behind them like floating fire, moving up and down like ghosts. "Leave me." Margaret runs her hands through her fire-red hair, straightening it, gaining some composure. "King Philip won't harm me. I'm of noble birth. You go." She gently pushes him away. "Save yourself."

There is no escape for him without Margaret, and there's no time to try to reason with her. He can't fathom the evil that Claude will perform on him, as well as his family and friends, if anything happens to her.

Margaret grabs his arm. "Did you hear that sound? Did you hear it?"

Thomas draws his sword. All he hears is King Philip's knights getting closer—their loud boasting, their laughing!

"I'm going to stop them. Please, my lady! King Philip will kill anyone to secure the Templar treasure, even you. He knows of your friendship with Jacques. Now go! Go, my lady! Go to the gate to the maze and wait for me. There's a boat on the other side. Now go! Go, my lady!"

"It sounds like a vielle," Margaret says, referring to a violin-like instrument. "Someone is playing the vielle." She's so excited yet confused; she's lost the power of rational reasoning. "Can't you hear it?" She hobbles in the direction of the maze. The stone floor is chilly on her bare feet, as her palm slides across the damp, cold wall for support, catching cobwebs that wrap around her hand as she goes. The music is so clear, so close. Jacques is the only person she knows who played the vielle, yet he's dead. Who could it be? Maybe she can find out who's playing if they get a little closer.

"Wait for me at the gate. There are deadly things down there you don't understand—strange creatures of the unnatural. You could get lost in the maze and die if you go in without me." In the darkness, he's unaware that she has already left him. He stands straight, whispers a prayer, and then carefully moves toward the advancing knights. He knows he's hopelessly outnumbered, but this time he can't run. Clarete borrowed some money from one of King Philip's guards and couldn't pay it back. Jacques would have given her the money, but she was too proud to ask him. King Philip's knights took her to debtors' prison, and Thomas did nothing to help her; he was too afraid. This time will be different.

Margaret reaches the steps to the maze and manages to carefully descend them, deep into an underground room. Her leg hurts, but her emotional high dulls the pain. The melody stops as quickly as it began. Confused, she pauses, wondering why she no longer hears the sound. She stumbles ahead. Maybe she just needs to get closer, a little closer to the maze, she thinks. There it is again, just a little pick, so quiet she can hardly hear it. She pushes forward, breathing heavily. "Only one person plays the vielle like that," she says, hoping Thomas will hear her. Her voice quietly echoes through the hidden passageways. "Only one, but it's not possible! It can't be!" She saw him die with her own eyes. "Jacques de Molay is dead!"

Jacques's senses are so keen now that in the depths of the maze he hears Thomas's cries of anguish as King Philip's knights take him apart a piece at a time.

Setting his Vielle down, he transforms into a vampire bat and flies through the caverns at an incredible speed, weaving in and out and cutting corners in a dazzling display of flying precision. His wings are beating twice as fast as those of a hummingbird. In the dark, his directional calls bounce off the stones, returning echoes that map the distance in a millisecond.

Margaret, startled, cries out, as something flies past her, brushing her face. She instinctively glances over her shoulder, but there's only darkness. "What is it?" she says rather loudly, savoring the sound of her own voice.

Jacques spots Thomas's mangled body on the stone floor. He's enraged that he didn't make it in time to help him, and his animal instincts take over. Morphing back into a vampire, he savagely attacks the seven knights, skinning huge chunks of flesh off their bodies with his razor-sharp fingernails. He snaps their bones while twisting their bodies into grotesque shapes. The bloodbath is so devastating and confusing that none of the knights understand what's happening. They become crazed defending themselves against the terror, madly swinging their swords in all directions, fighting and butchering one another.

Jacques takes Thomas in his arms and lifts his neck to his mouth. Maybe he can still save him, bite him, push his rich blood into him, and turn him into a creature of the night, but instead he hesitates and listens to his friend. "I'm dying," Thomas cries, holding his hand against Jacques's face, as he grows frantic from the massive loss of blood. "I saw you die," he wails. "This can't be. You can't be here. I'm speaking to a ghost." He pulls Jacques's face to his and feels his warm breath on his skin. "The veil between this life…the next life," he cries. "It must…must be lifting. I'm moving farther away from life on…this earth…yet I…I…" he says, choking, "can see you."

"I'm here, my friend," Jacques whispers. "Tell me what you want me to do."

"Leave me. Save Clarete. She's in the…debtor's prison. The king's summer palace. I failed her. Don't you fail her…my great friend." Jacques feels the last breath pass Thomas's lips.

He hugs Thomas's body to his own and runs his hand across his lifeless face and through his hair. Then he kisses his forehead in a final tribute to their friendship as he lays him gently on the ground. He planned to convert Margaret first, then Thomas, and then Clarete—the three people he trusts completely. If he could have gotten to Thomas just a couple of minutes earlier…Now, for all eternity, Thomas will be the true Squire of the Body for the Knights Templar.

Jacques hears what sounds like hundreds of rats scurrying behind the walls, squealing and scratching—wild with the smell of blood, the stench of death. He imagines, welcomes, their sawing jaws and gnashing teeth. He intentionally left all the knights alive, crippling their legs but leaving their arms intact so they would have to drag their bodies to distance themselves from the voracious rats or be eaten alive. This cruelty could only be called justice for the sins of a king and his soldiers. Had not the king himself declared, "Ye have heard that it hath been said, 'An eye for an eye, and a tooth for a tooth'?"

The knights' dreadful screams of pain fall on unresponsive ears. After the rats are done, the carnage will be so complete that only the priest who presides over the knights' burials will recognize their grossly mutilated bodies. His prayers will reveal the torments of hell to the dead knights' souls. Only the priest and Jacques understand and believe in the evil that now walks the earth: the vampire.

Jacques stands and, carrying Thomas's body, hurries back toward the maze.

Out of the sinister darkness, Margaret sees a strange illumination, a shadowed brightness ahead. She scarcely dares to hope that the glow is a light just ahead. She manages the gloominess of the last stairway and, following the wall for support, cautiously moves the short distance into a room. Never did she believe it possible to be so frightened, so utterly helpless, so alone, so cold. Not even when she was attacked by the wolves was she as terrified as this. She doesn't know what it is, but the room has a strange, ominous illumination about it. There are no windows, torches, sunlight…Then, to her horror, she realizes hundreds of sapphire-blue, pulsating glowworms are attached to the walls and ceiling. Their slimy bodies are wrapped around the metal bars, forming an outline of the gate that leads to the maze. Someone or something has smashed and mixed their remains, using them to highlight the letters on the wooden plaque.

BEWARE THE MAZE,
YE WHO DARE TO ENTER.
ONLY THE DEAD LEAVE.

Margaret's stomach heaves, and she claws at her throat. She concentrates in order to keep from vomiting what little remains in her stomach as she steps backward across an eternity of decomposing glowworms. Her terror fades, and what's between her toes crawls feather-soft around her ankles, ever so slowly inching up her calves, her thighs, and between them. They blanket her flesh, uncovering the innermost secrets of her being, and what was broken feels suddenly whole. Beads of desire form on her forehead, the back of her neck, and between her breasts as the warm tingling reverberates throughout her body. She runs her tongue around her lips, and her breathing becomes heavy. She feels safe, protected, emotionally hot. She exhales, lifting her white silk nightgown waist-high and fanning her nakedness.

Seeing a bench seat by the wall that's covered in royal-blue lamb's cloth, Margaret is overwhelmed by the need to sit. She smiles seductively. Jacques did this to protect her; she knows this. As the glowworms cover her body, she feels a new awareness of her passions. Their pulsating keeps rhythm with the beating of her heart; her fervor is amplified by theirs.

It's how they control you, she thinks. If you have a wicked heart, the glowworms will turn your malevolence back onto you, and you'll destroy yourself with your own hatred. If you have a good heart, they'll become one with you, elevating all your emotions, your consciousness, the genesis of love. An encounter with them tests a person, and Margaret has just been tested.

"Jacques is alive," she mutters. "Jacques is alive." She knows this as she sits down. There's nothing to do but wait for him. The worms will keep her company.

As she sits, she wonders what happened to Claude. After Jacques's execution, Claude took her to the de Molay castle, told her to wait in her room, and left. Maybe King Philip's knights killed him. For some reason that thought bothers her, and she feels a twinge of remorse. She takes a deep breath, thinking, wondering, running her hand through her hair. She had been so involved in Jacques's life that she hadn't realized she was attracted to Claude, and yet she believes that she is—in fact, more so than she could ever have imagined.

—⟋ⱴ⟍—

Outside on the battlement walk above the castle grounds, with the beauséant flying high over his head, Claude hacks his way through several invaders. Sweat and splattered blood drench his face. The weight of his armor crushes his chest, and he burns from the sun's heat on the metal. His breathing is labored, and his broad-brimmed kettle hat weighs heavily on his head. Blood from his enemies' wounds soaks the stone walkway.

He sees several more of King Philip's knights climbing a tall, wooden ladder a short distance away. He knows there's no way he can defeat them all. Lunging like a mad bull, he crashes into three knights and heaves them to their deaths on the ground several yards below. Then he mentally measures the distance to the doorway in the tower at the end of the battlement wall. If he can get there before the other knights climb the ladder and block his way, he can escape, but under the fortress of his armor, it's nearly impossible for him to run. A knight reaches the top of the ladder. Claude takes his kite-shaped shield in one of his massive hands and heaves it through the air, spinning it like a saucer. It smashes into the man's skull, sending him crashing down the ladder and into the dozen knights below. Reaching the enormous oak door, Claude throws his weight into it, and crashes it open just as night pulls the curtain down on the French countryside and transforms the fortress into a dark, forbidding, iron-and-stone beast.

A hard-shot arrow from a knight's crossbow tears through the back of Claude's chain-mail shirt, penetrating deep into his left shoulder, close to the heart, ripping flesh and muscle before lodging. The huge man staggers under the violent impact. His knees buckle, and he sucks in his breath. Instinctively he grits his teeth and stands, gathering his fighting spirit. "Only Claude de Lavoe," he spits out, "determines the time and manner of his own death." Stumbling down the steps, blood soaking the back of his chain mail, he wonders whether Thomas escorted Margaret safely away from the castle.

—ɯ—

Hearing the spellbinding music echoing through the hidden passageways, Margaret whispers, "Jacques, Jacques, is that you? I know it's you. I'm mad…I must be going mad, but I don't care. I saw you die…burned to death in the fire."

Still playing the vielle, he sits beside her. He's pale yet more handsome than ever.

Margaret lays her head on his shoulder. "Please don't stop. Please keep playing. I feel so content. I can't explain it, but I'm so filled with love having you here with me. I so want to hold on to the memory of you forever."

Jacques continues to play until he finishes the waltz. He places the vielle on the bench and kisses her deeply, savoring for eternity one last moment of human warmth, of her love.

"What's wrong, Jacques?" Margaret lightly strokes his face. "You seem so cold, sad…I'm so happy to see you. Yet how are you here?" she asks, her eyes reflecting the bewilderment in her voice. "With my own eyes, I saw you die."

"You saw someone else die that day," he responds. "Come." Taking her hand, he leads her through the gate and into the maze, stopping at different points, interpreting symbols carved into the rocks, following one tunnel and then another. The murky forms of the crawling things shadow them, attaching to the cave lining, their rapacious yellow-and-red eyes dotting the gloom like tumors. They will never attack Jacques. It's Margaret—the voracious insatiable scent of her skin—who signals their predatory instincts. Jacques holds her hand, storing in his mind the memory of its warmth. He takes her to the edge of the lake that reaches underneath the castle. Thomas's body, wrapped in a white robe with the Templar seal, is lying in the old rotting boat. Jacques tells Margaret about Thomas's death, and she feels a great sadness as he pushes the small skiff into the water. Even though its tattered sail is still standing, a breeze won't help. They watch as it drifts into the darkness, carrying Thomas's body to a watery grave.

Jacques turns and grabs Margaret, startling her. He embraces her, kisses her deeply, sucks the oxygen from her lungs. She manages a couple of lightly thrown smacks to his shoulders before she passes out.

"One day, my love, you will understand," he whispers, before gently sinking his fangs deep into her neck, ravishing the nectar of her life-force, inhaling the succulent scent of flesh, sucking out only enough blood so she won't die. He pushes the precise amount of his blood back into her veins through his fangs. Now Margaret will always be bonded to him.

He carries her back and lays her on the bench next to the entrance into the maze. "Sleep, my beauty. I'll be back for you. You're safe here."

5

Escape from the Summer Palace

A full moon, garlanded in red and orange hues, hangs in the darkened sky as gray, cottony clouds drift by. The cry of an owl echoes, teasing the silence. The trees lining the wheel-rutted road, their branches heavy with years of growth, shadow the land. A small, enclosed carriage pulled by two horses barrels across the French countryside. Jacques de Molay is dressed in a royal-blue jacket and gold pants, his red cape flying behind him. He snaps his whip, striking the horses, pushing them to run faster. The advancing riders behind him holler and shout into the darkness. Although Jacques can change into a bat or a wolf and disappear into the landscape at any time, he prefers the excitement of the chase. As a wolf, he could lie in wait and pick riders off one at a time, rip out their throats—now that's fun. Mithras, who is now Jacques's master, can shape-shift into any form. But the master has given Jacques and those he converts the ability to shape-shift into only three forms: vampire, wolf, and vampire bat.

The carriage is going too fast to make a bend in the road, and it cartwheels, smashing into a tree. The two horses break loose and run off into the night, still harnessed together. Catapulted through the air, Jacques tumbles into a thicket of blackberry bushes. "Ahhh!" he exclaims, lying among the thorns. "I must do this more often!" Unhurt, he stands, brushes himself off, straightens his cape, slicks back his long hair, and shape-shifts into a giant, steel-blue-colored wolf. It's an excruciating process—the rearrangement of his entire body, his senses, how he thinks, how he lives. His bones lengthen and break, changing shape. His flesh ruptures, the skull bones split and thicken, and his mouth elongates. His hands and feet twist into paws. Long hair grows rapidly, covering his body. The process completed, he casually trots into the woods.

Six horsemen wearing dark-red robes with gold belts and sky-blue capes with white stars ride up. The back of each robe is adorned with a naked, lion-headed figure of a man with the mouth open and fangs exposed. The creature stands on a globe decorated with crossed circles. His body is entwined by a green serpent, and the snake's head rests on top of the lion's horrifying head. Four blue wings speckled with silver stars, representing the four seasons of the year, lift up from his back. A gold thunderbolt is engraved on his chest. This is the symbol of their master, the god, Mithras.

Their horses are soaked with perspiration and hard to control. Guardedly the men scan the area. A couple of them dismount and warily walk up to the wreckage of the carriage, while the others post guard. Breathless from the hard ride, one horseman drags the sleeve of his robe across his face, wiping the snot from his nose and mouth.

"See anything? Is he there?" another rider shouts out. "Watch out! Keep together! He's Satan's blood! Could be anywhere!"

One of the dismounted riders cautiously surveys the broken carriage. "Damn full moon," he mutters while glancing up at the forbidding, dark-blue sky, chalked with black-laced clouds. It's an evil night, difficult to see anything in the darkness, and he shouldn't be here. He should be at home, protecting his family.

A man standing next to the carriage slowly lifts open one of the doors. Another walks toward him, pulling a cross from his jacket. When the first man accidentally lets go of the door, it bangs loudly as it slams shut. The sudden noise frightens the horses, and they panic. The horsemen struggle to regain control of their animals.

"Damn, that scared me!" shouts the man holding the cross. "Thought I was dead for sure!" He bends over and, holding the cross in front of him, fearfully looks inside the carriage. "He isn't here," he indicates to the head rider, who carries a gold staff in one hand. "Must've gotten away…into the woods. Must've run into the woods. God protect us. We can't let him get away. Demons walk tonight." The distant sound of a howling wolf tests their nerves.

"Mount up!" someone shouts. "Be quick about it. We must ride hard to catch him. Our god, Mithras, wants the Templar treasure. He believes Jacques de Molay will betray him."

Questioning the sanity of their task, the two Frenchmen hurry back to their horses. The moon slips behind another cloud as the fading sound of hoofbeats retreat into silence.

—⊗—

Standing amid a cluster of beech trees, Jacques gazes at a massive château of polished white stone and granite. A slight breeze ruffles the leaves, wafting his hair, which is now accented with a streak of premature gray.

A large party, celebrating the end of the Templars, is taking place at King Philip's summer palace. Handcrafted metal domes cap four turrets, one at each end of the castle. Oil-burning lanterns illuminate the night and blanket the lawn's rock ponds and manicured flower gardens in a radiant glow. Women dressed in ornate gowns of satin and lace trimmed in squirrel fur, their hair elaborately coiffed, are escorted by men wearing high-ranking military uniforms and costumes of gold and velvet. They parade into the palace. Horse-drawn carriages are parked outside and attended to by their coachmen. Some of the revelers are already leaving, as it's getting late.

All houses of French nobility have keeps of various sizes. Many people are imprisoned for minor offenses such as not paying a debt. Clarete, Jacques knows, is being held somewhere in the keep of this castle, and he's determined to find her. He walks toward it, blending into the night.

—⊗—

Staring through the window at the lavish ball taking place some distance away, Pierre-Louis curses his bad luck and wipes the tears from his eyes. He knew he shouldn't have listened to André, who said he wanted to go to Baron de la Force's summer estate and steal food. Turns out André and Pierre-Louis didn't end up going there at all but went to King Philip's summer palace instead. André, always confused, didn't know one place from the other. And now they've been arrested and thrown into separate rooms in the palace keep.

André has broken into other country homes, palaces, and mansions in the past and has never been caught until now. Regardless, one can't attribute this to his ability as a thief but, rather, to pure luck. These superfluent homes of the nobility are so large and have so many rooms that it's impossible for the guards to be everywhere at once. Also, André always eats the food that is left on the plates. More plates, more leftovers—who will notice? However, the magnificence of this pageant and feast is staggering, on a scale that he can't comprehend.

Before he was arrested a few hours ago, he stood in the banquet room, where he saw countless tables covered in white silk, set with silver plates, drinking cups of wood and horn, and gold and silver candlesticks. He staggered, stunned at all the grandeur, and then ambled down the hall and stumbled into the kitchen, which appeared to have the capacity to process, cook, and serve five large cows at once. Large, iron cauldrons bubbled with delicious-smelling soups, and stews hung by chains in enormous, stone fireplaces. Chicken, beef, and lamb were roasting on spits. Bowls of fresh apples, pears, and berries sat on the tabletops. The banquet is supposed to last fourteen days. André never had imagined, much less seen, such abundance. Closing his eyes and breathing deeply, he attempted to suck in all the delicious aromas. He stuck out his tongue, wiggling it around, hoping to taste the incredible flavors. He wondered where everyone was then quickly dismissed the thought. He wished his buddy, Pierre-Louis, were there—but he wasn't, so why worry about that?

André grabbed a large skinning knife from the butcher block and sliced huge chunks of meat off the spits. "Hot, hot, hot!" he sputtered, smacking his lips, attempting to eat the sizzling beef off the point of the knife. He grabbed a loaf of brown, day-old bread, ripped off a large chunk, and slapped the warm meat onto it. Pushing this way and that, he managed to stuff the whole thing into his mouth. Pieces dripping with juice hung out each side while he chewed; brown slobber dripped off his chin. He spotted a leather tankard full of ale, grabbed a copper skull goblet, filled it, and then stuffed a piece of hot beef into the brew to cool it off. Two oak barrels of wine sat against the wall. Hustling, enjoying himself beyond any scope of realty—caution clean forgotten—he grabbed three other goblets, dipped one into the stew, another into the soup, and the third into the wine. With a goblet of wine in one hand, and one in the other full of ale and pieces of meat, he tore into his drinking and eating like a hungry wolf, gorging himself. Food, slobber, and drink frothed from his mouth and spilled down the sides of his face. Attempting to clean his stuffed mug, he ran his arm back and forth across his cheeks, smearing the food and drink. *Burp, burp.* He lifted his leg and passed gas. "Ahhhh, yes," he muttered, grinning, "It don't get no better'n this." He relished the smell of his own farts—so much so that he lifted his leg and managed to squeeze one into his hand so he could hold the smell for a while longer. He would take another whiff on his way home.

Eventually, this was where the attendants and the guards caught him. His hair, face, and the front of his tattered shirt were covered in a mash of spirits and edibles. His filthy pants were down to his ankles, standing butt naked with a goblet of beer-soaked beef chunks in one hand, his salty dog in the other. He contentedly hummed a sailor song while he wiggled his butt around and attempted to piss write his name in King Philip's fireplace. Course, he never learned how to read, much less do the spelling. Grinning, he lifted the goblet high and toasted his captors.

Pierre-Louis shakes his head. They'll never get out of this one—never. It would take a miracle. Before he dies he has one wish. He wants a French woman to speak to him in French one last time. The words are so beautiful; they make him feel so good. He sniffs while wiping his eyes again. *Poor André*, he moans.

The royal guards have allowed Pierre-Louis to stay in the Chestnut Room, the waiting room on the masters' side of the prison. When he was arrested, he was able to bribe his captors with some francs he had saved. The money was supposed to be for both him and André, but the guards said no amount of money could help André. However, it was enough money to allow Pierre-Louis some freedom of movement inside the prison as long as he stays on the masters' side. Whenever the guards are drunk or absent from the building, which happens frequently, he sneaks down the narrow corridor on the masters' side to the end. Looking through the bars in the mud-caked wall, he sees André and Clarete in their rooms on the commoners' side of the hall.

Pierre-Louis still doesn't understand why he was arrested. He was near the perimeter of the property when he was found; he wasn't even in the palace with André. Claude must have had something to do with this. Shortly after the killing of Geoffroi de Charny, Claude must have told King Philip's men that Pierre-Louis and André were friends.

The orchestra is set up on a large outdoor balcony. Pierre-Louis has never heard an orchestra before. The music is tranquilizing, and he weeps again. The sound is a rare touch of heaven's virtuous world. He feels so sorry for his friend and wishes he could have done more. He knows the royal guards are treating André cruelly.

Pierre-Louis hears a noise behind him. Startled, he turns, yells out, and then stops. Standing in front of him is someone he recognizes, but he knows it can't be true. *Jacques de Molay was burned up in the fire,* he thinks. A low whining rises from his belly. "Oh-h-h-h! It can't be. Can't be. Oh-h-h-h!" He moves backward until a stone wall stops him. "Must be the ghost of Jacques de Molay! Real Jacques de Molay dead. I sees it meself," he cries.

Jacques places his hand on Pierre-Louis's shoulder, squeezing it firmly. "It is me, Jacques."

"Oh-h-h-h," Pierre-Louis continues to whine. "I must be dead. I must be dead. Everyone say you dead."

"Let's go find Clarete." Jacques grabs Pierre-Louis's hand and leads him down a short hall to the Disarming Room, the area where visitors give up their weapons. On the way, Pierre-Louis tells him that André is being held in a cell next to Clarete. Normally guards are on duty, but most of the knights are at King Philip's extravagant party. It takes a three-foot-long key, which only the guards have, to unlock the two massive oak doors with metal bars that separate them from the commoners' side of the prison.

The stone keep has two separate areas for prisoners. The masters' side, consisting of twelve rooms, is for nobles and others who can afford to pay the rent. Their wives or lovers, as long as they pay, are allowed to visit or live on the masters' side. The commoners' side and masters' side are divided by a mud-brick wall, as those on the masters' side refuse to view the conditions of those on the commoners' side. A hallway that the French guards use to patrol the building runs between the two areas.

The six rooms on the commoners' side have few openings for sunlight and fresh air, and visitors are rarely allowed. Clarete is being held in the second room, toward the end of the hall. This room is completely private so the guards can have their way with female prisoners, as can the male prisoners, as long as they pay off the guards. The guards are in the first room, at the very end of the hall, next to Clarete's. A large wooden door inside the room allows them access outside the building. Through this door they bring their ale, their prostitutes, and the perverted who seek evil gratification and are willing to pay for it. Room five: high treason, blasphemy, spying. Room six: murder, witchcraft, alchemy. In the fourth room, next to André's cell, are other prisoners, their bodies squeezed together without space to lie down. These are the walking dead. Their crimes: theft, begging, adultery, gambling, and debt. This is the guards' money room of horrors—where they bring the nobles, the wealthy, the ones who are sexually attracted to men, women, and children or get pleasure from inflicting pain on others, and the ones who have an erotic attraction to corpses or crave any other decadence imaginable. They often take their victims into the Disarming Room, which is completely private. The stone walls, the heavy oak door, and the solid wood shutters that shield the window bars muffle the screams and cries. In this room death is prayed for.

Unless they're rescued by someone who pays to release them, these prisoners eventually starve to death, stumbling around the center post in the room like a broken wagon wheel, all moving in the same direction, around and around, tripping over the dying and decaying bodies that have collapsed. Excrement and dried blood litter the dirt floor. The stink is unfathomable. Black rats by the hundreds run wild, eating the corpses clean in three to four hours. No one remembers the last time the rooms on the commoners' side were cleaned.

Strapped down on a table, André is in the Stone Room, a torture chamber for the unruliest criminals. There's a small hole in the stone wall between his room and Clarete's that André found. It allows them to talk and to hold each other's hand for comfort, a touch of soul in an ocean of hell. A loose rock slides perfectly into the space, concealing it.

"Guards hurt André bad," Pierre-Louis whimpers, as he wipes the tears from his eyes. He has always tried to be strong, envisioning himself as a leader of men, but now, with everything that's happened, he's very confused and afraid of dying. "He tries to help the girl, Clarete," he sputters. "Give her some bread, a little water. This makes the guards mad. They tie his hands behind his back. Throw the other end of the rope over the post in the roof. Tie weights to his ankles to make him fall faster. They drop him from the roof. Pull the rope tight just before his feet hit the ground. It sounded as if all the bones in his body broke. They do bad things to the girl…very bad. They take all her clothes away. Always watching her. They wait till she shits. Then they burn the shit red-hot…make her sit on it so Satan can't have babies with her. The royal guards drink too much ale…talk loud so I hear all this."

"André and Clarete," Pierre-Louis continues, pointing to the other side of the jail. "I hear them crying. One time I gets close. Guards not watching. I tries to speak to them, but it no good. I think Claude done all this. André overhear him betray all the Knights Templar—even you, Jacques de Molay. Claude betray even you. André hear all this."

Listening to Pierre-Louis's nervous yapping and the reminder of Claude's betrayal enrages Jacques, and he slams both of his fists into the metal bars of the two huge, wooden hallway doors between the Disarming Room and the commoners' side of the keep, again and again until the bars bend back. How could he have so misjudged Claude all these years? Several of Jacques's closest friends didn't trust him, yet he wouldn't listen to them. Now they're all dead. He can't bring back his friends or the Knights Templar, but he will kill Claude—or die trying.

Jacques grabs the large door handles, one in each hand, and effort-lessly rips the heavy doors away from their hinges, heaving one and then the other, sending them banging and crashing down the hall. He no longer seeks to be discreet. A battle is what's needed. The war with humans has begun. Claude will be the first to die. Jacques bends over and draws a deep line across the stone floor with his fingernail. A mark for eternity. A low moaning escapes from Pierre-Louis. The scratching of Jacques's fingernail sends shivers through his body. Everyone knows Jacques de Molay is a big, strong man, but how did he tear off the doors so easily?

After hearing the racket, two royal guards rush down the hallway with swords drawn. Jacques meets them and rips their arms from their shoulders and tears off their heads. Terrified, Pierre-Louis backs away as the crotch of his pants becomes wet. The last time he peed in them, it was from too much ale.

Jacques, holding Pierre-Louis, bites his neck. Pierre-Louis struggles briefly but lacks the strength to resist. Jacques wants him on his side, a vampire who will sacrifice all for the clan and not betray him. Pierre-Louis passes out from the blood loss.

"Rest, Monsieur Pierre-Louis." Jacques lays him on the filthy floor. "Your new life will be so much better than the old."

Jacques's keen ears follow the cries of André and Clarete, and he finds them immediately. All the other guards are at the party. After breaking the lock, he yanks the rusted gate open.

Clarete, eyes closed, huddles in a corner of the room with her arms wrapped tightly around her battered, blood-covered, naked body. Her tears have long since dried away. Again and again she has prayed for the salvation of death, but God has not listened.

"Clarete…" Jacques kneels next to her. "It is me, Jacques de Molay."

"Jacques," she moans, opening her eyes, blinking, attempting to focus them. The only light in the room comes from outside through a small gap in the mud blocks near a corner of the ceiling. "Jacques," she murmurs. "All say you are dead. Can it really be you?"

He takes off his jacket and covers her.

"Look," she whimpers, thrusting her head toward him to show him her scalp, which displays a map of scars from when the guards used a large, dull blade to carve it and tear the hair from her head. "They pissed on me too," she says, her body shaking as she recalls the trauma. "They beat me and called me a filthy trull. They even shaved off my eyebrows," she says. "My beautiful eyebrows." She runs her hand over the thin scabs above her eyes. "A great man," she says, weeping, "will never mix a magic potion and spread it all over my face and body now." Her cries swirl into heart-churning sobs. "I'll never be an admired lady and live forever." Struggling, she manages to pull herself to her feet and places her hand on the back of Jacques's neck so she can feel his Rider of the Sun birthmark. When they were children, whenever she had the opportunity to run her hand over it, the remarkable warmth of the birthmark made her feel secure. To touch it was a brief escape from an uncaring world to love and companionship.

Staring hypnotically into her beautiful but sad, hazel-brown eyes, Jacques leans in and gently bites her neck. Their blood mixes slowly, building her strength, attaching her spirit forever to his. He kisses her forehead while running the back of his hand across her cheek. "Rest. Your life as a vampire will be better than your life as a human."

Pierre-Louis is in a daze as he stumbles down the keep's corridor, his vampire gifts proliferate throughout his body. He reaches André's holding cell and manages to yank open the door. His body is acclimating to Jacques's potent blood assimilating with his. He struggles to process the sight of his friend slipping in and out of consciousness on the other side of the room. André is lying on a table encrusted with human remains and excrement, his hands tied behind his back. His shoulders are dislocated, his wrists broken, the lower part of his belly slit open. Several feet of his intestines are exposed, pulled out of his body and stretched onto a small wooden wheel fixed above him. Insects cover his face and belly and crawl inside all the open cavities, blackening his organs. "Poor André!" Pierre-Louis wails. "He no longer be able to drink the ale, eat the pork chop. Poor André." Feeling a whoosh of air, he glances over his right shoulder and sees Jacques standing next to him.

The other prisoners, peering through the metal bars positioned in the stone walls, beg Jacques and Pierre-Louis for food, for help, for freedom, anything. Their arms are raised above their heads, their moans and screams of pain deafening. It won't be long before the royal guards respond to the disturbance.

Jacques moves swiftly from Clarete to André, his blood supercharging their bodies. He watches as André's tortured intestines begin to wiggle, jiggle, twitch, and worm back into his body. The jagged gash from his chest to his belly button closes up and regenerates smooth flesh. These three and Margaret are the beginning of Jacques's army, the undying force of darkness, humanity's most terrifying nightmare. Their legions will grow so powerful that the human race will be pushed to the brink of extinction, living in fear, subsisting as primitives. Suffering, remorse, terror—the list goes on; Jacques is unmoved by the misery. He and his army will have their retribution. It will start here, tonight, at King Philip's summer palace. He releases all the captives, most of whom are diseased and starving. Then he walks up to the leather-covered oak door at the end of the corridor that leads outside. He kicks it forcefully, smashing it off its hinges.

The prisoners wander toward the light and the music, gorging themselves on the food and wine until they puke it up. The guards, using their swords as battle-axes, attack them mercilessly. The lavish party transforms into a landscape of gore and butchered bodies.

André snaps his rope bindings and, with his newfound strength, leaps from the table. Pierre-Louis catches him in midair and embraces him. Clarete joins them. The transformation is amazing; her formerly ravaged body is again beautiful and vibrant.

Mithras, is the vampire god of the entire world. He has churned into his searing pot of dark life the essence of the greatest predators, the deadliest creatures of the animal world. He has mixed these fearsome ingredients together to create the ultimate killer: the vampire.

Neither Clarete, nor André, nor Pierre-Louis understands the changes they're experiencing. They feel powerful but have yet to discover their uncanny new skills. They will hunt with the stealth of a tarantula and the speed and ferocity of the black mamba snake. Their jaws and teeth are wicked, like those of a piranha. They will join forces with one another in a natural pack, communicating through posture, scent, and voice with the cohesiveness of a family of wolves. Their loyalty will always be to Jacques because he is their father, their creator. These new, loftier, animalistic feelings have left them confused, although they do realize they are different now. Over time they will realize how much.

André and Pierre-Louis don't receive the gift of brilliance that is common among vampires. Even Mother Nature has her limits.

Jacques knows all who are in attendance at the lavish ball. In his anger toward Claude, he makes plans for the vampires to take over France, beginning at this ball. Pierre-Louis, André, and Clarete, like vultures, will pick those traveling alone, identifying them by the family shield carved into the side of their carriage. Those with castles and wealth who won't be missed right away will be the first. Jacques wants the power and prestige of the wealthy in order to grow his clan.

Clarete will be the bait, as she is now more alluring than ever. Her breasts, face, neck, and hands have gained an unnatural, celestial glow, accented by her long dark-brown hair and hazel brown eyes that seem to change colors depending on the light. Her vampire characteristics cause her to be alive to an unusual measure. The corners of her eyes and mouth don't appear to have an outline, and she's lost that mesmerizing smile. Like a wolf, her eyes have a fixed gaze. Silent communication now will be the mainstay of their lives.

Most of the nobles will be drunk, others fat, and all pompous. None will be expecting the beautiful, naked woman in the moonlight, and none will be expecting the horrors that will befall them. Pierre-Louis and André lie in wait in the woods. Once Clarete has the nobles' attention, they will do the rest.

Jacques has been away from Margaret for too long. He hopes she responded to his earlier directions and is still in the maze where he left her. After making sure she's safe, he'll find Claude and destroy him. He transforms into a proud, imposing, blue wolf with a streak of gray hair that starts at his left eye and shoots down his back; then he races off into the night.

Pierre-Louis, André, and Clarete pursue Jacques for a short distance and then, against Clarete's better judgment, hole up in a thicket of trees to watch the orchestra. The intoxicating music captivates them. Although Pierre-Louis and André are oblivious, Clarete notices a man and a woman of nobility talking and laughing loudly a short distance away. From their actions it's obvious that both are drunk. Sensing that this is a perfect time for Pierre-Louis and André to make their first kills, Clarete nudges both of them to attract their attention. They both ignore her, so she pushes them. Both of them take one step ahead but still ignore her. Frustrated, she grabs their heads and turns them so they're both looking directly at the man and women. She gives them a hard push forward and crosses her claws. *One can always hope*, she thinks.

The woman stumbles and almost falls, but the man catches her in his arms. She giggles and holds on to him for support. He tries to pull her close and kiss her, but she resists. "No, no, no…" She giggles while shaking her finger and pulling away from him. She takes a couple of steps but stumbles and falls to the grass. The man makes a futile attempt to catch her. Still giggling, the woman manages to crawl onto her hands and knees. "Don't sneak up behind me now," she says.

André strikes first, grabbing the man and sinking his fangs into his neck. He's a heavyset fellow and tries to struggle and break away, but he's helpless. While sucking his blood, André, like a lion, drags his prey into the cover and safety of the trees. All the ale the man drank cascades through André's bloodstream, and he feels a buzz coming on. He relishes his good fortune.

Pierre-Louis, forever the gentleman, reaches down and helps the lady up. She's still giggling and so drunk that at first she doesn't realize he's not her companion. Pierre-Louis easily lifts her into his arms. "Who...who are you?" she asks.

Pierre-Louis slides his tongue slowly across her neck, tasting the moisture on her skin, moaning with pleasure. "You've drunk red wine," he murmurs. "The Bordeaux and the Burgundies. You've drunk them all tonight. Oh, what a beautiful lass you are. Exquisite taste. Only on rare occasions have I had the pleasure of drinking such nectar of the vines."

"Who are you?" she asks again, sighing while running her hand through the sides of his mangy, scraggly, black hair. "So strong, such thick hair. Thank you for rescuing me from that fat creep. He's been following me all night. I wish it weren't so dark...so I could see you. I'll bet you're a handsome devil, aren't you?" She runs her hand over the top of his bald head, hesitates, and then giggles. "Where did the rest of your hair go?"

A French woman is speaking to him in French, and he could sure use a drink. Pierre-Louis grabs the woman's head and, after lifting it up to his, sinks his fangs into the soft flesh of her neck. She's whimpers softly, like a cat in pain. He continues to suck the alcohol-infused blood from her body until she's lifeless; then he gently lays her on the ground.

Clarete, Pierre-Louis, and André hear distant shouting. A couple of cooks from the summer palace, stumbling about in the carnage left by King Philip's knights and the escaped prisoners, have discovered the dismembered bodies of the royal guards. They also find that the commoners' side of the prison is empty. "Enemies of France!" they're shouting.

"Enemies of France!" Men gather in front of the château and form hunting parties.

"Let's go." Clarete grabs Pierre-Louis and André and shoves them ahead of her. "You've feasted enough tonight. All that wine and beer mixed in your blood can't be good for you. I've been around a lot of drunks. Nothing good ever comes of it. We need to go before they find us."

"I was thinking an after-dinner drink." Pierre-Louis pulls his arm away from her and points at a carriage that's being boarded by the high priestess of the god, Mithras, and three of her female assistants. Lifting his head and raising his arms high, he stares at the full moon overhead. He concentrates on it as only an animal of the night can. He trembles, and then convulsions wrack his body. His clothes tear away as he transforms.

Four horses pull the carriage away from the château.

When nature dictates, you are what you are, regardless of the animal your physical being assumes. Pierre-Louis has metamorphosed into a homely, dark-brown wolf with mangy, unkempt hair and a butt that's too large for his thin body. He gives chase, cutting across the French countryside. His strides aren't long, graceful, and majestic, covering several feet at a time, but short, choppy, and slightly sideways from his lack of natural grace and his overindulgence in wine.

As a wolf, André has long, brown hair, short legs, a tiny butt, a potbelly, a bulbous nose, heavy jowls, and a mouthful of blackened, rotting teeth. He resembles a bulldog more than a wolf. Howling at the moon, he bounds after Pierre-Louis.

Clarete shakes her head in disbelief and, lifting her arms over her head, stares at the moon and transforms into a magnificent wolf with velvety gray hair, accented by a streak of blond under each eye, as well as a sleek body built for speed. Stretching out, she races after the others.

André, head down, chases the carriage down the dirt road. Clarete, trying to catch up, is several yards behind him but has passed Pierre-Louis. The wine is taking its toll on him. She's fast, but André has too much of a lead on her. The horses pulling the carriage sense the pursuers and quicken their pace. The driver, realizing something is wrong—terribly wrong—glances over his shoulder and sees the dark outline of a wolf. Shouting commands at his four charging steeds, the frightened man whips them, pressing them on.

The four women are being tossed about inside the carriage. Hearing their driver's panicky outbursts, two of them look outside to see what's causing the uproar. André is so close to the carriage they can almost touch him. The women scream and slap the sides of the carriage, crying for the driver to go faster.

André leaps for the back of the carriage and turns into a vampire just as he reaches it. However, the alcohol in his body affects his ability to change, and one appendage remains a paw. He struggles to hold on to the carriage railing with his one good hand while scratching the wood with the other, attempting to get a grip. Caught up in the excitement of the chase, Clarete, in full stride, narrows the gap between them.

The six French horsemen who were chasing Jacques earlier in the night, ride out of the woods and onto the dirt road behind Clarete. She stops, turns, and watches them. They're advancing straight toward her, letting their horses out, pushing them to a hard gallop. The carriage is disappearing into the darkness. Clarete hesitates and then charges at the riders, hoping to distract them. It's the only way to save André. The riders close in on her. At the last moment, seconds before the horses trample her under their hooves, she darts off the road into the safety of the woods. Two of the riders separate from the group and follow her.

André stands on top of the carriage, his long, brown hair blowing in the wind. Defiant, he raises his fist in the air at the riders and then transforms into a bat. He tries to fly away, but his wolf's paw won't morph into a wing, and he crashes into the road. The riders cautiously walk their horses forward and encircle him. André tries to fly, to run, but he's trapped. His wolf's paw is much too large for his small bat body to drag on the ground, much less fly with.

The carriage skids to a stop, and the high priestess emerges. She holds a gold shield in her hand and wears a dark-red robe, a gold belt, and a sky-blue cape with white stars. The front of her robe is adorned with a tan, lion-headed figure standing on an image of the sun with crossed circles. She cautiously picks up André, who is still in bat form, and holds him high. The riders, seeing his deformity, laugh and torment him. For more years than they can remember, they've been hunting witches and demons for the church of Mithras, but never have they seen anything like this.

"And to think we were frightened of this pathetic creature," the priestess says, shaking André like a rattle. "So stupid. We must find de Molay and get the Templar treasure for Mithras. Jacques de Molay lives. This! This!" She gives André another shake, drops him to the ground, and climbs back inside the carriage. "Kill it," she hollers as the carriage pulls away.

Circling him, the riders cut the air with their whips, tearing gashes across André's body. The horses throw their heads and paw the ground. In seconds, Andre will be stomped to death under their hooves. While he's breathing in dust and the stench of his own blood, he can't help wonder why there's never a drink around when you could really use one.

Farther down the road, Pierre-Louis howls at the reddish-orange full moon and trots into view, momentarily distracting the riders. Clarete leaps out of the woods, dodges between the horses, and scoops André up in her mouth. Eluding another horse, she vanishes into the cover of the woods on the other side of the road. The infuriated riders curse the night and chase after her.

The moon is beginning to fade over the horizon. In a couple of hours, the world will be graced by the radiance of the sun and a new day. A gorgeous, velvety gray wolf with a streak of blond fur under each eye trots gracefully across the French countryside. A bat rides on the back of her neck, holding on to her hair with one webbed limb while an enormous wolf's paw dangles from his other side. Pierre-Louis, a short distance behind, lifts his furry leg and pees on a bush.

6

MARGARET TURNS THE BUTCHER

Claude, mortally wounded, gasps for breath. An arrow from the cross-bow tore through the muscles in his shoulder and penetrated his lung. With blood soaking his surcoat, he drags his sword in one hand and with the other supports a torch as he winds his way down a hallway and into a trophy room. Taxidermied mounts of antlered red deer and wild boar, along with wolf hides from all parts of the known world, line the exquisitely decorated walls. A wooden plaque with hand-carved instructions for how to hunt unicorns hangs over the massive fieldstone fireplace. Pushing on the rustic, oak beam mantel, the wall swings open. Struggling from his wounds, he finds his way behind the fireplace and stumbles down a wooden staircase that leads to the keep. Along the way he almost falls several times. His blood-starved, weakened body wants to give up. It's only his sheer determination and brute strength that keep him going. If he's going to die, he will have company.

Prisoners have been held in the keep since the castle was built. Rumor has it that it often served as Claude de Lavoe's playpen. Jacques heard whispers about Claude's unusual talents, but in his position as Grand Master, Jacques was off to other parts of Christendom so often that he was rarely at the castle. Besides, everyone knew that if Claude found out that anyone had told Jacques, Claude would have butchered them.

For many years, hideous torture was the way of life here. Prisoners guilty of nothing more than poverty or hunger were starved to death on the bread-and-water diet. Their bodies were so ravaged that they were unable to feed themselves, much less fight others for their miniscule ration of food. Some were shackled and left in isolation to die. These victims were often eaten alive by rats and finished off by parasites and disease. Faces were disfigured, and empty sockets glared where eyes once showed.

Attempting to satisfy his insatiable appetite for inflicting pain, Claude personally rubbed the bottoms of prisoners' feet with fat grease and then held their feet up to the fire, burning them until the bones fell out, leaving them to crawl on all fours. Death was then a blessing. Their bones were picked clean by the rats that littered the floor.

Claude's preferred piece of equipment was the torture rack, which gave him complete control over the prisoner, prolonging the suffering as long as needed to satisfy his perverted sense of gratification. The rope was tied to the wrists and ankles of a prisoner and attached to a roller with a handle at the end of the table. Claude turned the crank at his chosen speed, stretching the legs and arms of the victim. The victims' anguished cries aroused him, and he kissed their cheeks and ran his tongue along their ears, whispering obscenities as they begged for mercy. He turned the crank until the cartilage in their joints cracked and they screamed and thrashed their heads and begged for him to stop. Instead he kissed them passionately on the face, neck, and body, crying with them, his tears mingling with theirs. He greeted their pain like a great love. When he kicked a lever on the torture rack, wooden ratchets slapped over the cogs. The rack cranked upward into place, banging the victim's body back and forth, snapping cartilage and ligaments, pulling bones from their sockets. Claude's ecstatic screams echoed their horrific cries of death, and with each death, he felt a great loneliness.

Now Claude struggles down a passageway that runs beneath the castle. Breathing laboriously, he stops and leans against an impenetrable, rust-covered steel door. He can't rest; King Philip's knights are right behind him. After taking a key from his wide leather belt, he unlocks the door and stumbles inside. He holds up his torch. The light shines across the large dusty room, revealing treasure chests of gold coins and fine jewels stolen from the people he has tortured and killed over the years. This room represents a lifetime of work—false promises of freedom to his victims if they told him where their wealth was hidden. And he always ensured their journey to death was longer and more agonizing when they finally did.

He stumbles through the treasure room and into a burial crypt where several bodies of Knights Templar have been laid to rest. Rotting, wooden platforms with dead and decomposing bodies are stacked one on top of the other. *I will die here*, he decides, *among other Knights Templar.*

He leans on his sword for support and struggles to hold up the torch, his wounds forcing him to cry out in pain. "What was that?" he murmurs. He swears he heard something. Faint, but it was there. With a shaky arm, he holds the torch up higher. "Who goes there?" Only he knows of this room; he killed the craftsmen after they finished building it. A woman's voice whispers from a far, dark side of the room. For the first time, as his life reaches the end of the road, Claude knows fear but only for himself. He hasn't one regret for the evil he's inflicted upon humanity.

"Claude, Claude de Lavoe, I have walked the keep and seen your work," a veiled voice coos. "Your life is ending. Do you wish to sleep with the dead or live with the undead, with Jacques de Molay? You choose. I can grant either."

Recognizing Margaret's voice but feeling it somehow is not her own, Claude collapses to his knees, his strength failing. Pleading for his life, he lies. "Yes, yes, what you speak is true. I did what I had to do. My treasure here…" he stammers. "I never told anyone about it." He believes that if he can convince this evil, this devilish being, this living darkness to let him live, he can manipulate Margaret into revealing the hiding place of the Templar treasure and the Ark of the Covenant. She must know where they're hidden. "I've tortured and killed people, yes, yes," Claude confesses, "to protect the order…to protect Jacques. I saved him from the monks of Vosne-Romanée when they plotted to kill him. I killed Geoffroi de Charny when I found out he had betrayed Jacques. I tried to save him," he pleads, "from King Philip. Jacques is a Templar like me. We lived together, fought together. I want to live!" Collapsing, he drops the torch, and the room darkens with the dying light.

The shadowed outline of a woman dressed in a sleek, white nightgown quietly moves across the floor until she stands over him. Her body is silhouetted in the last whispers of the flame's light. She crouches and, holding Claude's head in the palm of her hand, lifts it and stares at him with haunting brown eyes. She smells the skin on his neck. Her lips are pressed together, almost smiling. Then she licks them and touches the tips of her fangs with her tongue. She knows Claude will be attached to her forever. He's a determined man, never detoured, and he always gets what he wants. Yet because of her love for Jacques, she's resolute in believing she's strong enough to resist his beastly physical advances. Also he's Jacques's best friend; Jacques will be pleased with her for turning him.

The torch flickers a couple of times and then goes out, leaving the room in pitch-darkness.

7

BEWARE THE MAZE

Claude and Margaret have killed more than a hundred of King Philip's knights, drinking their blood, moving in their midst quickly from one to another. Some they enjoyed for only a couple of drinks; others they sucked dry while holding their next victim captive. The louder the screams of terror, the more violently they hunt. They stalk their victims, playing with them, choosing the time and place for each kill. One hides in wait while the other pursues the confused, disoriented knights, chasing them, herding them into the maze like cattle to slaughter.

Terror-stricken knights, pushing and shoving, attempt to escape Claude and Margaret, crowding inside the walls at the entrance to the maze. They're enraptured by the pulsating, bluish glow of the phosphorescent worms. The glowworms drop from the stone ceiling and land on the knights, covering them, making their uniforms glow. The knights are caught up in the rapture of it all, and a soothing, relaxing feeling overcomes them. But the worms are able to sense the knights' compulsion to kill, so they become this compulsion to kill, boring under the men's skin and penetrating their vital organs. The screaming knights are driven mad, fighting and clawing at one another, running down the stone passageways that lead through the maze, a rectangle with thirty-one inside walls, right corner in, left corner out.

Bisu, the dwarf god, has roamed these halls of stone for more than one hundred fifty years. He was captured in Egypt during the Crusades and brought back to the de Molay castle, where he has lived ever since. He is a grotesque creature, four feet six with an enormous head and oversize features. His eyes are round and yellow, and his blue tongue is as thick and long as a giraffe's. His belly rises from his middle like a large, lonely mountain. Coarse, camel-like, red hair covers his face and hangs from his bloated cheeks to the bottom of his chin, rolling under his neck and lying on his shoulders in a matted blanket. The Dark Shadow Gods of ancient Egypt carved exquisite tattoos of the world's deadliest creatures into his molten-gray skin: snakes, jellyfish, piranhas, spiders, frogs, octopi, lizards, bears, wolves, bats, birds of prey, crocodiles, alligators, lions, tigers, worms, wasps, ants, mosquitoes, and hornets. His bald head is covered with yellow spaghetti-like lines; the nests of glowworms lie just under the surface of his skin. A forty-foot, two-thousand-pound anaconda, the Snake Guard of Darkness, is the force of chaos, an ancient, canary-yellow serpent with an orange-tinted head and cream-colored belly. The snake's massive head and tongue cover the toes and the right foot on Bisu's body and then wrap around his ankle, covering his right leg, encompassing his ass and thighs, and running down his left leg. The tip of its tail covers Bisu's left foot.

Hearing the cries of the approaching French knights, Bisu kneels on the ground and lifts his hands in the air. His tattoos rip from his body, leaving seeping wounds. They morph from tiny drawings into life-size creatures and rush into the maze. Wasps and hornets burst from the teardrop nests on the sides of his neck into a buzzing swarm. Spitting cobras and vipers disappear into the rock walls. By the hundreds, mosquitoes, flies, spiders, scorpions, and poisonous frogs spring from their painted nests on Bisu's hideous skin and blacken the inside of the maze.

The more creatures Bisu sends to attack his enemies, however, the weaker he becomes. He'll heal when the beasts return to their nesting places. If they don't return, he'll die. Finally he sends out packs of black rats from their dens in the lower-leaf litter of the forest habitat and the tombs and pyramids of ancient Egypt. This is the cleaning crew that will devour the flesh from the knights, leaving nothing but bones.

The anaconda, the Snake Guard of Darkness, is so large—and the mutilation of Bisu's body so great when it leaves him—that he can only send it away by itself; however, he holds the glowworms back. There are already so many in the maze that a few more won't make a difference.

The lake where the castle sits backs up into areas farther down some of the paths in the maze, filling them waist-deep with water. Intermingled with Bisu's creatures, spiders, various venomous snakes, and eels imported from exotic places make their way out of the cracks and crevices and slip into the water, their sheer numbers making the water boil. The snakes and eels attach to exposed areas of the fleeing men's bodies and crawl inside any exposed orifice—eyes, nose, ears—and feed on the flesh, driving the men insane.

The outside walls of the maze have small crawlspaces that begin half-way to the ceiling, built to provide the lost with a false sense of freedom. The panic-driven knights climb through the crawl spaces thinking they've discovered a way to safety. Thousands of flesh-eating vampire bats live in the deep caverns that follow where these walls of despair lead. The terrified knights hear the rustling of their wings, a deafening noise. The bats' black bodies look like a violent thunderstorm crashing toward them. The swarming bats blanket the screaming knights, sucking them dry of blood. Hundreds die inside the deadly, unrepentant walls.

Claude, using his great strength, is ripping out throats, breaking necks. The passageways are awash in blood. He transforms several knights into ghastly, nightmarish, deformed beings with crippled bodies and torn faces. He's building his clan, his followers. These living dead are physical reflections of his unchecked wickedness, sexual proclivities, sadistic compulsions, and narcissistic self-absorption; they are his Demons of Distortion.

Eventually his butchery stifles Margaret's spirit. Buried inside her is a kernel of something warm and alive, a nugget of love hidden deep within the recesses of the vampire embodiment. An echo of what she once was touches her heart, and she retreats to her room in the castle.

The glowworms, sensing Claude's great evil, end their attacks against King Philip's knights; combine their bodies into large, yellow, ultraviolet, pulsating balls that radiate light; and hurtle through the passageways of the maze toward him. His ruthless perversions and blooming hatred, the grotesque butchering, and the impaling of King Philip's knights—these are an intense magnetic force that attracts them.

The massive impact of the glowworm balls sends Claude crashing back-ward into the walls of the maze. The worms cover his body, crawling into his nose and ears and blanketing his eyes, his mouth, any orifice they can find. As he struggles to stand, his ear-piercing cries of pain rip through the passageways as he tears at the glowworms. He can feel them, the parasites beginning to eat, their sharp teeth burrowing into his skin, the radiation from their squirming goo burning his flesh. Behind him he sees a large wave of glowworms moving toward him. Even Claude, with all his vampire gifts, his iron skin, his acidic blood that razes any invading species, feels excruciating pain. Regaining his self-control, he races through one passageway and then another and another and out of the maze, tearing the worms off his flesh, rubbing his back against the stone walls like an itchy bull, peeling in disgust the remaining glowworms from his body. The damage to his face has been done, however. It's deeply pitted with large, black pockmarks and jagged scars, a curse to his formerly rugged good looks. Claude, the indestructible alpha vampire, has tasted mortality.

Moving through the rest of the castle, Claude, in his repugnance, continues his slaughter of King Philip's knights; he doesn't need Margaret for this.

The remaining knights flee the castle. King Philip realizes something has gone terribly wrong and positions himself in front of them in hopes of slowing their retreat. His stallion rears up, pawing the air, hooves flashing. It's hopeless.

—✠—

When Jacques returns to the de Molay castle, he sees more dead French knights than he would have thought, but he also has been gone for some time and knew Margaret wouldn't wait for him. He checks her room first; after a night of feasting, she will want to rest. He finds her seductively lying on the divan. Her lips, the edges of her cheeks, and the front of her dress are stained with blood.

"I was gone too long." He sits on the side of the bed next to her and runs his hand through her thick, red hair. "I was concerned about you." He leans over and kisses her forehead. The killing of Claude will have to wait.

Margaret suggestively runs her hand across one breast and down her side. Never has it felt so good to be in control. Jacques can smell her; his nostrils flare. He grabs her, lifts her up to him, and kisses her deeply, sucking the blood from her fangs, relishing her sweetness, each swallow fueling their passions. She lays her head back, daring him to bite, to drink her blood. She grabs his hair, wraps it around her hand in a fist, and yanks his head down. She pushes his head against her neck and then pulls it down to her breasts. They madly scratch, claw, and bite, ripping flesh from each other's naked bodies.

Their lovemaking burns through the night. It will be the last time either will feel the moisture of sweat on their skin.

"Come." Jacques takes Margaret's hand. "We must rest somewhere safe." He sees more dead bodies along the way but believes it's only Margaret's work. He's concerned that he hasn't seen or heard any of King Philip's knights, but sunlight is already pressing on the morning, and they need to bed down. He'll search the castle tomorrow night.

They cross the courtyard to the white-marble chapel of the Knights Templar. Here they were always able to worship without disturbance from outsiders. The building is circular, the white-marble exterior polished to a high glisten. Three ornamental lakes, octagon shaped with exceptional rock-work, decorate the landscape. Weeping willows hug the manicured grassy banks, dipping their long branches into the serene ponds, home to water lilies, perch, trout, and carp. Flowered shrubs shelter the firecrests and wood larks as well as the roses. Daffodils, lilacs, dwarf shrubs, and other bushes whisper enchantment.

The lakes are fed by a channel of water that leads to the sea; stunning, bluish-green waterfalls bedeck each of them. Each lake boasts oak, beech, and holly trees strewn among violets, irises, and lilies, and the statues of two Knights Templar guard each body of water. The Templar cross, in crushed rubies, is inlaid on the blades of their silver swords, while the tops of their silver shields and breastplates are outlined with black mother-of-pearl highlights. One knight of each pair has outstretched arms, and both statues are accompanied by a bronze war-horse, symbolizing the order's vow of poverty.

Arched stone doors lead to rooms with vaulted ceilings and walls adorned with panel paintings and frescoes of ships, Knights Templar in battle, and the Blessed Virgin Mary holding the Christ child. Metal, camel-shaped incense burners sit on gold stands, their aromatic fragrance permeating the rooms. Jacques's uncle, Master de Lezines, and other masters of the de Molay house—all of whom were his ancestors—lie in crypts in the mausoleum attached to the chapel. At night the white structure is illuminated with countless lamps and torches, their luminosity radiating hope and sanctuary for the weary and lost.

King Philip and his retreating, humiliated army move by, leaving plenty of berth between themselves and the chapel, believing any disturbance of the dead will leave them cursed, mad—perhaps even suicidal.

Jacques takes Margaret's hand and leads her into the Room of Penitence. It is here where the Knights Templar have sought absolution for their sins, suffering for their imperfections. Many have whipped themselves with leather straps until their naked bodies brimmed with blood—only then can they can bring themselves to believe God has forgiven their iniquities.

A statue of a Knight Templar dressed for battle stands against one of the walls. The knight wears his chain-mail shirt, with its long chain-mail sleeves, hand coverings, leggings, and hood, as well as shoes covered with chain mail. Over his armor is a white cloth surcoat adorned with a red cross so he can easily be identified in battle. On his waist hangs a great helm sword in a shiny brass scabbard.

A life-size ivory statue of the Crucifixion, with Jesus and the two thieves hanging on crosses, is displayed behind a gold-plated altar with ivory legs. Jacques pushes a concealed release on the statue, sliding it back on the floor and revealing a priest hole. He and Margaret follow the spider web–infested, chiseled-stone stairway to a chamber with ice-blue granite walls and floors.

Jacques pulls a heavy iron chain that hangs from the ceiling and watches as the statue slides back into place, enclosing them in the chamber. He locks the chain in position so the priest hole can't be opened from above. Then he walks over and taps one of the granite slabs. "Behind this is an underground passageway back to the castle," he tells Margaret. "Just push here, and it swings open. The Egyptians didn't forget anything."

He points to two crypts—one black, one red—on the floor. "Master de Lezines had these made for me and whomever I eventually would marry. He always planned ahead. He wanted to make sure all the de Molay masters were buried here. He had a friend, a stone maker and craftsman, chisel them out of solid granite. Yours is the red one. You will sleep here, my love."

"I turned Claude," she suddenly says, while Jacques is pushing open the lid. "He was wounded, dying, looking for you."

"You did what?" Jacques shouts angrily. "You turned Claude? Claude the Butcher! He betrayed us. He betrayed the Knights Templar. He destroyed all that was sacred to us. *I* turned *you*. You have my blood in your body. You are mine." He grabs her by the shoulders. "I gave you eternal life."

"Please, please, Jacques, you're hurting me!" Margaret cries. "He's always been your closest friend. I thought…I thought I was helping you. I thought it would make you happy. I'm sorry. I'm—"

"He's no one's friend," he spits out, before releasing her. "You should have let him die. Now he has your blood in his body—he's attached to you. Claude will stop at nothing until he has you all to himself. This will never go away—*never*—until either Claude or I dies. It's the only way it can be resolved. You are the trophy." He opens the lid on the coffin. "Lie down now. Rest," he says, helping her inside. Then he pushes the lid shut.

Now Jacques knows why he saw so many dead bodies, why King Philip's army was retreating. Margaret had help. Claude will be looking for the Templar treasure, and Jacques will have to challenge him. He'll have to kill him—but how? "There's a lot to do tomorrow night," he mutters to the silence, before crawling into his casket and sliding the lid shut.

Bisu drops to his knees on the stone floor of the maze, the ragged skin around his open wounds oozing blood and pus. He lets out a low moan and raises his arms—a call to the creatures of his skin. They return one by one, the snakes and birds and fierce cats reduced to ink drawings as they slap, slap, slap to their home on his flesh. The beasts have fed well on King Philip's defeated knights, and they rest easily—and as they rest, Bisu heals and regains his strength.

Although Bisu is a born killer, he kills to live, like a bear or wolf. He is the guardian of the nests on his flesh and will risk all to protect his creatures. Abandoned as a baby, he was placed, screaming, by the Dark

Shadow Gods of ancient Egypt, into a pool of boiling water mixed with dried blood, the graveyard dust of lost empires, and the mummified flesh of wild animals. To these antediluvian ingredients, they added herbs, spices, and precious stones. The gods then carefully brought the water to a precise boil, uttering spells so the creatures that grew from the baby's skin could travel in the worlds of both the living and the dead. These creatures must return to their nests on his body regularly so that they may survive. In this perfectly symbiotic sharing of skin, Bisu is as dependent on these creatures as they are on him. Upon returning well fed, they revitalize the dwarf god.

Mithras, the White Wolf, the Ghost Child, captured Bisu, his centuries-old foe, in Egypt decades ago. Using unearthly secrets that were hidden by the occult gods in forgotten cities, lost to the desert's ever-shifting sands, Mithras, commanded the assistance of gigantic, yellow-and-beige, camel spiders. They speedily wove adhesive strands of silk into threads of sticky spider webs, which they then wove into large sheets.

These bloodthirsty, venomous, shadow chasers—predators of the desert—attacked an unsuspecting Bisu in the pitch-darkness of an underground cavern. Several charged him, delivering painful bites with their chopping jaws, distracting him, while others dropped the woven sheets of sticky webbing over him. Quickly racing around him, they wrapped him tightly in a viscid, gooey, impenetrable cocoon, rendering him and all his sycophant creatures helpless. They chained him to the floor of a prison wagon, covering his head in a camel- leather bag so he could neither see nor hear. Mithras, took Bisu to Jerusalem to help him defeat the French and German knights and win the battle for Damascus. Once the battle for Damascus was over, he planned on killing Bisu, to butcher him like a hog and feed his flesh to the spiders.

The French and German crusaders, in alliance with Jerusalem, failed to conquer Damascus, ending the Second Crusade. Bisu was rescued by Lord Guarin de Molay with the help of Jude the Great and several Knights Templar. He was then taken to the de Molay castle in France, where he now protects the maze. Bisu is loyal to his creatures, Jacques de Molay, and Jude. Nothing else matters. Life to him is a whisper's fading breath, death a vanishing shadow.

8

SOMETHING NOT QUITE FROZEN

Still seething while Margaret follows him, Jacques glances up at the heavy, blue, night sky. A nearly full, yellow moon glowers at the countryside. An owl lifts its wings and flies over the castle walls. The crickets are louder than usual; perhaps they're trying to warn him. He lifts a torch from a stand, its flame barely licking the air, and walks around the outside of the chapel, lighting the few lanterns that still have oil. He wishes there were more, but at least he will be able to see their brilliance. "This will have to do." He scowls as his torch flickers out before he tosses it away, scaring a pheasant running through the tall grass.

"Why did you light the lanterns?" Margaret asks. "I don't understand."

"This may be the last time I witness the beauty of this place. This night—I may be the last of my family to walk this ground. Three hundred years—the de Molay house."

"Please, Jacques, don't fight Claude," she pleads. "He'll listen to me. Although my blood is in his veins, I love *you*."

"No." Jacques holds up his hand. "A de Molay never runs from a battle. My family is bound by honor."

Margaret is silent. Jacques raises his hands above his head and stares at the moon, concentrating. He hasn't told Margaret exactly what he's planning to do. If Claude defeats him, he doesn't want that butcher to have any reason to take his wickedness out on her. She must be left out of this.

Margaret watches as Jacques shape-shifts into a wolf. His senses of sight, smell, hearing, and taste are dramatically heightened. He trots through the grass to the top of a small rise a short distance away. She wants him to run and hide; she will protect him from Claude. She would do that for him. It's her fault Claude has life, and she feels something akin to shame for the betrayal. *Claude.* Jacques can't defeat him; no one can. She knows what he has become. Only she can protect Jacques from him.

Jacques paces before finding just the right spot on the ground to stand, and then he howls at the moon. It's a long, forlorn, mournful howl, a summons to a life-and-death battle. It's a call to his loyal followers—Clarete, André, and Pierre-Louis—the wolf pack that will hear him and come running. He will need their help tonight to defeat Claude.

Jacques's cries touch something liquid in Margaret, something not quite frozen. She imagines something sad and far away. Is he saying farewell to this place, to all he's ever known? She wonders whether she'll ever see him again, if he'll become a lone wolf, leave, and never be heard from or seen again.

Pierre-Louis and André, in wolf form, sit on their haunches and watch Clarete, who's standing next to a small lake and loathing her unbeautiful appearance. Unfortunately, the water is smooth and infinitely clear. Clarete's reflection is lucid and bright in the light of the moon. The tapping of a woodpecker on a black pine tree echoes loudly. Wistful, she slowly flicks her tail a couple of times and walks away.

Clarete is the hunter in this wolf pack, exceptionally skilled at tracking prey, never confused by the terrain, focused. She is humble about her success, however, and never takes a position she can't defend. One mistake, she knows, can cost all of them their lives. Her philosophy, learned in debtors' prison, is this: "Always take the pain to gain life."

Jacques's howls for assistance tear through the night, and the wolves lift their heads high and listen. Several frightened geese paddle toward the bank on the other side of the lake. The three wolves have been hunting down King Philip's knights and turning them. It was Clarete's idea—convert the best men in France to their ranks, and the vampires will be indestructible.

She growls for Pierre-Louis and André to follow her. It's a long way across the rolling countryside to the Templar castle.

Putting her gorgeous head down and stretching out, she covers huge swaths of ground with her graceful strides; she hopes she's fast enough to help Jacques defeat Claude. For all of them to live, Claude must be killed. Determined, she'll do it herself if necessary.

—〰—

After Jacques's wavering howls have ended, he trots back down the hill and morphs into a vampire bat. Margaret follows his lead and also transforms into a bat, and the two fly deep into the dark labyrinth of passageways to look for Claude. They eventually find him standing in a cavern that's covered in mosaics and carvings. His clothes, hands, and fingers are covered in dirt. He's been digging away at the stone walls, looking for the secret door that's hidden some distance away at the other end of the chamber. Jacques wonders whether Claude could ever find it, even with his vampire powers.

Four of Claude's Demons of Distortion, their faces and hair splattered with bloody saliva, are fighting over and gorging themselves on the bodies of an unfortunate farmer and his wife who lived a short distance from the castle. Several more of Claude's demons are out hunting. Another five are already dead. They watched Claude transform into a bat and, wanting to follow their master, attempted to do the same. Their grotesque bodies became twisted in the process, and they were thrown into violent convulsions and perished. Claude wanted it that way. Complete control. He is their god, the master of their world. Only he has the power to change.

Alarmed when they see Jacques and Margaret, the demons grunt and slap the dead bodies, possessive of their kills. Claude doesn't turn around but continues to dig. He already knows. His keen hearing picked up Jacques and Margaret's distinctive sound patterns several minutes ago. He's been plotting how he can kill Jacques and have Margaret and the Templar treasure all to himself. He's surprised Jacques found him as quickly as he did. He knew their paths would eventually cross, but Jacques, even as a vampire, is pathetically weak, so it must be pure luck.

Claude believes that he has surprise on his side, that Jacques and Margaret are ignorant of his betrayal. All he must do is be patient, set Jacques up, choose the precise time and place when Jacques least expects it, and kill him. Then his followers can fight over the leftovers. Margaret will be difficult for a while, but he already has hunted with her and has seen her other side. He's watched her lick the blood off flesh and revel in the arousal. Yes, it may take some time, but he knows she'll come around. Claude has ignored their presence long enough and reluctantly turns to greet them, but he's frustrated that his work is being interrupted.

"Jacques, Margaret. At least some of us Knights Templar survived King Philip and his betrayal." He slightly nods, barely acknowledging Margaret's presence. No need to let Jacques know there's anything between them. He guesses Jacques knows Margaret converted him. There was no one else who could, at least to his knowledge. The thought of her lips against Claude's neck must be tearing Jacques apart.

All of Jacques's muscles are vibrating with anticipation, taut, preparing for Claude's next move. He glances at the demons and their butchery. Rats are gathering for the scraps, but getting too close, one quickly becomes a morsel for one of the demons—head, body, and tail.

What Claude has done disgusts Jacques. As part of the animal kingdom, he despises degenerative mutations of any kind. Vampires are supposed to be proud, leaders of the pack, not freaks of nature. He knows the demons' life-spans will be short; he can smell it. They are dying animals, their disfigured bodies fraught with disease.

Margaret looks away from the sight of the demons. She inhales, and they smell like rotting fish. Jacques takes a step back. He knows he's faster than Claude, but in this confined area, he won't be able to move very much. Claude, with his superior size and strength, will have the advantage. Also, including the demons, it's five against one. He hopes Margaret won't try to help him. She must stay neutral. Who knows what madness Claude will try on her?

"You seem uneasy, Jacques." Claude cautiously stands up and steps toward him, pressing him. He senses something is wrong but isn't sure what it is. He entered the subterranean passages and caverns earlier as a bat. He believes the Templar treasure is in this maze, somewhere amid the old, broken wagons and the skeletal remains of slaves. Yet this place may be a diversion; it was almost too easy to find. He knows he'll have to keep Jacques alive long enough to find the hiding place. Grunting, he shakes his head in frustration while thinking, *the old master, Lord Guarin de Molay, who designed the maze, was a genius of confusion. The treasure could be anywhere.*

"It's the new body," Jacques answers. He's surprised Claude hasn't attacked him, but then it dawns on him—only Pierre-Louis and André knew that Claude betrayed Jacques and the other Knights Templar. Claude isn't aware that he knows, which buys Jacques time. "Difficult to adjust to," he says.

One of the demons rips an arm off one of the dead bodies and offers it to Margaret. She cringes in disgust. "I'm leaving," she states, and turns toward the exit.

Claude angrily grabs the demon and rips out its throat. Its body shakes in death throes, splattering yellowish-brown blood on the other three demons. They're momentarily confused—all the dead demon did was offer Margaret their most prized possession: food.

"We'll split the Templar treasure equally." Jacques uses the distraction to revise his strategy. "A new time, a new beginning. Agreed?" He quickly turns and follows Margaret toward the staircase. "You're looking in the wrong place."

Claude is momentarily confused; Jacques gave in too easily. He wanted justification to attack him, but he'll go along with this. If Jacques tries anything, Claude will kill him, feed him to his pets, and take Margaret for himself. He'll return later and resume his search for the treasure. "Agreed," he responds firmly.

Now that one demon has perished, it's now four to one. Margaret won't take either side.

The three remaining demons, dragging the mutilated bodies behind, follow Claude, Jacques, and Margaret. As hideous as the demons are—hairless, with sallow skin, black eyes, puffy gray lips, and long red fangs like those of a saber-toothed tiger—they're a reflection of Claude's sadistic deviances. They possess his great strength, impious rage, and determination to survive at all cost.

The night feels weighty to Jacques, as he, Margaret, Claude, and the demons walk across the dark countryside toward the chapel. Most of the torches have burned out, leaving a struggling few that the shadows are quickly erasing.

Jacques understands that everything—his life and the future of vampires—depends on what he does next. He slowly distances himself from the others and walks to the top of the ridge where he called out to Clarete, Pierre-Louis, and André earlier. A bloody moon fills the sky with blackish-orange blotches. He inhales deeply, filling his lungs with fresh air, flexing his muscles, preparing himself for battle. With or without Clarete, Pierre-Louis, and André, the time is now.

Claude is lagging behind, habitually on guard, a precaution he's learned from all the battles and wars in which he has fought. He's been killing since his youth. Never trust anyone, he's learned. Always look for the slightest warning. Jacques hasn't gone far, but the fact that he's wandered away at all bears questioning. Since they left the castle, Jacques has been leading them directly toward the chapel. *Perhaps the treasure is hidden there, hidden among his ancestors' dead bodies.* Claude didn't think of that before and believes it's rather ingenious. *Those imbeciles. Their belief in God. It's the last place anyone would think to look. Even King Philip kept his army away from the chapel.*

Claude has always believed he's special, chosen for a greater purpose. Now a vampire with his own adherents, he's a god. He'll build his own army and defeat the kings of Europe, become the Caesar of a new, more powerful Roman Empire. No one will be able to stand in his way. He picks up his pace, closing the distance between himself and Jacques. He's so close to finding the treasure; there's no way he's going to let him escape. He motions to his demons to move in front of Jacques and cut him off.

Jacques intentionally leaves his back exposed, waiting until Claude, driven by his greed, arrogance, and sense of superiority, is within striking distance.

Call it woman's intuition, animal instincts, or the will to survive—Margaret suddenly understands why Jacques has been acting the way he has. He wanted Claude to underestimate him; he wanted to get him outside, where he stands a chance. He never intended to show Claude the hiding place of the Templar treasure. Not wanting to bring attention to herself, she gazes into the sky, brushing her hair away from her face, and casually moves through the tall, green grass toward the demons, positioning herself between them and Jacques. Somehow she'll keep them away from him, make it a fair fight. How...she doesn't know.

The wind is blowing hard, a gale force cracking and breaking branches in the black pines a short distance away. Stags with towering antlers—as well as does, roe, and birds—scramble, seeking shelter in the forest's thickets.

Jacques—muscles taut, nostrils flaring—waits until he can smell Claude behind him; evil has its own stink. Using all the gifts of speed and strength the god, Mithras, awarded him, he attacks by turning around and throwing his body full force into Claude's. The impact is a colossal earthquake.

Claude absorbs the blow from Jacques, but his body is unable to withstand the aftershock. The wind is knocked from his lungs, and his powerful legs buckle. His confidence is shaken.

The two vampires tear up huge clumps of dirt and grass, plowing deep furrows in the earth as they crisscross the field in their brawl. Claude grabs Jacques in his massive hands, using his brute strength to break him, but Jacques is much too fast. He spins away, racing up Claude's back, ripping out chunks of flesh, leaving tendons and muscles exposed like strands of loose-hanging rope.

Normally Claude's vampire body would heal immediately but not when hurt by another vampire. His body reacts, bleeds, and feels pain as if he were human. Jacques slams into Claude again, but this time the big man is ready. Blood pumps out of his damaged arteries, spraying into the night. Although his strength is failing, he manages to smash Jacques to the ground. Claude howls for his demons to help him.

Margaret holds the three demons back. Whenever one of them attempts to move past her, she strikes him in the chest with the palms of her hands, screaming, "Let them fight! Let them fight!" while shoving him back.

The memory of what Claude did to the demons' other friend is still fresh in their minds, so they move cautiously. But as they're the embodiment of Claude's hatred and evil, they must respond to their master's calls for help. One of the demons brutally strikes Margaret across the side of her head, knocking her down. At first she struggles to get up, but then she falls back, holding her face—she can't focus. The thought of those pathetic demons touching her sends chills throughout her body. There's no way she can help Jacques now, and she's distraught. As vindictive as a wolf, she fixes in the hunter crevices of her predator mind a mental picture of the demon that struck her. She will never forget him. Someday, she vows, he will suffer the consequences of the she-wolf's revenge.

With Margaret out of the way, the three Demons of Distortion, like marauding grizzly bears, charge at Jacques.

Claude moves, giving his followers room. As he attempts to regain his strength, his anger surges. "Not like this!" he screams. "Not like this. I won't die like this." He stumbles to a chestnut tree and, using his immense strength, breaks off a large, pointed limb. With limb lance, he'll take Jacques down.

Margaret, recovering from the blow, has moved farther away from the fight and is sitting on the ground, her knees pulled up to her chest. She feels torn between the one who gave her life and the one to whom she gave life. She can see that Claude is gravely injured. If he dies and the demons kill Jacques, what will they do to her? She loves Jacques, but Claude is much larger and stronger, more dominant than Jacques. She's torn between vampire loyalties and wolf instincts in a conflict that will consume her for most of her existence. If she had a choice, before she would have chosen Jacques, but he didn't confide in her when he summoned Clarete, André, and Pierre-Louis to help him, and jealousy is abundant in all her forms. Maybe she could have helped. And yet Jacques's forlorn cry on the hill cut her more deeply than a vampire's fangs. Margaret sits paralyzed by the onslaught of conflicting feelings.

The last lantern at the chapel flickers out. Jacques flexes his muscles, moving from one fighting stance to another, spitting on the ground, challenging the demons. Sunlight creeps toward the horizon. It's all come down to this; he just needs an opening.

The demons attack him first. Jacques moves fast, but there are too many. Whenever he leaps to capture one, another leaps at him and tears at his flesh.

Sucking up his pain, Claude rejoins the battle, swinging violently at Jacques with the tree limb but missing. Then he connects. The impact sends tremors through Jacques's body. Two of the demons manage to grab Jacques and hold him between them, immobilizing him. The third one grabs him from behind. Claude motions to them to spread-eagle Jacques while he's standing, so he'll be completely defenseless.

Tree limb in hand, he swaggers up to Jacques. "I'm going to run you through, Jacques de Molay," he boasts loudly. "I'll watch you die. Welcome to hell."

Jacques meets Claude's glare and shakes his head defiantly. As he glances toward Margaret, the thought of what the demons will do to her sends a shudder through his body. He raises his head high. "If hell is where we finish this, so be it." He spits blood-red saliva onto the ground.

And then the howls tear through the night, and three wolves launch from the forest through the creeping fingers of morning light. They're massive animals with tails raised like banners. The Demons of Distortion are distracted and loosen their grips as Claude rams the limb toward Jacques, but Jacques twists ever so slightly so that the lance misses his heart and lodges between his ribs. Crying out, he drops to his knees and then collapses to the ground. As the glaring eye of sun begins to lift over the horizon, Claude, believing Jacques is dead, slips into the dark safety of the chapel's mausoleum.

The wolves, somewhat protected by their thick coats, ignore the rising sun and hurtle their bodies like wrecking balls, smashing into the demons and tearing their bodies and necks apart with ripping jaws. At first the demons are no match for the ferocious wolves. However, they quickly adapt to the new fighting style while managing to struggle free and follow their master.

Margaret's skin begins to burn, and she crawls over to Jacques. She gently runs her hand over his face, searching for life, for tenderness. He grabs her arm. "Help me, Margaret…please." Blood spills from his mouth with the words. "Don't let me die like this."

"Only if you promise me you'll leave this place," she whispers. "Go far away. Leave France. Never come back." She pushes him with her hands, rocking him back and forth so he doesn't fall asleep. He may never wake up. "Promise me now, before we both die."

As a Knight Templar, Jacques was a fearless warrior and a brilliant strategist. The only death he feared was death with dishonor—and dishonor wore multiple masks, including the face of a fool and a coward. The Templar code that shaped him as a man was in his bones, and, even awash in the cold blood of a vampire, he still follows that code. To stay now and face Claude in his weakened state would be to play a fool. To leave before the fight is finished would be cowardly. But Jacques understands that a battle must sometimes be sacrificed for the greater victory of the war. So he wraps his powerful hands around the tree limb that's sprouting from his chest and, with his remaining strength, slowly pulls it out and heaves it from his body. A river of blood pours from the wound, and his skin smolders in the rising sun. As he places his hands firmly over his chest and applies pressure to the injury, minimizing the blood loss, his rejuvenating powers abruptly heal him. He knows that he needs time to plan and that he has an eternity to defeat Claude, so he must leave, as Margaret has requested.

"I promise," he mumbles. "I do."

Kneeling, Margaret places his arm over her shoulders and then, grasping for every ounce of strength, helps him struggle to his feet and drags him to an overturned war wagon a short distance away. The wagon is their only chance for protection from the rising sun. If they stay out here much longer, they'll be burned to dust. Jacques stumbles and falls, his great weight pulling both of them to the ground.

"Get up," Margaret hisses. "Get up! How dare you quit!"

Eventually they make it to the wagon and crawl underneath it. Margaret grabs an end panel that's lying on the ground and slides it into place, shutting them in. The sides of the wagon protect them from the lethal rays of the sun, and for the day, the wagon is their casket.

Margaret cuts her neck with a razor-sharp fingernail and presses Jacques's face against the wound, her blood wetting his face. The Rider of the Sun birthmark feels cold to her touch. Worried, she pushes harder against the back of his neck. The birthmark has lost all its warmth and sensitivity; it's ice cold. She knows he's dying. "Drink," she commands. "Drink and live."

The blood drips into his mouth, and he tastes its strength. He sinks his fangs into her neck, his body jerking from the energy blasting through his system.

Margaret allows him to drink freely until she feels the cold life return to his body. It takes great effort for her to shove him away from neck, the nipple, but she must, or he'll drink her dry. Jacques immediately falls into a deep, relaxing sleep, breathing heavily as his body heals.

Margaret crawls around the inside of the wagon, pushing dirt and grass against the exposed edges, blocking even the slightest ray of sunlight. Then she lies down and gazes into the closet-like darkness, crossing her arms over her chest. She feels the awe of complete fulfillment. She has given Jacques life, and only she knows. It's her secret, her devotion, her commitment, her passion, her repayment for a debt of unbridled love and life that he gave her freely. Hopefully he will leave France tonight.

The wolves—Clarete, Pierre-Louis, and André—chase Claude and the demons to the chapel mausoleum. As the sun's rays begin to warm the leaded glass in the heavy oak door, Claude opens the door and then slams it shut behind the demons, locking the wolves out. The wolves race across the courtyard and take shelter from the sunlight inside the castle's walls. They will try to find Jacques tonight.

When evening falls, Margaret lies quietly, digging her nails into the thick grass, as Jacques slips from beneath the wagon and closes the panel behind him. She considers following him but only for a moment. As far as Claude knows, Jacques is dead. If Margaret disappears, Claude will seek her out and find him. So her work is here. She draws a hand across her face, brushing her eyebrows, letting her fingertips rest on her lips. She has seen a side of Jacques she never knew existed—dashing, exciting, so strong that she burns at the thought of him. He almost defeated Claude. What will he do now? He's all alone.

She turns onto her side, resting her head on her arm, listening to the splashing of the garden's waterfalls, wishing to reach Jacques with her thoughts. She holds her palm against her face and inhales deeply. The Rider of the Sun birthmark has left a lingering scent of dying dreams on her hand. She gave Jacques her blood and with it a new life, just as she gave Claude life. They are both of her, and that knowledge makes her full. She will love Jacques for eternity. For now she must deal with Claude.

9

CLAUDE THE ROMANTIC

Over the next century, Claude converts legions of men into Demons of Distortion. Through his absolute power and command of the night, he controls travel across vast swaths of the French countryside. The scourge of demons casts a dark umbrella of terror over the land.

He eventually locates the hidden door in the maze and breaks through it to find a vast, empty cavern where he was certain he'd find the Templar treasure. In a vengeful rage, he raids remote villages and slaughters the inhabitants, making it look like the work of a marauding tribe. Jacques de Molay is dead—Claude is certain—and he took the secret location of the Templar treasure to his grave. Embittered, he shakes his head, finally realizing that Margaret never knew where it was hidden after all. At one time Claude and the guardians of Mithras planned to form an army of demons that, under his leadership, would control all of Europe and push their influence eastward into Russia and Asia and south toward Africa. Without the Templar treasure, this is no longer possible, and the disruption of this plan fuels the furnace of his rage.

Margaret has seen Claude and the demons butcher hundreds of men, women, and children and leave their bodies to turn black with maggots and rot in the sun. She knows his evil and initially tries to hide from him in her family's manor outside of Paris.

Claude, bellowing his anger and frustration, ravages the inside of the country home, searching for her. He tears out entire walls and ceilings, destroying everything, leaving nothing except the exterior stone walls and roof, but she is nowhere to be found.

Margaret has managed to elude him for years, and she eventually travels to northeastern France, where her family, the Passavants, once had their fiefdom. She was the only child and the common heiress to the barony of Passavant, but she waited too long to exercise her inheritance rights after her father died, and thus she lost her baroness heritage, land, and title. Margaret understands that Claude knows all of this, which is part of the anger he directs toward her. He aspired to nobility; now he'll never be a baron.

Claude has his connections: the underworld, the children of darkness, his vampire clan, the night crawlers, and the silent, dark souls suspended in time. Through these connections he eventually finds out where Margaret has escaped to and follows her. It's at this time, possibly because of the long journey and the time he spends by himself thinking, that he realizes how much he misses her. Perhaps it's the routine of shape-shifting from a vampire into a wolf and running until tired, and then morphing into a vampire bat and flying until exhausted, and then beginning all over again. Maybe it's his being alone for the first time since his childhood. He recalls his years as a street orphan after he was abandoned at five years of age, waking up alone in the middle of the night, shivering from the cold, his body stiff from sleeping on rough wooden floors in deserted buildings. When these deeply buried memories rise up, they're excruciating, and they inspire more memories, and then he relives his wretched childhood—the hunger and beatings and begging for food. Back then, the adults in his life routinely cut him to shreds with harsh words and heavy fists. This was all before he met Geoffroi de Charny and the Knights Templar, who found him wandering the streets and took him in.

It's when he's haunted by his past that Claude decides he wants to be with Margaret for the rest of his life and never battle the malignant spirits of loneliness again. Just outside the otherwise deserted keep of the Passavant castle, where he knows she's living, he picks some black-and-white irises.

Each night Margaret sneaks out and flies a long distance away from the estate and takes her fill of blood. No one can be aware of her presence there, as she'll be hunted down and killed. Either a stake will be driven through her heart, or her head will be chopped off.

For Margaret nothing compares to the kill: sucking the blood out of a person who's completely helpless. The heart grows desperate, as blood—and therefore oxygen—are drained from the body. Breathing becomes a wet, noisy gasping, and then no breathing occurs, and still death waits to strike. And death works patiently, stripping the skin of heat, coloring the arms a molten blue or purple, collapsing the body, and confusing the eyes before snapping away that last breath. It's at this point that Margaret likes to whisper Jacques's pledge into the ears of her victims: "Your life as a vampire will be much better than your life as a human."

She's clearly surprised to see Claude when he walks into the keep with a bouquet of lovely flowers. He holds them high, at arm's length, for her to see.

He hopes she likes the flowers and the clothes he's wearing: a white silk shirt and red-velvet trousers with a matching full-length red cloak that's trimmed in fox hair. After shape-shifting into a wolf, he chased the fox down and killed it himself. He glances out the window at the orange-glazed moon that casts puffy shadows and lends a party flavor to the night.

Margaret casts her head toward him, flipping her long red hair. She knew he would eventually find her, and had an escape planned. However, watching him inside the tall, fieldstone, guard tower reminds her how truly dashing he is. Yes, she takes a deep impassioned breath; she knows he is— and even though she's tried to elude him for so long, she wants him badly and gives in.

The first time Margaret has sex with him, he's so aggressive and rough that he hurts her badly. Afterward, he realizes what he's done and feels remorseful. He holds Margaret in his massive arms, gently brushing her hair, and cries for forgiveness. He weeps and tells her how sorry he is and promises he'll never do it again. When, like a small child, he begs for her forgiveness, Margaret finds she truly loves him. However, she knows she must do something to protect herself, just in case he tries to harm her again.

"Claude, my love, my one true love," she murmurs, running her hand softly across his face, "promise me we'll love each other as wolves, like the animals we are. Never as the Ventrue again. You can chase me. I'm fast." She smiles. "You'll have to catch me. I'll be tougher, quicker, and able to withstand and enjoy your aggressiveness. We'll be a mated pair and stay together forever." Margaret, saying those last words, thinks of Jacques. She sighs. It's time for her to move on.

Claude likes the idea. If it gets old, he'll just go back to the old way. He can't lose.

Margaret caresses his face, smiling at him. "Be proud of me. Be good to me. Be patient. You'll have everything you've ever dreamed of. You'll be the alpha male, and I'll be the alpha female. We'll be the alpha pair and build vampire alliances from which no one will be safe."

Claude agrees, as he loves Margaret and wants to be with her.

"Let me rest," she says. "My body hurts." She turns her head in Claude's lap and closes her eyes. She feels good about their agreement; under the circumstances it's the best she can hope for. She doesn't tell him that female wolves only stay in heat and mate for roughly two to three weeks in late winter. At that time her fur will be much longer, very dense, and fluffy, affording her the protection she'll need from his sharp fangs and claws. Most importantly, her speed and agility will allow her to escape if he gets too rough with her.

Over the next three hundred fifty years, they work together and build their love for each other. Their vampire clans and wolf packs eventually control large slave-trade routes extending from Europe to Russia to the Baltic countries and Asia. There's a particular demand for blond girls and young boys, both of which are considered exotic luxury items. The Demons of Distortion, along with the wolf packs, raid villages and scattered communes, continually building their network. Over time the Demons of Distortion start to suffer from a mysterious fever, and the smell of death, similar to that of rotting fish, permeates their skin. Red marks blotch their faces and necks, and their bodies turn in on themselves, attacking their own organs and tissues so that their skin shrivels. They endure excruciating stomach pain and piss and shit all over themselves. Claude's freaks of nature are dying and, with them, his control of vast expanses of land and slave-trade routes. Claude has been so involved with Margaret that he doesn't do what's necessary to replenish his ranks. The demons have cannibalistic instincts, eating the flesh and internal organs of their victims, and they don't convert enough followers to fill their dwindling ranks. Claude's mutants, with their short life-spans taking their vast toll, decrease by the thousands. By the time he comes to grips with the problem, it's so far-reaching that it's impossible to counter. Feeling he needs the power to deal with the hopeless situation, he once again blames the person closest to him and channels his anger toward Margaret. He loves her, but he can't keep the locks on his most perverse, damaging feelings, and over time he isolates, withdraws, and becomes increasingly manipulative and violent.

Over the next fifty years, they each build their own vampire clans separately. Margaret tries to work with Claude and continue to be a pair of alpha wolves, but he's incapable of trust and continues to lose control. He continually goes off on his own, even though it pains him deeply to do so. Margaret is relieved that he takes his few remaining Demons of Distortion with him. She has never been comfortable with their hungry looks and deformed, grasping hands. Now he spends all his time with them.

Claude allows Margaret's clan to exist but limits its growth by betraying their daytime resting places to rogue priests and bands of Gypsy trackers.

Years later he goes to Margaret and, on his knees, begs her forgiveness for betraying her clan. She grants him this. Claude, however, discreetly continues to betray her vampire followers.

In 1445, Vlad Dracul took by force from Bulgaria to Wallachia around 11,000 to 12,000 Gypsies. The trackers are the rogues of the Gypsy clans. Tired of being persecuted, turned into slaves, working in the gold mines or the salt mines, they've escaped to the immenseness of the Russian wilderness. Overtime they've become the best hunters in this remote, mountainous country. They are talented, tough, outstanding men with uncanny, natural abilities. They've trained themselves to move secretly through the most difficult terrain; experts in tracking, hunting and survival. Their hair is always worn long, believing it transmits energy to their brain, making them more aware of their surroundings. To continually prove their prowess they raid crypts, graveyards, and mausoleums and kill vampires by driving stakes into their hearts, burning them, or chopping off their heads.

After what she believes is the death of Jacques, Clarete escapes Claude's vengeance by fleeing to Italy. Pierre-Louis and André retreat to areas of France uncontrolled by Claude and lurk outside of pubs and lavish nobility parties, attacking the most intoxicated people in order to savor the alcohol in their blood. When he's not drinking, André shape-shifts into a wolf. With the blood of Jacques de Molay and Mithras, rampaging through his veins, all it takes is a couple of fights for him to establish his dominance as an alpha wolf. This is something that has never happened to him before. He's always been the downtrodden fellow, the wimp everyone picks on. Except for Pierre-Louis and Jacques, he's never had another friend. So, being André, he takes full advantage of his newfound position. One day, while trotting across the countryside, irritated by an itch, he decides to stop, lift his leg, and take a piss on a large French blue Scotch pine tree with long needles. It's open, with full branches spreading out. Finished, he backs his butt into the tree's needles and prickly cones, swishing it back and forth, scratching one of those irritating itches that seems to move. "Awrrroooo! Awrrrroooo!!" Oh, it feels so good. If life were any better, he'd howl at the moon during the day. *Oh, yeah,* he remembers. *Only comes out at night.*

Even in their drunken state, Pierre-Louis and André manage to convert numerous individuals to vampires and werewolves but not in numbers of any significance to cause Claude alarm.

Jacques disappears into the vastness called Russia. For several years he hunts to satisfy his lust for blood, and he converts hundreds to the vampire cause. But he can't forget the man he once was—a leader of knights from an order of honorable, courageous men, a leader from a proud, privileged family. And now he has become an animal, waking from murderous dreams to think only of warm flesh growing limp in his jaws. He'll slay anyone with the misfortune to cross his path, while he remains immune to their pleas and screams. Many of these victims are the poor, the isolated, the unlucky—the people he once proudly served to protect under the emblem of the Order of the Knights Templar. Killing has become Jacques's nature, but he has grown to despise this nature, and so he is a vampire conflicted.

Over the ensuing decades, his mission becomes to convert only the poor, the defeated, the hungry, the oppressed, the downtrodden. Their new lives as a vampire, much better than their old lives of a human, will be his redemption. His impressive size, powerful physical attributes, mixed with the pure blood of Mithras—the White Wolf, churning through his veins, allows him to create monster vampires: giants that are more than six and a half feet tall and weigh up to three hundred pounds. Their hair, like Jacques's, fans out from the tops of their heads to their ankles. His army, which he has named the "One Hundred Twenty," can easily defeat ten thousand battle-hardened soldiers. Their formation is the Roman military's manipular system, with three lines of forty vampires each—very flexible, highly mobile. Although Jacques has converted thousands of individuals, all except the One Hundred Twenty eventually lose their way and succumb to the temptations of evil. All the vampires look to Jacques as their leader, but only the One Hundred Twenty walk with him. Their movements across Russia take them to Romania, a country that lies directly between the two powerful forces of the Kingdom of Hungary and the Ottoman Empire.

For nearly a thousand years, Constantinople has blocked Islam's access to Europe. In 1453 Constantinople falls to the Ottomans, sending shock waves through Christendom, as Europe is now threatened by the Turks. In 1456, with the support of Hungarian military and political leader John Hunyadi, Prince Vlad III, also known as Dracula, assumes the throne of the Romanian region of Wallachia for a second time and begins his reign of terror. In 1459, on St. Bartholomew's Day, Vlad has thirty thousand merchants and wealthy boyars impaled in the city of Brasov. Ten thousand are impaled in the Transylvanian city of Sibiu in 1460. In 1461 Mehmed II, conqueror of Constantinople, orders his invading Ottoman army to retreat when they encounter twenty thousand impaled Turkish prisoners hanging naked, upside down in the trees on the banks of the Danube River. Eventually this area comes to be known as the Forest of the Impaled. The Turks finally succeed in forcing Vlad III from power in 1462. With the support from the king of Hungary, however, Vlad regains the Wallachian throne once more in 1476.

That same year Jacques and the One Hundred Twenty take shelter in the deserted Poenari castle in Wallachia, which borders the principality of Transylvania to the north. Ransacked by the Ottoman Turks in 1417 and abandoned more than fifty years ago, the castle has fallen into decay. The formerly fortified ramparts and towers are crumbling, and the interior passageways and tunnels lie in ruins. The castle is perched high atop sheer cliffs, close to the Făgăraş Mountains and a canyon in the Argeş River Valley. Its location made it difficult for the Turks to capture. The invaders had to climb 1,480 steps just to reach its walls.

A bluish supermoon fills the cloudless, starlit sky, illuminating mountain peaks capped in ice that spills down into a frozen teardrop pool that never melts. The hanging moon seems unusually large, as if one can touch it. This is a night of illusions.

Jacques takes his position at the head of the One Hundred Twenty, who have gathered in the courtyard of the abandoned castle. This is a weekly ritual. In a show of his vampire strength, he leaps to the top of a deserted mausoleum so all the vampires can see him.

The One Hundred Twenty shout while beating their chests.

"What is the Blood Law?" Jacques yells, standing tall above them, holding his hands up.

"Life!" they shout. "Convert only the poor, the sick, the persecuted, the hungry, the weak, the downtrodden!"

"What is our promise?" Jacques screams.

"The life of a vampire must be better than one's life as a human!" His army's loud voices blister the night.

"What is family?" Jacques hollers, strutting back and forth on the wall. He enjoys firing up his faithful followers.

"We will defend the One Hundred Twenty to the death!" they shout back, continuing to beat their chests. "*Aaseeebooo! Aaseeebooo!*"

"What is the punishment for breaking the Blood Law?" Jacques yells, before morphing into a wolf and howling at the supermoon.

"Banishment for life!" the One Hundred Twenty roar back in unison. "No one is above the Blood Law." The clan transforms into wolves and becomes a storm of howling, snapping fur as they race out of the crumbling castle and into the night.

Most nights Jacques is accompanied by other vampires from the One Hundred Twenty, but tonight he leaves the castle alone. He's anxious, restless, looking over his shoulder as if he's being followed. His dreams have recently been tormented, but he doesn't know why. The sky, he thinks, reflects his mood; teal-and-gray clouds shadow the dark night. Something has been calling him unceasingly—long, smoky fingers snaking into his thoughts. He wanders without knowing where he's going and then finds himself in a place of stone and rubble from a long-since-abandoned and forgotten settlement built against the rock wall of a mountain.

A large outcropping of quartz lies in front of him. One cluster is twice his size. Thunder and lightning scream across the dark sky, and then the heavens open and release a river of rain. The water runs down the huge quartz stones, creating electrical charges. The vapors illuminate and grow, materializing into the luminous form of a beautiful child, his face the fire of light. His hair is curled and yellow like a lion's. One eye is white like billowy clouds on an enchanting day; the other is black, piercing the depths of hell.

Jacques is astounded. Vampires hate water, but right now he's impervious to the rain. He steps back, attempting to wipe the water from his face, to clear his eyes. The rain continues to drench the countryside.

"Jacques de Molay," Mithras, the Ghost Child, calls. The voice creeps from the quartz and encircles Jacques. "You betray me. You and your brotherhood, converting only the castaways of life, sucking the blood from the traders of the unfree, the masters of the weak, the conveyers of evil, leaving their lifeless bodies to rot in the sun. I hold your soul. I hold your life in my hands." The child holds out both hands and then, smiling, clasps them together, causing Jacques to collapse breathlessly to his knees. As the Ghost Child squeezes his hands tighter, pressing them back and forth, Jacques thrashes uncontrollably on the sharp stones and mud like a dying animal. He musters all his strength and slowly pulls himself to his feet against the thunderous current.

"Mithras," Jacques says when he finally pulls himself to his full height. "What do you want of me?" His strength is returning, and the rain is beginning to lighten.

"You shame me, Jacques. You and your brotherhood. I can kill you—all of you."

"Then why don't you?"

"I need you. You will go to Transylvania. There is someone there who will be my greatest disciple. Someone more evil than even Claude de Lavoe. Already this man has killed and tortured thousands of innocents: Prince Vlad III. You will make him mine, and my power will be unstoppable. Then perhaps I will forgive your transgressions."

Jacques knows of Vlad III. The prince's reputation for evil and his reign of death and terror have spread throughout Russia. His cruelty is boundless. He has destroyed entire villages, burned fortresses, and conducted infamous mass executions in which he impales multiple victims at once. His weapon of choice is a sharpened, well-oiled stake the size of a man's arm that is planted in the ground or held by an executioner. The victims are hoisted upright with ropes, their arms tied above their heads. They're momentarily suspended above the ground and then released; the weight of their bodies drives the sharpened spike through them, from anus to mouth. Death is always gruesome, agonizingly slow, and extremely painful. He has had infants impaled on stakes, forced through their mothers' chests—dying mothers left holding their dead children. Sometimes he strings his victims naked between two horses and impales them. The cries and screams of tortured victims provide the background noise for Vlad's lavish banquets with his royal court. The decaying, mutilated corpses are the landscaping of the nearby villages, the stink saturating the air.

"No," Jacques says, and Mithras, claps his hands together and swings them back and forth, which hurls Jacques to the ground. He presses Jacques into the earth just by motioning with his hands, and Jacques sinks like an enormous ship in the ocean. When he finally stops, Jacques crawls from the hollow in the earth to his knees and painfully forces himself to stands up.

"You aren't in a position to bargain," the Ghost Child snarls. "You broke once—I will break you again, but next time your suffering will be eternal."

Mithras, glows so brightly that Jacques must avert his eyes.

"But I am generous with those who serve me," he continues. "Your soul is my eternal prisoner. Anything else I will give to you."

Jacques isn't fooled by the offer. Once Vlad is converted, Mithras, will no longer need Jacques. He will destroy him completely, so he begins to bargain. "Vlad will be your greatest servant, your greatest vampire," Jacques says. "None can equal him. Not even Claude can match his evil. I am nothing. Release my soul from your bondage, and I will give you what you want. Free me, and still I will have no home, no rest. My eternity will be purgatory. The fact that I cannot live and cannot die should please you."

The Ghost Child slaps his hands. "I won't ask again," he shouts angrily.

"Then kill me," Jacques moans, his head hanging. "Without me you have nothing. Only I can convert Vlad into what you want. Only I. Of all the vampires, I'm the only one who has your pure blood flowing through his veins. We have a deal—I gave you my soul. You made me, only me, one of yours. I come from you. All other vampires come from me. All are stepchildren. Even you, the White Wolf, must keep his end of the pact."

The silence is huge and heavy, and Jacques is barely able to raise his head. The Ghost Child raises his arms, and something lifts off the thorny flowers of his hands like a phosphorescent moth. It grows and billows and hangs in the air, a dusting of glass, and then, in a flash of wings, it goes to purgatory. Mithras, observes this pathetic servant, his ambivalent knight of the darkness. This giant once was the Grand Master of the Knights Templar, but he has proved to be a disappointment. Vlad, with his unlimited capacity for evil, will be the better servant, a true prince of the night.

"Vlad will be my true son, the son of the underworld—Dracula. I agree to your terms, but if you fail, your soul will return to me," the Ghost Child says before he fades back into the stone, taking the rain with him.

Jacques and his Russian vampires, the One Hundred Twenty, cross the treacherous Borgó Pass in the Romanian Bârgău Mountains, the gateway to Transylvania and the realm of Vlad III, Dracula. It's a country of forests, the Carpathian Mountains, the Danube River, and rustic landscapes. The high hills and meadows are lush with wildflowers and wandering spring-fed streams. Wolves, bears, lynx, and wild boars roam the forests; eagles and owls capture the sky. Fortified churches, where people seek protection from invaders, front tiny villages of walled homes to protect the inhabitants and cobbled courtyards. The nights are beginning to cool, and the countryside is awash in the warm colors of autumn.

Jacques and his brotherhood have morphed into wolves and are moving quickly across the countryside. Through the underworld they've received word that a large Turkish army has invaded Wallachia and is pushing toward Bucharest. They've also heard that Vlad is moving out to meet them with a much smaller force. Jacques and the One Hundred Twenty have laid out their battle plans. Once again they'll arrange themselves in the manipular formation, which will provide them exceptional maneuverability on uneven ground. Each vampire occupies a three-foot-by-three-foot killing square. If one of the vampires in the front line falls behind, his spot is immediately filled by a vampire in the second line, and then the vampire in the third line moves up. The three-by-three-foot killing squares are always maintained, and everything living dies. To the vampires, the Ottomans are invaders, a scourge that must be destroyed.

In the distance they see glimmers of the army's campfires. The Ottoman cavalry and infantry are spread out across the countryside. They've chosen an unsuitable area to rest, as the woods and marshy ground restrict the cavalry's movement. Using the element of surprise, Jacques and his army launch their attack as wolves. As they fan out and race through the encampment, the Ottoman soldiers huddle in fear next to their fires. The wolves rip out their throats with a slash of their powerful jaws and burning teeth. They disappear into the darkness with such speed that the Turkish soldiers believe they're being attacked by blood-drenched demons. The frightened horses buck and bolt away from their cavalrymen, throwing them to the ground. The burning embers of their campfires are scattered by the vampires' onslaught. The fire quickly spreads out of control, mushrooming into larger fires with flying sparks igniting countless tents. The clothing of the confused soldiers catches fire so that the men become screaming human torches.

Jacques breaks away from the pack and transforms into a vampire bat to search for Vlad's camp. It doesn't take him long to find it. Vlad's small force is positioned between the Ottoman army and Bucharest, where he plans to stop the Turks from invading Europe. Vlad's tent is easy to spot; it's black and emblazoned with a coat of arms consisting of a black eagle with its head turned over its shoulder. The bird holds a cross in its beak, and a crescent and star appear on either side. Two guards are positioned in front of the tent. Jacques lands at the back of the tent and crawls under it to where Vlad is sleeping. After materializing back into a vampire, he lies beside him and listens to his steady breathing. He smells the musky, sour scent of his skin.

Jacques has heard so much about Vlad the Impaler and his reputation for cruelty that he looks him over, glancing up and down the length of his body. This man with this sagging cheeks and mangy, grey-streaked mustache is the roaster of children, so macabre and wicked that even Mithras begs his service. The hands with thick fingers bent in repose have cut the breasts off women and impaled hundres? thousands? on the stakes surrounding his castle. Even the Ottomans call him Kazikli Bey, the Impaler Prince—the only creature, other than Satan, whose evil frightens entire armies into retreating. Jacques is surprised at how tall but thin Vlad is. He's not a handsome man, with thin eyebrows, pointed ears and deep scars running across his face. His thin, black hair hangs past his shoulders. Jacques knows he's breaking his law—the law of the One Hundred Twenty. Vlad isn't of the poor, the sick, the persecuted, the hungry, the weak, or the downtrodden—but this is the price Jacques must pay if he wants Mithras, to release his soul.

The heavy animal skins that cover the tent flap in the strong wind, drowning out Vlad's brief scream as Jacques pierces his neck with his fangs. Jacques covers Vlad's body with his own so he can't struggle, and his blood roars into the impaler's veins. The prince's body shudders and then surges as he transforms into something darker and more sinister than even he himself could imagine.

"All will call you Dracula," Jacques whispers into Vlad's ear, over and over. "For eternity, when men talk of evil and darkness, they will think of you, and they will call you Dracula."

Jacques doesn't know that he's been followed, that he's almost always being followed. The One Hundred Twenty are a careful bunch. They always send a sentry after him to protect him, their master and leader. However, on rare occasions Jacques does slip through their watchful eyes. This night is no different. Tonight the sentry, a vampire wolf, lies flat on his stomach, legs stretched, hidden in the tall grass. He saw Jacques enter Vlad's tent, and with his penetrating eyes, he made out the conversion of Vlad in the thin light of the campfire. The sentry rushes to tell the rest of the One Hundred Twenty that Jacques has broken their law.

—⟋⟍—

It is Dracula who stands outside of Vlad's tent later that night, but to the untrained eye, he is the same. Upon closer inspection, however, it is as if he has been perfected in steel. The scars are stripped from his face. His hair is blackened, curling in waves, his eyes ignited. When several of Vlad's spies tell him Ottoman soldiers are deserting their camps and fleeing the area, he mounts his black horse effortlessly and orders his army to attack. The cover of darkness will give them the edge they need to defeat the Turks.

Jacques's brotherhood withdraws to a deserted village some distance away and waits for him. When he arrives, he knows something is wrong; his clan broke off their attack of the Ottomans much too early. When he walks into the walled area of the church courtyard, the One Hundred Twenty surround him. One of his first converts is Petya, also known as "the Rock." At seven feet tall and 350 pounds, he's a muscular mass of strength and power.

Petya steps out of the circle of vampires. "Vlad III noticed that the poor, the beggars, and the cripples had become numerous in his land," he begins, speaking loudly and with command. "He issued an invitation to all these individuals to come for a lavish feast, claiming no one should go hungry in his land. When the poor and crippled arrived in the city of Târgoviște, they were ushered into a great hall, where a fabulous feast had been prepared for them. The guests ate and drank late into the night. Vlad then made an appearance and asked them, 'What else do you desire? Do you want to be without cares, lacking nothing in this world?' When they responded in the affirmative, he ordered the hall boarded up and set on fire. None escaped the flames. He explained his actions to his citizenry, claiming that he did this so these people would no longer be a burden to others and stating that no one in his realm would be poor. You, Jacques de Molay, told us this truth of the man known as Dracula. He's the opposite of everything we believe. You have broken your own law, the Blood Law. Dracula's blood is now one with yours. It flows through your body. You know the punishment for breaking the law. You are banished from the brotherhood forever."

The Blood Law is the law, and Jacques accepts that expulsion is the price he must pay for his soul. He assures himself that this isn't the end, that what he's enabled he will eventually stop. The road to redemption is long and twisted.

As the circle of loyalists opens, and those whom he protected and who protected him in all their various mutations snarl and gnash their fangs and beat their leathery wings and turn their backs to him in disgust, he knows hell isn't a place you can depart. A soul cannot be bought with the lives of innocents—the ones he condemned when he empowered the evil in Dracula. Although his soul is his, he believes it's forever doomed. As he walks into the thick cover of the forest, his name is lifted from the tablet that lists the One Hundred Twenty. "The Templar treasure and the Ark of the Covenant," Jacques says, as turns back to his clan, "are hidden in the Ural Mountains. Follow the voices in the wind. They will lead you there. Help the guardians protect it."

As time passes, Jacques hears that the Turks counterattacked near Bucharest in December 1476 and defeated Dracula's small force. It's said that the Ottomans found Dracula's resting place and drove a stake through his heart, killing him. The Turks then decapitated him and sent his head to Constantinople, where they displayed it on a stake as proof that the feared impaler finally was dead. Jacques's relief is dimmed by the knowledge that Vlad's body never has been found.

10

THE CHILDREN OF SIRIUS, THE SOUL OF ISIS

AD 1501

Jacques has just crossed the border into Russia on his way to the Castle of Odin in the Ural Mountains. He sits down on a hillside that overlooks a long valley leading to a distant lake. He feels the cool wind against the side of his face and inhales the invigorating night air. He gazes at the lonely, blue-gray moon in the black night. Its faint light appears like steps across the hushed water, and once again he's the lone wolf. He thinks about those he used to know—André, Pierre-Louis, and Clarete—and wonders whether they're still alive and what has become of them. Most of all, he wonders about Margaret. What has happened between her and Claude? Are they lovers? If it weren't for Margaret, Jacques would be dead now. He owes her his life—an impossible debt to repay.

Gazing at the distant stars, he reflects on times past. So much has happened—will he ever see her again? What about the impenetrable Claude? Is he the alpha male in Margaret's life? He's heard on the winds of time that Ivan the Great, who unified Russia under one leader and tripled the size of the country, is still alive. He's one of the longest-reigning rulers in Russian history. Jacques's uncle, Master de Lezines, and Ivan I of Moscow were great friends. He wonders about Jude and the last of the Knights Templar and if they made it to the castle of the Norse God Odin. So many were ruthlessly tortured by King Philip and the Church. So many lives were taken. So many sacrificed so much to protect the Templar Treasure, the Ark of the Covenant—and him. Was it all worth it? He must see for himself. He knows he must be careful on this journey—if the One Hundred Twenty find him, they will try to kill him—but it's worth the risk. Finding out the answer is the only thing that will erase these thoughts of tribulation from his mind.

During his travels he keeps away from all areas with populations or towns of any size. He lives off deer, elk, rabbits, and the occasional human. He transforms into wolf form when he hunts and buries the remains of his prey. What evidence he fails to cover, the bears, wolves, and birds scavenge. To avoid being seen, he slides into the shadows and disappears into the night. However, even with all his precautions, people still see him move across the dark countryside beneath the citrus moon, and stories travel among the peasants from one remote village to another of an enormous vampire and a massive, blue wolf. Talk turns to hunting parties and tracking, but then the talk remains talk.

Russia is a huge country, and it takes Jacques five months to reach the Ural Mountains. The range is in the west and runs approximately twenty-five hundred kilometers from the Kara Sea in the north to the Kazakh Steppe along the northern border of Kazakhstan in the south.

As Jacques approaches the range, the mountains appear like a great, gray curtain hanging from the stars. The tops of the snowcapped peaks are smothered in a haze that drifts down onto the jagged cliffs, which are blanketed in firs, pines, spruces, birches, maples, oak, and elms. The exposed rock along the ridges has been weathered smooth and flat. Alongside this immense range, grasslands blush with red, yellow, and white flowers that meet the high tundra, and thick forests fall away into deep valleys. The respective landscapes are home to reindeer, brown bears, beaver, wild horses, foxes, and moose. Jacques hears the calls of various birds, including grouse, cuckoos, and songbirds such as the nightingale and redstart. Abundant rainfall trickles down the mountainsides, feeding lush meadows, cool, clear-water streams, placid lakes, and endless rivers that nourish the Russian Empire. Jacques stands, gazing at the huge expanse of mountains, and begins to second-guess his reasons for coming here. What if Jude and the others are dead? Are the One Hundred and Twenty out there somewhere? What if their entire trip had been a failure and all was lost? He nods slowly. *There's only one way to find out*. Shape-shifting into a great wolf, his thick fur the color of blue steel, his piercing, bright-blue eyes probing the bliss of the landscape, Jacques lopes easily across the wild, remote countryside toward the Castle of Odin. He's waited nearly two hundred years for this day, and he quickens his pace. He's a wolf searching out members of the pack. He wants to reach his destination before sunup.

The Castle of Odin is a massive structure of stone blocks and wood, with curtain walls thirty feet tall and ten feet thick. The castle sits on a wide bend of the Pechora River, with a bird's-eye view of the surroundings. Part of the river has been rerouted to provide a deep, wide moat to protect the castle from invaders. The bailey between the castle and the moat has been cleared of all brush and trees. This is a killing field, with nothing left that one can use as a shield for protection. A thick, iron-plated, wooden drawbridge is used to cross the moat. A narrow stream, cascading down the steep rocky cliffs, supplies fresh water, which is carried to the inhabitants by stone waterways to each floor. It's used for bathing in wooden tubs, as well as cooking, washing, and drinking—before it flows under one of the thick walls and into the river. Some of the windows are made of crystal, lime-green glass. The first floor of the castle is beaten earth, while the second floor or great hall, is made of wood and supported by stone vaulting. Four large, stone fireplaces provide heat. In the corner of the room stands a large statue of Odin mounted on a pedestal. He has long hair and a beard and wears a skull helmet with horns that was hammered and molded from gold. He holds a silver-tipped spear in both hands and wears a robe that hangs down over one shoulder, revealing a strong, muscular physique. The chapel hasn't been used for centuries and is in a serious state of disrepair.

The back of the castle is built into a mountain. Long passageways have been chiseled into the stone, some of which are escape routes to the other side of the Ural Mountains. Others lead to the maze, which is home to inconceivable beauty as well as unfathomable horrors. Most of the vile creatures that live there were brought by sailors attempting to find a north-ern passageway across the top of the world. Defeated by the cold and ice, some of these sailors were lucky enough to find safety in the waters of the Murman Sea. It remains ice free year around due to the warm North Atlantic drift.

The keep, the front of which is shaped like a half circle, is seventy feet tall, with six-foot-thick walls and narrow windows. The rounded back half of the keep was built into the mountain. The stairwells are curved in a narrow, clockwise direction so that attackers coming up the stairs would have their right shoulders against the interior curve of the wall. This made it nearly impossible for them to swing their swords with their right hands, which was generally a warrior's sword hand. The uneven design of the stairs caused invaders to stumble and fall in their attempts to ascend, and it made them vulnerable to counterattack.

Jacques reaches the castle's moat a couple of hours before the sun rises. As a vampire he stands and gazes at the castle, impressed by its massive size and how it appears to be an extension of the mountain. Nothing has ever breached the castle's mighty walls. He surveys the area and sees no guards, no movement. Normally, he would try to conceal himself, but he's far enough away that no weapon they have could reach him. He wonders whether his greatest fear has been confirmed, that Jude and the Templars are all dead. Or is it a trap? Maybe the One Hundred Twenty know he's here and are waiting for him. Suddenly the entire front wall of the castle is illuminated with pale-blue men, each with shoulder-length, white hair. Their bodies are crisscrossed with large, blue, pulsating, blood vessels radiating a deadly, high-energy light. They look like living torches standing on the battlement platforms. The men cast a phosphorescent blue, night-fire beam that fulgurates light into darkness and resembles the blazing trail of a comet in the night sky.

The heavy drawbridge is lowered and drops into place. Jacques, recognizing the glow of the worms of the Nile, walks across and waits at the edge of the bailey for whatever will happen next.

The huge, iron gates to the castle are pushed open, and one of the men walks out alone. "Jacques de Molay," a familiar voice not heard by Jacques in two centuries says, breaking through the silence.

Jacques immediately recognizes Jude the Great and waits for his old friend to approach. There's really nothing that can be said in a situation like this. So much time has passed; so much has happened. Jude's golden hair is pulled back behind his head; braided, it falls to his waist. He's wearing a tan leather toga of deer hide that hangs over his right shoulder and reveals his heavily muscled upper body. Laced leather is wrapped around his calves, and on his feet are leather moccasins. The movement of the glowworms under his skin literally makes his flesh crawl with their bluish light.

"We all call ourselves the Children of Sirius," Jude says as he approaches Jacques and unexpectedly gives him a huge bear hug, his deep-blue eyes inspecting the friend he thought he would never see again. Jacques, reacting to his wolf-pack instincts, accepts Jude's advances heartily, sniffing his flesh to make sure this blue-skinned man is really him. Satisfied, he wraps his long arms around his old comrade's shoulders.

"Don't worry about how I look," Jude continues, while stepping back. "I won't hurt you. I have complete control over them. Sirius is the sky's brightest and most beautiful of all stars. We call it the Enchanting Star. It blinks many colors. We, the Children of Sirius, Dog Soldiers—" he says, nodding toward the line of glowing, blue-colored men, "shine the same colors. Yellow as the light of day, blue as the night. Green—neither full light of summer nor full darkness of night. We become the color of blood when we prepare to attack. See? See?" He points at the stars as they walk toward the castle. "The one twinkling just below Orion's Belt—that's Sirius; that's who we are. The Dog Star is the symbol of power, the Heavenly Wolf. You and I—all of us—are bridged together by the blazing face of the wolf." He turns and looks at Jacques. "It's good to see you, my friend. I—we—" He waves his hand toward all the figures standing on the battlement platforms. "Many of them are your Knights Templar. All of them are now called Dog Soldiers." Arms outstretched, Jude reaches toward the sky. "About half of us have survived. Age only improves the wine. Many of us have families with the female forest dwellers. We've heard all the tales of your death and your rebirth as a vampire, as well as what happened with Margaret and Claude. I never trusted him, you know." Jude stops, turns toward Jacques, and places a hand on his shoulder. "How many times did I tell you? But you never listened. Come." He waves his hand. "You, us—we're now one with the great mysteries of the heavens. Sirius, from the time of ancient Egypt, was worshiped as the Star of Isis. Isis shines and mingles her light with that of her father, the horizon. For now you are with the Dog Soldiers, the watchmen of the heavens. If it weren't for you, we'd all be dead. You own our hearts."

"Where did you find the wisdom to know all this?" Jacques asks. "This was never learned in France."

"The Potion of Life. The worms that inhabit our bodies. They are one with us, sowing a higher consciousness. There is much to show you."

"What about the One Hundred Twenty?" Jacques inquires. "Do you know who they are?"

"Everyone knows who they are," Jude responds, as they walk through the iron gates and into the courtyard. "They live on the other side of the Urals. The Ob River, the Gulf of Ob. It's very cold, frozen for nine months out of the year. They know you're here. We have a truce with them."

"Knowing the One Hundred Twenty as I do," Jacques answers, "I don't believe what they've told you. They must be planning something."

"And so we'll deal with it then," Jude responds.

"The Ark of the Covenant and the Templar treasure?" Jacques asks. He's been worried about them for two centuries.

"Safe," Jude answers. He points at the castle walls. "The Children of Sirius, the Dog Soldiers, your Knights Templar welcome you." Holding his hands above his head, he claps loudly and then motions to the guards to open the two huge, black, steel-reinforced doors that lead to the inside of the great building. A large number of women and children file outside and stand in a line. The women are made up of two groups of individuals. Some have the same golden skin as the men; the others are the forest dwellers, with dark skin and stocky builds, and they are shorter than the other women. Their eyes and their thick, straight hair are either black or brown, while their faces are broad and flat, with small, protruding noses. The children display their mothers' characteristics.

"The survival of our people is our most sacred mission," Jude says, rubbing his fingers across his lips. "I'll never forget what you said to me." He pauses while looking at Jacques. "Back in France, when we saw each other last, you said, 'When the time is right, you'll know…when their flesh has melted and blended with yours. Through their feelings you'll sense when to do the same to the strongest, the fastest, the brightest, the most determined and trustworthy men you've chosen for your new Templar army.'" Jude stops and turns toward the castle. "Watch!" he hollers.

The Dog Soldiers—more than two hundred of them at their positions on the wall—turn and focus their attention on Jude and Jacques, who are standing in the middle of the courtyard. Inhaling, they force the expanding blood vessels covering their pale bodies to rhythmically pulsate an effulgent blue light, setting off an electrical charge that flashes from their bodies. Their eyes cycle from yellow to blue to green to red and then back to yellow. Turning and twisting and throwing their hands and arms in the air, they generate massive surges of power around their bodies and above their heads. The light dances off their illuminated forms and triggers what looks like a massive thunderstorm, with blazing, jagged lightning bolts that blast through the dark, torrid sky. The children take burning sticks from two bonfires, and hustling around the courtyard, they light black gunpowder fuses.

Jacques can't believe his eyes. What are these strange bursts of colored flames appearing high in the sky? The booming noises sound like cannons firing. He's never seen anything like it, such a spectacular show of force and power. The incredible display lasts half an hour and ends with the Dog Soldiers creating a splendid rainbow of multiple colors that reaches from one end of the castle wall to the other. Jacques is impressed; now he understands why the One Hundred Twenty live on the other side of the Urals. He would too.

Jude gestures first toward the women and children, then at Jacques, and finally at the Dog Soldiers standing on the castle walls. "This is the man I've told you all about," he announces. "None of us would be alive today if it weren't for him. He died, and now he lives. The Star of Isis—the bringer of life, of energy, of light—brought him here for all of us." He waves his arms at everyone inside the castle's curtain walls. "Will any of us ever see him again? Only the Star of Isis knows."

An attractive woman with straight black hair and dark eyes walks across the courtyard toward Jude and Jacques. She's wearing a handmade, brown blouse and a tan leather skirt. A young boy, who looks to be around five years old, with long, blond hair and piercing blue eyes, runs ahead of her.

"My wife and son," Jude explains. "I bought her from a ship captain and freed her. I call her Biuy, which means 'my precious stone' in Chinese.

The explosions in the sky—they're from the Chinese. My wife and the ship's captain showed us how to make them from black powder. They call them fireworks. My son's name is Loiza Zhou," he says, as the boy leaps into his outstretched arms. Jude is beaming. "This is the friend I told you about," he tells the boy. "Remember him always."

Loiza Zhou rolls his head and stares at Jacques.

The women and children, showing their respect, and thrilled about the night's events, begin a high-pitched wailing.

"Come." Jude motions to Jacques. "We haven't much time before sunrise."

Jacques drags his right foot backward across the ground and presses his right hand horizontally across his stomach. He holds his left hand out at his side and several times turns in different directions, giving a deep bow of respect, showing his gratitude to the Dog Soldiers and the Children of Sirius. Finished, he follows Jude down the dark, mysterious passageways that are consistently cold and damp from the seepage of rainwater and moisture from the mountain. The corridors run from the keep and the maze, connecting to subterranean chambers where Dog Soldiers, blanketed in grayish-black cobwebs, stand in hibernation. During this time their skin takes on a glutinous quality that attracts animals of every kind and species. Rats, foxes, wolves, mice, flies, snakes—none are excluded. Trapping their bodies in the sticky membrane, the Dog Soldiers digest every creature that comes into contact with them.

"How long can they live like this," Jacques asks?

"Forever," Jude responds. "Unless their food source dries up. But, they need so little to live. Every sixty days they rotate out and are replaced by another group of Dog Soldiers. We do that so they don't lose contact with friends and families."

"What about the maze," Jacques questions. "Is it finished?"

"Building it wasn't the problem," Jude answers. "A maze isn't a maze without Bisu."

Jacques follows Jude and several other Dog Soldiers through a long series of secret tunnels and winding galleries that takes them underneath the Pechora River to a natural, gigantic, underground cavern hidden by pine-covered rolling hills above.

As they step out of the passageway and into a subterranean field of green algae, the Dog Soldiers quickly spread out, light a few torches, crawl up the high limestone walls, and take seats on the ledges. Jacques, feeling the cool dampness of the stone, glances around the vast underground chamber. He immediately recognizes the tiny glowworms radiating their luminescent blue light. It's accentuating the cave's fantastic stalagmites, stalactites, stone pillars, stone curtains, birds, plants, and animals in a wonderland of incredible shapes and sizes. Large, cylindrical, white crystals litter the floor and lie in piles, as if a giant left his stacks of firewood unattended.

Peering out and over the quiet, underground lake, Jacques shakes his head while rapidly blinking his eyes because he can't believe what he's seeing. There in front of him, on smooth, ripple-free, white water, sits a large, ghost ship partially hidden in the dimness of the bluish, smoky haze misting across it. The white sails of the three masts are set, waiting for the next gust of wind. The French flag hangs lifelessly from the aft sail. Through a crystal in the cavern's ceiling, the moon glowers down on the ship like an enormous, white eye. *How*, Jacques wonders, *did that ship sail in here? It's impossible!*

The Dog Soldiers light several more torches, which cast a pastoral glow across the white water.

Jude walks up and places his hand on Jacques's shoulder. "What do you think, my ageless friend? This is the ship that carried all of us to Russia."

"I've never seen anything like it," Jacques replies, picking up a stone and then stopping, deciding not to skip it across the water. He turns and looks at Jude. "Everything is too perfect…how?" He raises his hands, questioning.

"We had a lot of time on our hands. A couple of hundred years." Jude wipes his blond hair away from his face. "We took it apart, piece by piece, and rebuilt it here. The Templar treasure and the Ark of the Covenant are on board." He claps his hands three times and shouts, "Jacques de Molay and Jude to board ship!"

A long, sturdy, wooden gangplank is lowered from the vessel for them to cross over on. "How safe is this place?" Jacques asks, as they walk across the water to the ship. What's to prevent a betrayer from giving this all up?"

"These guards that you see—" Jude points at the various Dog Soldiers. "They're what's left of the Knights Templar who left France with me. Only they know what's here. They built this. You know them all. They have powers beyond imagination. Like you advised me so many years ago, I chose wisely. None of the other Children of Sirius know of this place. Look at the water. See the blue reflections in it?"

Jacques nods.

"Watch," Jude says, grabbing several raw pieces of meat lying on the deck railing and scattering them across the lake. The water begins to boil like heavy gravy in a hot steel pot. Enormous striped snakes, several feet in length, with slanted, orange eyes, are attracted by the smell of blood and break the surface. Their sharp fangs rip one another's flesh as they fight over the meat.

"We've bred them using the glowworms of the Nile," Jude explains. "They're extremely deadly. Two drops of their venom will kill thirty people. An underground stream feeds the lake. They follow that into the Murman Sea, where they eat. They breathe like we breathe and can stay underwater for only a short time. They return here between hunts because it's dark and safe. If they're injured and need help, they crawl out of the water and wait in the cave for one of the Dog Soldiers. We smear their wounds with the Potion of Life, healing them. They never harm us."

Jacques is heartily welcomed on board by the Dog Soldiers. They all follow Jude down a ladder and into the cargo hold of the ship, where the Templar treasure and the Ark of the Covenant are stored. Jacques, after inspecting the area, stops in front of a small room built of rough-cut cedar. Hesitating, taking a deep breath of anticipation, he pulls back the green veil. There the ark sits in all its wondrous glory. It's a chest made of acacia wood, overlaid with pure gold inside and out, with a crown of gold around it. On top of it stand two cherubim at the two ends, facing downward toward the ark, with outstretched wings that spread over the atonement cover. Four rings of gold are attached to its four feet. Through the rings, staves of shittimwood, overlaid with gold, for carrying the ark, have been inserted and are never to be removed. A golden cover, the mercy seat, adorned with golden cherubim, has been placed over the ark. The entire structure was beaten out of one piece of pure gold. Everything is still there, exactly the way it was in France almost two hundred years ago. Back on the ship's deck, Jacques tells Jude and the Dog Soldiers, "The treasure and the ark are safe. Everything is at it was."

"We have set black powder," Jude says. "My wife showed us how. She calls them explosives. Much more powerful than fireworks." He walks back down the plank. "If we light the fuses, the explosives will blow a hole so big in the cavern wall—" he pauses, letting the thought sink in, "that the ship will be able to sail out to safety on the underground river that feeds the Murman Sea." He points to one of the walls in the cave. "See? Up there, the fading light on the stones? The sun is going down. We've been in here all day, and you didn't notice. This cave is a world unto its own."

"The time has come for me to leave," Jacques says. There's nothing more that he can do here. He has found out everything he wanted to know—even more—and it's good. Jude has everything under control. He misses Margaret. It's the wolf in him. She saved his life. Wolves mate forever. He also believes the One Hundred Twenty will do everything in their power to kill him, which puts everything at risk that Jude and the Knights Templar have built. It's time to go back and deal with Claude.

"We understand," Jude replies as they exit the cavern. "There, in that direction." He points eastward. "The large mountain that's taller than all the others."

"I see it," Jacques answers.

"That's the Mountain of the Dead," Jude continues. "It's where they land their flying ships. They fly through the air faster than a great wind and as silently as an empty cave. Mighty warriors, the vampires from the stars."

"Vampires in flying ships?" Jacques asks attentively. He's never heard of anything like this, but how can he forget Mithras? It all makes sense.

"Even the One Hundred Twenty are no match for them." Jude stares at Jacques for a moment. "They bring their captives—strange yet human-like creatures—here. They turn them loose and then hunt them down. We always find their dead. We've watched them get into deadly fights over their kills. They've been here as long as we have. They know we're here, but for some reason they leave us alone. Someday that may change, and so we wait." He places his hand on Jacques's shoulder. "Just go south, the way you came. You'll be all right. Stay far away from them. Their weapons aren't of this world, and their numbers are far greater than ours. If they catch you and think we were spying on them, they'll destroy the Children of Sirius, and all will be lost. No one will know we ever lived." He puts his arms around

Jacques and gives him a hug. "Where does your long journey take you from here?" he asks.

Jacques places his hand on top of his friend's. "I follow the path that beckons me." He swallows, thinking about his friend, the Knights Templar, and all that they've accomplished. "You've done so much, protecting the treasure, the ark. Saying thank you seems so, so trivial." Believing he'll never see Jude again, he leans down and kisses him on both cheeks. He tips his head back and then drops to one knee, giving him a good-bye gesture of respect. Shape-shifting into a wolf, he trots away.

The moon's shadowed light owns the starless night. A freezing wind blows. A narrow stream runs through the rocky, snow-packed ground. Large stones and fallen, broken trees litter the area. A small lean-to built from rough, hand-cut logs is supported by two cedar trees, one on each side. The sloping roof extends all the way to the ground; thus the roof itself forms the rear wall. Jacques pulls back the elk hide that hangs across the front of the structure. Inside, on the frozen ground, sit four lifeless creatures the likes of which Jacques never knew existed. Even in their hunched-over positions, they appear tall and slender. After crawling inside he brushes the light flakes of snow off them. Their blue suits are stretched tightly around their bodies. The vessels running through them are filled with a blood-red liquid. They have a thick, course, fleshly tissue that wraps up to the tops of their foreheads and thick hair, gray as dust that hangs in braids down the backs of their necks. Their ears are pointed like those of a cat.

Jacques kneels down next to one of the males. The blood has been drained from him, leaving a hollow, mummified skeleton with wrinkled, black skin, a shrunken face, and empty, yellow eyes. He tips his head back and sees several deep fang marks in his masticated neck. He checks the others and sees they've all been bitten numerous times. *This is what they do*, he realizes. *Keep them alive and share feedings. The lean-to keeps them hidden from the other vampires.*

Seeing streaks of blood on the female's skin, he leans over and licks the residue off her neck and feels an almost undetectable whisper of breath on his face. How? He can't believe it. Somehow, she's still alive. Her loss of blood—it seems impossible. He quickly bits her on the neck, sucking the little blood she has left, mixing it with his. He drinks it down while pushing his own back into her body. That tiny bit sends an unbelievable emotional charge through his system. He's never experienced anything that compares to it. It's incredible—like tasting emotions or having feelings or mood swings, but multiple times stronger. Suddenly Jacques has become extraordinarily conscious. He wonders what love tastes like—as well as anger, desire, excitement, rage, passion, sadness, joy, warmth, and on and on. These are the same emotions he hasn't felt in years, but they're much more dynamic and impressive than when he was a human.

Using his sharp fingernails, he quickly cuts open the front of her suit, pulling it down over her shoulders and firm breasts to her slender waist. Her body looks like a human's. He leans back and watches, fascinated. Like a wolf watching a helpless rabbit. *Shall I let it live or kill it?*

Her heart flickers and then begins beating steadily. His blood pumps through her veins and begins to warm her body, energizing it, immediately turning her sooty flesh to a translucent pink color, glowing beneath with violet-and-white light. First, one finger twitches and then another. Her long, heavily braided, hoary hair mutates and shines like gold. She quietly lifts her head and stares at Jacques while running her tongue across her sensuous, violet lips, her bright yellow eyes questioning, wondering what's going to happen next. She's remembering the inconceivable torture and pain the alien vampires put her and her counterparts through and wonders when he will kill her. She fears it won't happen quickly. The other vampires dragged it out until they drank every emotion out of their bodies, creating an endless aqueduct of flowing pain and agonizing torment—feelings of love, hope, and promise deluged by their evil, leaving an empty shell of hopelessness. Tears of anguish form in her eyes. She prays she will die quickly.

Jacques turns and, sitting in the snow, puts his hand on the Rider of the Sun birthmark, which is oscillating with the same emotions. Now he understands why the vampires hunt these space creatures. Their blood causes them to feel again, with emotions hundreds of times greater than a human's. Once sipped, the vampire's thirst for the blood is an eternal, enslaving addiction that cannot be satisfied. Fortunately, Jacques savored only the slightest drops of blood, just enough to leave him with the taste of emotion. Kneeling over he pulls her space suit back up and over her shoulders. "You are going to live," he says, while staring into her beautiful yellow eyes, like the summer sun high in the sky.

—w—

A heavy breeze blows, slapping the branches in the fir trees, casting dark shadows across the haunting, full moon, which the austere sky has turned to a violet, shadowed black. Wolf Jacques, attempting to take a shorter route, unexpectedly reaches the top of a ridge overlooking a valley on his third night. Not wanting to be seen, he shape-shifts into a vampire, crawls under some brush, and lies on his stomach, spreading his body out. Two of the vampires' orange ships are on the ground. They each have four paw-like feet and are covered in reptile-scaled skin with flashing lights of glittering stars, a moon, and a glistening white sun with a rainbow effect that seems to shine through everything. The ships have a tail and the flat head of a snake, their piercing red eyes reflecting the evil within.

The starships' high-energy particle-light sensors, observing any change in the environment surrounding them, scan and record the blue wolf's various energy fluctuations as he walks into their space. Running the data through their immense species catalog, they identify him in a millisecond as a nonexistent species on earth, which sets off the internal alarms, waking up the two spacecrafts to high alert, their laser-particle floodlights illuminating the area.

Jacques immediately knows he's set off some sort of warning system, but before he can react, he's surrounded by eight heavily armed vampire space creatures. Not sure of what to do next, he watches, waiting for a break.

Before Jacques can move, they trap him in a cage of white light that forms around him and sucks the energy from his body, rendering him helpless.

—w—

The vampires are extremely tall, and they walk on two feet. Their brownish-green hide appears lustrous but tough like the skin of a lizard. Instead of hair, running crossways over the tops and down the sides of their heads and necks, are stiff folds of skin, which also form their cheeks and ears; these folds are a vanilla color with orange streaks. Their dark-blue, catlike eyes are slightly larger than those of humans, and their orange lips, accented by white fangs, are thin. Their arms, legs, and hands have a very muscular appearance. The language they're speaking sounds very course and guttural, filled with deep growling and hissing noises, which Jacques seems to remember, but doesn't understand. All are wearing ash-gray, loose-fitting, high-collared suits with dark- and light-blue straps that wrap over the shoulders and hook into belts.

They know Jacques had to have shape-shifted from a wolf into a vampire, but they don't understand how he did it. Their history tells stories of their ancestors and how, thousands of years ago, they could shape-shift into different life-forms. Over the centuries, through evolution and the physical enhancement of their bodies—raised to a higher degree, intensified, magnified with performance-enhancing drugs and the transplantation of maximum-force, powerful muscles from other species—they have lost this ability. However, they haven't missed it. They are the Vampire Empire, conquerors of galaxies, destroyers of all. Nonetheless, they believe it might be worthwhile to study him, to do a whole-body transplant with this creature—transfer the head of one of their seriously wounded to his body. This would give one of their vampires a functioning host body while keeping his personality and memories intact.

The vampires are so assured of their catch that they begin to argue among themselves as to how to deal with him.

Jacques, gathering his wits, knows they aren't watching as he realizes the space between the narrow cage bars is just wide enough apart for a vampire bat, standing upright, to squeeze his little body through. Deciding the least expected is his best escape plan, he transforms and quickly flies away.

The starships' high-energy particle-light sensors observe the change and scan and record Jacques shape-shifting into a vampire bat; however, their species catalog identifies the creature as a nonexistent species in Europe, which shuts down the ships' alarms as the onboard computers report a system malfunction and the cage doesn't adjust to his smaller size.

—◊—

Some distance away the One Hundred Twenty are waiting for Jacques. To them, he is the great betrayer. Everything they believe in—the Blood Law—he sacrificed for his own selfish desires. Appearing to watch them, thousands of fireflies pepper specks of yellowish-blue light into the dead of night.

Jacques doesn't hear a noise, but a sixth sense tells him he's being watched. He also knows it's very dangerous and he's outnumbered. Quickly shape-shifting into a vampire bat, he attempts to fly out of harm's way. Behind him, the darkness fills with a swarm of large vampire bats that chase him.

Jacques is not only fast, but his mind quickly calculates his position by echolocation, and he orients himself to his surroundings at superfast speeds. He flies complex patterns, zigzagging through the trees, around rocks and other obstacles, and he pulls away from the other bats. Up ahead he sees the entrance to a long deep valley. He angles downhill, taking advantage of gravity—but then something vehement rips him painfully out of the sky and sends him crashing into the cold ground. He is tangled up in fishing net, and his thrashing only tightens the net's hold. The One Hundred and Twenty must have hung it across the entranceway into the canyon, guessing that's where he would fly. How right they were. He transforms into a wolf, hoping he can fight and chew his way out, but the One Hundred and Twenty prepared for this. As soon as they reach him, they also transform into wolves and attack Jacques. Fangs bared, they begin tearing at him, but they're quickly stopped.

Petya the Rock, a monstrous, silver wolf, walks up and growls at the others, ordering them back. He slowly circles around Jacques a couple of times, measuring him, relishing the thought of the kill. He snarls at the other wolves to pull the net off, freeing his victim. He orders other vampires to post guard so that Jude and the Dog Soldiers will not surprise them. Shape-shifting into a vampire, he stands tall, all seven feet and three hundred and fifty pounds of him. Thick, rugged, powerful muscles surge across his shoulders and ripple across his stomach. Dancing about, jacking his mighty legs high like a prancing horse while beating his chest, he challenges Jacques.

"What is the Blood Law?" Petya yells, standing tall, holding his hands up.

"Life!" they shout. "Convert only the poor, the sick, the persecuted, the hungry, the weak, the downtrodden!"

"What is the promise?" Petay screams.

"The life of a vampire must be better than one's life as a human!" the One Hundred Twenty's loud voices shatter the night.

"What is family?" Petya hollers as he struts back and forth, firing up his followers.

"We will defend the One Hundred Twenty to the death!" they shout back, continuing to beat their chests. "*Aaseeebooo! Aaseeebooo!*"

"What is the punishment for breaking the Law?" Petya yells.

"Banishment for life!" the One Hundred Twenty roar back in unison. "No one is above the Blood Law!"

Jacques, free of the fishing net, shape-shifts into a vampire. From a lying position on the ground, he leaps up and attacks Petya, catching the giant off guard, knocking him off-balance. The fight carries into the early morning. Many times during the bloodthirsty battle, Jacques is quicker and occasionally gets the better of Petya, ripping chunks of flesh out of his body. Whenever this happens the other wolves viscously attack him, protecting their mighty hero. Eventually Jacques is so damaged, with broken ribs and torn flesh, that fighting is impossible, and he falls down. He attempts to stand several times, but he can't. His blood loss is great, and he's slowly dying.

Large flocks of eagles, hawks, and other birds of prey, attracted by the noise and the smell of blood, crisscross the sky. When they land, their numbers blanket the trees. Their excited gawking rattles the air as the early morning sunlight begins to cast its gleam across the land.

Unexpectedly, Jude the Great walks out from the trees and into the open clearing where Petya and Jacques have been fighting. "I have seen," he challenges loudly, pointing aggressively at Petya and the other vampires. "One Hundred and Twenty against one. You shame yourselves." He spits blue saliva onto the ground. "Now," he points at his chest. "It's still One Hundred and Twenty against One!" The yellow glowworms ripple across his skin like rapids, cascading along all the muscles of his body, charging them. His eyes shine like Sirius. His yellow day-flesh pulsates to fighting red. The red glowworms crawl from his ears, lie inside his lips and between his teeth, and stretch out of his nose.

Petya steps back. He doesn't understand how Jude got through his guards, but he'll deal with that later. Once again, it's time for his faithful followers to demonstrate their loyalty to him. He commands his three most prolific killers, "Attack!"

Jude draws his sword, waving it while his body radiates a fiery red light, as hot as burning coals, that incinerates the grass and brush all around him, leaving the ground charred black. The heat scorches the skin of the three attacking vampires and burns their eyes. Their long, red hair shrivels and falls away, leaving them bald. Their screams burst the ears of mortal species in the valley. They stumble blindly, and blood pours from their mouths and noses.

Jude, stepping forward and swinging his sword, chops off their heads, one at a time. Like chickens that have had their necks wrung, the dead vampires hop and spin around, pumping their legs before falling, kicking and thrashing, to the ground.

Petya, his fellow vampires, and Jacques are beginning to burn in the morning sunlight. The other wolves want to try to separate Jude from Jacques and finish him off before the sun breaks free of the horizon, but Petya stops them. They've run out of time. They need to leave now or burn. And he believes that Jacques's fate is sealed—that the vampire is dying. *Not even Jude can save him*, Petya thinks. He's wondered for a long time about Jude and the Dog Soldiers and how powerful they are. Now he knows.

"Until next time!" Petya shouts, pointing at Jude. "Until next time."

Jude, his flesh flashing like a volcano spitting heat, hoping that there is still time, cools his body down to daytime yellow, grabs Jacques, and drags him into the heavily tree-shadowed forest. Several Dog Soldiers, their flesh the green of neither day nor night, are impatiently waiting for him. They've been watching—just in case he needed their help. Not even Jude, whose flesh is pulsating to green, knew they followed him, but he is thankful for their loyalty.

"This way! Hurry, hurry!" the Dog Soldiers shout as they hustle up to Jude and, grabbing Jacques, help carry him into the thickness of the dark forest. On the way, their bodies adapt to the colors of the flora, becoming virtually invisible to the naked eye except for their translucent-like movements. They know they don't have much time. Jacques's body is hot and his breathing ragged. Beads of sweat are starting to form around his lips and forehead, and he's beginning to slip in and out of consciousness.

Four of the Dog Soldiers run ahead to a small, log-and-stone, fur-trapping hut and cover the two tiny window openings with grizzly bear hides to keep out the sun's deadly rays.

"He's dying! We need blood!" Jude demands loudly, while anxiously waving his hand in the air and staring at the shack. "I didn't bring him here to watch him die!"

"We have live rabbits," a Dog Soldier shouts as they carry Jacques inside the hut and lay him on the hard dirt floor. A shaded lantern that hangs next to the brown-and-reddish-stone fireplace is lit by a Dog Soldier. Several frightened, grayish-brown, fur-spiked, wide-eyed rabbits are hanging from the roof's support beams by brown leather straps tied around their back legs. Another Dog Soldier hurriedly cuts down two of them and hands one to Jude who rapidly slits the screaming animal's throat with his long-handled skinning knife. He grabs the back of Jacques's head and presses the flesh of the animal's bleeding neck against his face. "Drink and live!" he commands. "Drink and live!"

Drink Jacques does. A few swallows at first and then ravenously sucking the rabbit's body dry. Jude tosses that rabbit aside and grabs another one the Dog Soldier has just skinned and holds it against his friend's mouth. Jacques, breathing deeply, takes a couple of drinks of the warm blood and then rips the quivering rabbit out of Jude's hand and begins ferociously gorging himself on the warm, raw flesh, ripping and tearing the meat with his sharp teeth until nothing remains except broken bones and scattered scraps of flesh. Taking a deep, cool-headed breath, he looks hungrily at the other rabbits hanging above him and knows he'll eat another two or three before dark. He'll need their strength to carry him through the night. The rest he'll turn loose.

"How?" he asks Jude, feeling stronger, sitting up by himself. His face, hands, hair, and chest are red with wasted blood. "Where did you come from?"

"Over the last two hundred years, I and the Knights Templar have learned how to mask the colors of Sirius," Jude responds. "We blend into our surroundings so that not even the animals know we're there."

11

THE RENAISSANCE MAN, LEONARDO DA VINCI

AD 1503

André and Pierre-Louis are still lurking around remote areas of France, raiding pubs at night. André has invented a new game that Pierre-Louis participates in called "tipping a few." One of them holds a drunk person over his head, upside down by his ankles, while the other one, kneeling, bites the person's neck and drinks his blood. One particular night, after a great deal of boozing, André leans his shoulder against a tree for balance so he can take a piss.

"I've told you this hundreds of times already—vampires can't piss so good," Pierre-Louis reminds him.

André babbles, "I keeps forgetting. Too much booze, not enough snoooozze. Ahhhhh, yes," he moans proudly. "I can still shake it."

"I hears that one before, too. Forget how many times," Pierre-Louis pipes back. "Not much shaking going on," he tries to sing in his high-pitched, howling-wolf voice while wiggling his big, gelatinous, bouncing butt around, performing ill-conceived, uncoordinated moves. He and André have tried on many occasions to drink so much booze that the impact of the alcohol will make them think they're having fun, but it never works. Vampires are never supposed to get lost, but they always do when drinking too much. This happens to them most nights of the week and sometimes twice a night. Once, they got plastered four times during a total eclipse of the sun. Half the people in France were drunk, running around, screaming and shouting, praying, asking God to forgive them. Prophets were predicting the world was coming to an end. Pierre-Louis and André didn't have to chase anyone. Most people were already on their knees. All they had to do was lean over and bite them.

André, his small, bat ears laid back, his short tail sticking straight up, was furiously beating his tiny bat wings, attempting to fly fast enough to keep up with the eclipse and remain in the darkness. However, the rays of the hot sun began to emerge with the passing of the moon, causing his hairy legs and body to smoke.

Two peasants, mystified by the eclipse, saw a strange puff of black, punch-drunk soot, zigzagging, whirling, wobbling through the air. "Look! Look!" one of the excited peasants hollered while shaking his hand and pointing. "It's a bat outta hell!"[4]

It was the best night out André and Pierre-Louis can remember.

After Jacques's departure from France, Clarete wandered to Italy, where she made a home among the ancient ruins of the Roman Empire. Over the years she's learned to speak Italian, Russian, English, Spanish, Portuguese, and several other languages fluently and has become more Italian than French. She's watched as the more powerful city-states annexed their smaller neighbors and as adventurers took to the seas in large sailing ships and discovered new worlds.

Now, at the beginning of the sixteenth century, the country is in the midst of a cultural movement, the Renaissance. Individuals are involved in intellectual pursuits, educational reform, and scientific study. This period is perhaps best known for cultivating the great geniuses, including Botticelli and Michelangelo—and Leonardo da Vinci, the original Renaissance man. The Renaissance eventually will encompass all of Europe, closing the door to the Middle Ages.

For many years, the rapes and physical abuse Clarete suffered in the French debtors' prison have been throbbing wounds, even nearly two centuries later, and the pain has made her fierce and ruthless. She lies in wait in crumbling temples or the falling arches of the Colosseum, ravaging unsuspecting peasants who happen by. But the killings do nothing to ease her pain. The feel of her fangs penetrating soft, warm skin and the taste of hot, sticky blood are twigs on the fire of her rage.

Italy is a country with some of the most varied, scenic landscapes on earth. It's shaped like a boot, with the Alps at the northern end, the Adriatic and Tyrrhenian Seas flanking either side, and the Mediterranean Sea at the bottom. The country boasts rugged landscapes, great forests, alpine lakes surrounded by snowcapped mountains, coastal plains, and tiny independent villages separated by difficult travel conditions, various dialects, and mutual mistrust. More than 75 percent of the country is mountainous or hilly. This diverse land is home to roe deer, lynx, brown bears, wild boars, wolves, and foxes. The captivating alpine sky nurtures the black grouse, golden eagle, and wood grouse.

Clarete drifts through various city-states toward northern Italy: Milan, Treviso, Brescia, Cremona, Mantua, Bologna, Piacenza, Venice, and others. She transforms into a bat and flies into these areas, undetected, using the cover of night, attacking the first people she encounters, drinking her fill of blood, and converting her victims into vampires. She goes on wild killing sprees, slashing necks with her razor-sharp teeth, tearing gashes across the bodies of old women pulling water from wells or young farmers plucking the ripest fruits from their vines. With claws like sharpened glass, she rakes her hands across their bodies, leaving them mutilated and then discarding them to be discovered the next day, a testament to her rage. She pours her pain into her victims through the venom that is her blood, scratching agony into human bodies. She wants all to suffer as she has.

The Church and others hunt down Clarete's vampire followers, killing them in the most gruesome ways, while she quietly moves into the countryside, morphing into a wolf and slaughtering sheep and cattle. Over time her legend grows, and people begin to watch for her arrival. At night, sentries peer into the darkness for anything strange, unusual.

This night, a watchman stationed in a bell tower spots vampire-bat Clarete, flying into the village. After grabbing two meter-long, oak logs that hang sideways, he pushes them into the copper bell, banging out the alarm.

More than a hundred villagers with their galaxy of torches lighting up the night sky chase the enormous bat, pushing Clarete south to the rural area surrounding Florence, the cultural center of Italy. From now on, she adapts her tactics, killing only animals, and only to satisfy her hunger. The lack of passable roads and communication between villages and hamlets makes it easy for her to remain undetected for several years, until a wedding takes place between a well-bred bride and a wealthy landowner from separate villages.

The wedding is a six-day feast, with storytelling, singing, and dancing in sweet concert. Guests breakfast on meats, boiled eggs, bread, pastries, and wine from the vineyard and sup on roasted chicken dressed with reattached feathers for effect. At some point the dowry is exchanged. The women wear colorful scarves to cover their hair so they won't outshine the bride. This bride wears a red-belted gown of green wool with long, red, voluminous sleeves. A matching red, silk scarf winds around her neck and through her braided, brown hair and then floats down her back. The groom wears a green, wool shirt; black, knee-high boots; a black doublet; red hose; a red robe as an overgown; and a brimless, scarlet cap.

The wedding is an opportunity for villagers to exchange news and catch up on gossip. The men discuss weather, crops, and dead sheep and calves. The dead animals all have torn throats, as if they were attacked by wolves, but they're all oddly bloodless. The villagers have often seen a woman, eerily beautiful, wearing a turquoise dress with shoulders bared, her hair flowing behind her as she leaves the scene of the killings.

"Who is she?" they ask one another. "Where does she come from? Does anyone know her?"

On the third night of festivities, the woman is spotted, and several men follow her to an ancient cemetery where a witch is buried. It's a clear, moonlit night, and the ground is littered with bones. Many of the skulls are split by flat stones that have been driven through them so the blood will drain out. If vampires cannot suck the blood out of freshly buried bodies, the corpses cannot rise from the dead. Seventeen spikes—an unlucky number in Italy because of its association with death—have been driven around the witch's body and into the planks to which she has been nailed. They wanted to make sure she never rises from her grave.

Hiding behind a cluster of trees on the side of a small, brush-covered hill, the men, with help from the full moon, watch as Clarete pulls open a small, bronze door and disappears into an earth-brown stone crypt. This is her home. It's where she's been staying, along with witches and other nightmares of the dark, for the past several months. It's where she feels safe. Other young women are buried here in shallow graves with no coffin or shroud, surrounded by seventeen dice and other sinful games—such as cards or games of skill and strategy—that they were forbidden to play when they were alive. The locals stay away from this malevolent place.

Clarete relishes the cool, still-as-death air. On some nights the damp, putrid odor of decomposing flesh rises from the soil, an evil smell that drives her mad with the desire to kill. This is one of those dark, wicked nights.

Earlier that evening she ran down the most magnificent animal in all of Italy, a male red deer. The large buck ran for its life but was no match for the redoubtable she-wolf. Clarete leapt, transforming back into her human form, with snarling lips and giant fangs. Her thick, brown hair cascaded down her back as she extended her powerful arms. She forcefully landed on the back of her prey, staggering it, digging her sharp, swordlike fingernails into its hide, ripping the skin back. The buck cried and stumbled, struggling to keep its balance.

With her left arm wrapped around its shoulder, Clarete rode the animal while sinking her fangs into its neck and tearing its throat out, drinking its blood. She bulldogged the buck to the ground in a swirl of excitement, like a tornado ravishing everything virtuous and good in its path. She sucked the buck dry and then tore off its skin with her powerful fingers. She dug out the eyes and the tongue, savoring them. She tore the legs from the carcass, snapping the bones, ripping and devouring the meat, leaving her covered in blood and mangled deer flesh. When she finally appeased her prodigious appetite, she smashed the buck's rib cage with her fist and ripped out its heart. She slowly wiped it around her face, smearing its blood on her skin, paying tribute to the great animal before slowly feeding on it. The assault left her exhausted, and she transformed into a wolf and walked slowly back to the graveyard.

It's a black, full moon tonight with a blanket of light-blue rays spreading out around and crawling over its edges. Inside her crypt, Clarete howls a low, forlorn cry. She thinks of her pack, André and Pierre-Louis, and their hunts together. She wonders about Jacques, Jude the Great, and her family, as well as her old hunting grounds in France. Those days seem so very close, and yet it's been nearly two hundred years since she's been with her friends. Where will her solitary trail lead? She drops her dispirited head and lets out another quiet, melancholy howl.

Normally Clarete would immediately have sensed the men hiding on the hill, but she's sick from eating the rabid deer. It must have become infected within the last hour before her attack; otherwise, she would have tasted the difference and spat out the poisoned blood at the first bite. After hanging up her dress, she fans the dirt off the stone body shelf and lies down on the cool slab. She'll feel better shortly.

The men rush back to report to the villagers.

"The woman is a witch!" someone shouts.

"A vampire!" cries another. The villagers are thinking of the spikes they'll need to kill her.

"We know where she sleeps," another man says, raising his fist in the air.

They shout scripture to one another, and it tastes like blood. "No one shall be found among you who makes a son or daughter pass through fire, who practices divination, or is a soothsayer, or an augur, or a sorcerer, or one that casts spells, consults ghosts or spirits, or who seeks oracles from the dead. For whoever does these things is abhorrent to the Lord. Thou shalt not suffer a witch to live."

"Amen!" they all cry out, their voices rising to a fever pitch. "Amen! Amen! Time to kill Satan's child."

It's a dark, dark, sticky night, with nearly black clouds that hide the stars and the moon. A cool wind blows, ahead of the approaching thunderstorm.

Drunk from the wedding, the men carry crosses and torches and shout blasphemies to the Devil as they march righteously to a killing—it seems somehow fitting to celebrate this way. Their cries quiet down as they approach the graveyard and search for the small, stone crypt where Clarete rests. Quietly, a couple of the leaders throw a fishing net over the tomb to prevent their prey from escaping. Three others, carrying German and Italian muzzle-loading rifles loaded with silver balls, position themselves around the tomb. It takes several men numerous tries to pry open the ancient, bronze door, awakening Clarete. She has never used the door to leave the burial chamber, so now she transforms into a bat and flies through a small opening between two stones, only to find herself caught in the fishing net.

This isn't their first vampire hunt, but it is the first vampire bat they've ever caught. Their other victims were mentally challenged women or other females they'd condemned, hunted down, and killed.

Clarete transforms back into a vampire, screaming and fighting against the netting, tearing it with her hands and teeth. She strikes two of the villagers, who tumble off the crypt's roof, but two others manage to hang a cross on the fishing net next to her body, and she drops powerlessly to her knees. The men drag her to the ground and place her on a wooden plank. One of them drives spikes through her hands and feet—in crucifixion position—outlining her naked body, pinning her down, seventeen spikes in all to ensure she won't rise from the dead. The men then load her into the back of a wagon.

They drive the wagon fast, with several riders following. They rush toward Florence and the essential blessings of a priest so they can kill Clarete properly. Without a blessing, they worry she'll feed on the bodies of the dead, gathering strength until she rises from the grave. Then she'll return to take revenge on them and their families, creating new vampires and spreading the scourge.

Gusts of wind stir the branches in the trees that pepper the hilly countryside. A cool rain falls, soaking Clarete's captors and their horses. Lightning and cracks of thunder rip across the incensed sky. The rain falls harder, turning the road into a trail of mud, slowing the wagon and the riders. Blasts of wind snap the limbs off trees. The riders hunker down, chins on their chests, hats pulled low, their visibility limited. They attempt to wipe their faces, but it doesn't help; they can't keep up. Their cotton shirts are waterlogged and dripping.

The men believe the storm is a curse brought by the young woman they captured, one of the Devil's chosen, but there's nothing to do but press on. They can't chance releasing the vampire because a plague will curse their families forever. One of the riders considers killing his two young daughters if they don't get Clarete to a priest. Only his prayers can spare the girls from the evil scourge that will befall all of them.

Jagged, white lightning like human blood vessels flashes in the sky, illuminating the outlines of the mountain creek they must cross. Using rope, four riders tie their steeds to the wagon's team of horses and edge them into the fast-moving current, helping to pull the wagon behind them. The other riders cross and wait on the other side. The night is frighteningly dark, with the wind and rain making it worse. It's impossible to see. A rush of water roars toward them, sweeping away everything in its path, headed for rocks and branches. The wagon is slammed in the side by the debris washing over it. The impact tossing the driver into the swollen creek, sweeping him away in the strong current.

The plank to which Clarete has been nailed is carried away by the raging torrent and sent downstream, rolling over and over, crashing against jagged rocks and broken tree limbs, dragging her along the shore. Her naked body is bashed and bruised, the spikes ripping through her flesh.

The horseback riders alongside the ferocious stream can't let her escape. The plank flips, burying her face in the surging water. Clarete gasps for air; she's drowning. Then the fishing net, intertwined with the cross, is torn from her body by a large tree limb rolling by. Regaining some strength, she pulls her hands up, tearing her palms through the nails. She yanks the spikes out of her feet and pulls herself to dry land. Her regenerative powers instantly heal her injuries.

One of the riders has a leather cap the size of his finger over the barrel of his muzzle-loader to keep the powder dry. He quickly pulls the rifle out of its heavy cowhide case, lifts it to his shoulder, and fires. It's point-blank range, but the turmoil surrounding him throws his aim, and the bullet rips into Clarete's shoulder, missing her heart and knocking her to the ground. She struggles under the impact of the silver bullet, which, because of its purity, has the power to kill her. The riders, spreading out, pursue her.

Clarete stumbles up a footpath through the olive groves, the silver slowly sapping her strength like a sponge absorbs water. She hears the hoofbeats of the horses behind her. Through the rainstorm, her vampire vision enables her to see the light from a lantern inside a farmhouse a short distance away. Unlike many houses at the time, where people use thin strips of horn or linen soaked in tallow to make a translucent window, this house has glass windows, so she knows the owner is well-off. But the riders will look for her in such an obvious, visible place, so she breaks off the path, struggling through a thicket of trees and edging up a hillside. She hopes the riders' pursuit will take them to the farmhouse, and she'll lose them in the storm.

An earsplitting lightning bolt rips across the heavens, illuminating the sky. Clarete sees a cave, partially hidden behind a thick growth of under-brush. The opening is just large enough for her to slide through. Her eyes quickly adjust to the dark, gloomy place. She hears bats, the sounds of crickets, snakes, and lizards, and the wild storm fuming outside. Finally she feels safe. She collapses against the side of a rock and checks the bullet wound in her left shoulder. She has to get it out somehow or she'll die. The silver is like a deadly poison, eating its way through her body. She needs blood, raw meat for strength, but first she must rest. Tomorrow night she'll have to eat, or her vampire hunger will turn on her like a disease, eating away at her body so that she may live, but killing her in the end. After brushing away the stones and smoothing the dirt, she lies down on her good side, curling her naked body, pulling her knees to her chest, and clos-ing her eyes. She has chosen a spot close to the opening of the cave so she can hear any visitors.

The year is 1503, and Leonardo da Vinci has moved back to Florence, only twenty-eight miles from Vinci, his childhood home. Vinci is a tiny hamlet surrounded by the Tuscan hills, a landscape of vineyards, fruit-laden olive trees, rolling meadows, and green trees. Leonardo from Vinci was born on April 15, 1452, in a cinnamon-colored fieldstone farmhouse three kilometers from Vinci, in the rural area of Anchiano. He stands around five feet eight and possesses mannered elegance. He's dashing, with thick, luxu-riant, reddish-golden, gray-flecked hair that rolls down to his shoulders. His chest-length beard falls in waving cascades. He enjoys bright colors—the bold shades of red, blue, green, and yellow—and wears tunics and hose to match his personality. He spends much of his time at his childhood home. He loves the countryside, the wild animals, the birds, the streams, the feel-ings of newness each day brings. His is an idyllic, observing nature, which fuels his vision of creativity, his infinite curiosity, his inventiveness.

Leonardo sits at a square, oak table and works on a sketch for a painting he calls *The Battle of Anghiari*. The battle took place in 1440 between the Milanese and the victorious Florentines. It's a drawing of a desperate battle between two charging horse cavalries amid the smoke of cannons and dust. The steeds hurtle their magnificent bodies into one another, savagely ripping one another's necks apart with their teeth. It will be Leonardo's most ambitious—and possibly his greatest—work to date, an immense painting that will be some sixty feet across when completed. He will work on it at the council hall of the Palazzo Vecchio in Florence, where it will take up an entire wall. The painting will represent his innermost thoughts about the evils of war and the violence of man, which he describes as "the most beastly madness."

Leonardo is left-handed and uses mirror writing, moving from right to left in a script most easily read in a mirror, to make notes about his painting. In front of other people, he easily can adapt to normal—right-handed— writing to avoid seeming sinister, the word the Church uses to describe left-handed writers. The Church considers left-handedness a cause for suspicion and accuses these "wrong-handed" writers of consorting with the Devil, condemning them to death by execution. Leonardo has never told anyone his secret.

On this night, he slides his olive-oil-burning lamp closer for better light. The lamp, he believes, is one of his more useful inventions. Now he can choose the time he wants to work, day or night. He is the first to enclose a wick in a glass tube filled with olive oil that sits inside a water-filled glass globe. The flame, protected by the globe, burns steadily, as it's not affected by the movement of air. It also produces better illumination due to the magnification of the light by the water.

There's a bang, bang, banging at his door. As he gets up from his work, he wonders who it could be on this windy, stormy night. "This had better be important," he mumbles as he opens the door.

The riders' cotton shirts, saturated with rainwater, hang from their bodies. It's been a long, arduous night. Their horses stomp nervously behind them, exhausted, their bodies heaving. The sun is creeping over the horizon, light conquering the dark fury of the tempest, and the rain has eased up.

"Signor Leonardo," one of the tired riders begins, breathing heavily, his voice gravelly from the hard ride, "we's been chasing a witch." He sniffs and spits, whipping his arm across his wet face. "Most a' the night. Maybe a vampire. Don't know for sure." His horse paws the ground and throws its gray head back, jerking the reins. "She's a bad one, she is. One a' the worst. Put seventeen nails in her, we did. Right to the board." He puts his hand against his nose, leans over, and blows it. "Lost her in the creek. Bad, bad water took the wagon and busted it up. Have you seen her? We tracked her to here." He sneezes and wipes the rainwater from his face again. "Know a place a witch or vampire could hide around here?"

Everyone in the area knows Leonardo and where he lives; his reputation is larger than life. "I've been cooking some soup," he responds while looking the riders over. He's wrapped in a light-blue cloak and wearing a dark-blue wool cap pulled down over his ears, along with one brown slipper and one blue slipper, and standing under a small extension of the roof that's keeping him dry from the light drizzle that's falling. "I'm getting old," he says, his voice strong and assertive. "Needed something to warm the belly. Get some sleep. I don't believe in vampires or witches. Wouldn't know one if I saw one and don't know where one would hide. I've seen some frightening people in my lifetime—couldn't tell the difference."

He's convinced the stories of vampires and witches are just another way for the authorities to keep the populace under control. By keeping the public afraid of imaginary nighttime creatures, the government can pretty much do as it wants during the day.

He scratches his behind and the back of his leg. *Could be fleas, lice, bedbugs, or all three,* he thinks, *but they sure itch.* He shakes his head in frustration. He can't believe he keeps forgetting to ask one of the seamstresses in Florence to weave him a ticking mattress cover. *I've got to get rid of these bugs somehow.*

"Get yourselves home before you get the sickness," Leonardo tells the men. "That'll kill you faster than these mythological demons you're chasing."

Another rider moves his horse close to Leonardo, causing him to step back toward the house. The man impatiently injects himself into the conversation; he's very direct and controlling. "I shot at her!" He holds his muzzle-loader above his head for Leonardo to see. "With a silver ball. I think I hit her but couldn't tell. The storm—so much evil protecting her.

She could be dying and looking for a place to lie down—some shelter. Where could she hide around here?"

Leonardo has grown weary of this conversation. "You go look where you want. I'm going to eat that soup. Should be done."

He doesn't tell them there's a cave a short distance away that he used to play in as a boy—a deep, dark, scary place where great monsters lurked and made his childhood imagination run wild. He watches the riders leave, following the muddy path through the olive groves. He's excited as he steps back inside. A large smile crosses his heavy face, which is etched from years of concentrated thought. He hasn't felt this way in decades; he hasn't been inside that cave since he was eleven years old. "What if there really is a vampire hiding there?" He chuckles softly. "Maybe she'd let me paint her portrait." He laughs, forgetting about the soup while pouring himself a cup of wine. "You're a foolish old man, Leonardo," he says, smiling. "Such great fun." He takes a sip of the wine while walking to his bedroom. Time to take a nap, rest up for his adventure.

—◊—

As the sun is setting, Clarete is awakened by the sound of someone approaching the cave. Her sensitive hearing picks up the sounds of footsteps and the bushes at the mouth of the cave being pushed aside. Then she sees the flickering of a torchlight and the face of an elderly man peering inside the cave. Her animalistic instincts go on high alert. She stands and moves off to one side, against the wall of the cave. Her body burns from the pain of her bullet wound. Just a few more minutes, and it would have been dark enough for her to escape. She doesn't want to kill anyone. If a dead body is found, the entire countryside will be looking for her. She decides to lie down, play helpless like a wounded deer, and see what happens. After all, it's only one old man.

Leonardo steps into the cave, his heart pounding with excitement; coming here frightens him, just as it did when he was a child. Holding his torch high, he takes a couple of cautious steps inside, and the sight of Clarete leaves him shaken. She's naked and curled up on the ground. He raises the torch higher, peering into the darkness, looking for others. Several bats, startled by the light, fly out of the cave, taking him by surprise, and he stumbles, almost dropping the torch. Catching his breath, he places his hand over his chest and smiles; his heart's still pumping. He loves this cave and the feeling of being eleven years old again.

Clarete, carefully watching him, takes a deep breath. She knows her only chance to live is for him to help her.

Leonardo kneels next to her and gently places his hand on her shoulder, moving it slightly to see whether she's conscious. She moans, blinking her eyes, gazing up at him. "Don't move, my child," he says, concern lacing his voice. "I'm something of a physician. I've spent countless hours studying human anatomy." Holding the torchlight closer, he follows the length of her naked form, analyzing the wound, the fresh blood on her shoulder and chest. He can't help but think how beautiful her body is.

"Strange," he mutters. Her body seems to glisten, which reminds him of something, but he quickly forgets what. He has painted several portraits in his life but no one quite as perfect as this. He takes off his blue cotton shirt and wraps it around her wounded shoulder, tying it tightly to stop the bleeding.

Placing his arm around her waist, he encourages her to stand, but she resists, looking up at him. She doesn't have any eyebrows, he sees, and of course he wonders why.

"No, no," she mumbles. "The hunters will be back, looking for me. They'll kill me. I need to stay here in the dark, where they can't find me. Please don't tell them." Clarete looks at Leonardo, her eyes meeting his. The torch illuminates his face. He's a handsome man for his age, his face nearly free of wrinkles, with a distinctive nose and a slightly receding hairline. He possesses an air of dignity, and his enormous self-confidence is apparent in his bearing. His penetrating, blue-gray eyes provide a comforting softness.

"I have a wine cellar," he responds. "You would be safe there during the day. It's not much, but only I know of its existence. There's a small bed there where you can rest. Sometimes I go down there to relax when it's hot outside, to think about things." He nods reassuringly. "It's much cooler there. Please, my child. You'll die if you don't let me help you. The walk is all downhill."

"I can't go out there," Clarete responds faintly. "The riders will see me. Kill or capture me. They think I'm a witch."

Leonardo, holding the torch, walks to the entrance of the cave. Pushing the bushes aside, he peers out. "The sun has gone down," he replies. "You'll be safe. Please, child," he pleads. "Let me help you."

"All right." Clarete sighs. "All right." She knows there isn't another choice.

"Put your arm around my neck," he says, as he wraps his arm around her waist. "You'll have to try to help me. Not as young as I used to be." He can't believe how strong she feels as she pulls herself up and her skin… so soft and smooth yet unusually firm. The way it seems to shimmer in the torchlight is glorious. It reminds him of the spider-silk cloth woven in Florence and other cities in Italy. Only the nobles or the very wealthy can afford to luxuriate in its rare, exquisite aura. *How can this young lady have skin of such a rare quality that looks and feels like spider-silk cloth?* he asks his analytical self.

Gasping for breath, Leonardo does his best to help Clarete down the very steep hill, which is rough going in places. The torch he's holding casts scattered shadows on the rocks and trees. The sweat from his forehead burns into his eyes. It blurs his vision, making it difficult for him to pick the best places to step in the weed-infested path. Clarete has a painfully strong grip on his shoulder, which he finds surprising given her condition. Several times they stumble and almost fall, but Leonardo is determined to get her to the safety of his house. When they finally struggle through the front door, he's exhausted, breathless. He's amazed that she's still with him, that the loss of blood hasn't killed her. He gently lays her on his bed and lights the three oil lanterns in the room.

Hurrying through the house, he grabs the kitchen bucket, which is almost full with drinking water, as well as a bottle of whiskey, a sharp skinning knife, two sewing needles, thread, and a gray-blue cotton nightshirt.

"This is going to hurt," he cautions, while sitting on the edge of the bed next to Clarete. He heats the skinning knife's razor-sharp blade over the flame of an oil lamp that sits on a small wooden table next to the bed. Several years ago he came to the conclusion that heat purifies objects. He also believes anything being used to seal an open wound should be purified.

He's experimented with needles and thread and has stitched the wounds of horses, cattle, and sheep with great success.

"I have to dig the muzzle-loader ball out of your shoulder," he says, holding up the knife so she can see it. You may pass out from the pain and also bleed a great deal. It's going to hurt; the knife blade is hot. Scream if you must."

"I understand," Clarete mumbles.

Leonardo presses the knife into her shoulder. The burning blood hisses from the heat of the blade. He keeps digging, cutting deeper, until he's able to get under the silver ball and lift it out of her shoulder. He sets it on a cloth on the table next to him.

Even in Clarete's weakened state, screaming from the pain, she manages to force blood away from the wound so her vampiric regenerative powers won't heal her too quickly; otherwise, Leonardo will realize something is very unusual about her.

Leonardo, after dipping a handful of cloth into the bucket, washes the wound, pours whiskey on it, and then stitches it closed with the needle and thread. Most surgeons during his time believed in bloodletting, but he isn't one of them. Throughout his tireless years of observation, whenever he saw animals or humans lose blood, they became weakened and in many instances died. That was enough proof for him.

Clarete acts as if she has fainted. Now that the silver bullet has been removed, her vampire blood quickly seals the wounds. Her body already is beginning to mend, getting stronger. All she needs is nourishment.

After inspecting his work, Leonardo tears his gray-blue nightshirt into strips and wraps the wound. Satisfied, he covers her naked body with a light-green cotton blanket. *Hopefully she'll live*, he thinks, while pulling closed the tan curtain that hangs over the window so no unexpected visitors might see her. Leaving the room, he takes the silver ball with him. He'll look at it later, melt it down, make a paperweight.

He finds her to be a most unusual woman. But of course he's a man of the world. He's been to Rome many times, including the port of Civitavecchia, and he's seen strange animals and treasures and people from all parts of the known and unknown world. And the oddities are always the most interesting. *Ah, yes*. He grins. *How exciting*. God has been good to him, bringing such an unusual creature into his life. And to think those idiots thought this beautiful creature was a vampire or witch. So ridiculous. He prays she will feel better in a few days.

That night, while Leonardo is sleeping, Clarete quietly sneaks out the front door and into the darkness. She kills two wild rabbits, drinks their blood, and eats them raw.

The next morning, just before sunrise, Leonardo checks in on her and finds her sitting up, looking very fresh, the blanket wrapped around her. He smiles to himself. His operation went much better than he expected. He lays three nightshirts on the bed next to her. "Personally I like the red, but the dark blue and green are nice also." He offers Clarete stale bread along with some vegetables he's grown in a small garden. "I don't eat meat. I call myself a vegetarian." He smiles. "You should try some."

"I'm not hungry," she declines weakly. "I just need rest. Help me to the cellar, please...in case the men come back."

Leonardo believes it's much too early to be moving her; she might tear out the stitches, but a promise is a promise. He helps her up from the bed and slowly walks her to the other side of the room. "This will only take a minute," he says proudly, as he walks back to the bed. "I designed it myself." He pulls aside the reddish wool rug on the floor and pushes on the bed. It slides toward the wall, lifting a trapdoor in the floor that was hidden beneath the rug. He picks up the nightshirts and helps Clarete down the stairway, which leads under the floor and into the old stone wine cellar. Leonardo lights an olive-oil lamp that sits on a flat stone shelf. It's a small room; the bed and four barrels of wine—three red and one white—are lined against one of the walls. Clarete, acting faint, sits down on the bed. Leonardo points at a stairway at the back of the room. "It goes to a small room behind the fireplace that leads outside," he explains. "A person can come and go without anyone ever knowing."

"You're very kind," Clarete responds. "I don't know what I would have done if you hadn't helped me." She lies down on the bed.

"What is your name, my child?" he asks. "I think it's only polite that I know who I'm letting stay in my home." He grins broadly.

"Clarete...Clarete Lisa Ménehould," she answers.

"Very interesting," Leonardo says, as he takes a brown wool blanket from the foot of the bed and pulls it over her. "Very unusual name, Clarete Lisa Ménehould. Rest, my child," he says, as he leaves the room. "I'll check on you later." He thinks it's remarkable that she's doing as well as she is. She must be very strong.

—⁂—

Over the next two weeks, while Leonardo believes Clarete is recovering, he travels to Florence and works on his project, *The Battle of Anghiari*. He doesn't realize that she healed immediately after he stitched her up, and that she's acting as if she's human so as not to betray her true nature.

Outside the house is a small chicken coop. Next to it is a rabbit pen. Leonardo, concerned about Clarete's well-being while he's gone, has a farmer down the road deliver chickens and domesticated rabbits. Nothing makes her mouth water like live rabbit. The farmer also kills, butchers, and salts a fattened pig that he's reared. No meal is complete without ham, blood sausages, and black pudding on the table, which Clarete, skipping the pudding, devours raw when Leonardo isn't home. Two apple trees provide fresh fruit, which she feeds the rabbits to fatten them up.

When Leonardo returns from his trip, he questions her one night while sitting at the table. "Clarete," he says, "I find it strange that you won't eat with me. Why is that, my child? Is my company so uninteresting?"

"No, not at all," she answers. "You're such a brilliant man...I thought you understood my reasoning. There never can be two settings on the table at once. What if the riders come back? What if they force their way into your house?" She picks up Leonardo's dirty dishes and carries them to the washing station. She uses sand to scour the dishes and soapwort made by boiling roots and leaves together to clean them. "If they see two settings on the table, they'll know you've been lying to them all this time. They'll kill me and perhaps even you."

He and Clarete always sit together after the sun has set. This arrangement allows him to concentrate on his work, *The Battle of Anghiari*, during the day and gives Clarete the opportunity to rest in the wine cellar. On several occasions the vampire hunters who were chasing Clarete return, searching for her. The men believe they and their families will be tormented and die horrible deaths unless they find and kill her. Their persistence reassures Leonardo that he made the right decision in letting Clarete hide in the wine cellar and agreeing to let her keep just one setting at the table.

The trips Leonardo takes to the council hall of the Palazzo Vecchio in Florence to work on *The Battle of Anghiari* allow Clarete to secretly hunt and satisfy her need for nourishment—blood and raw meat. She preys mostly on wild rabbits and rats. It's a living but not much of one.

It is during one of these nights, bored, with nothing to do, that she goes into Leonardo's study to look at his work and get a better understanding of the exceedingly accomplished man who saved her life. It's a small room, like the rest of the rooms in the cottage, except this one has two large windows—one facing north and the other west—which maximize the sunlight that flows into the study. Everything is well arranged, organized, and put together. The walls are red, signifying the blood of Christ. Paintings, ceramics, and sculptures are displayed. All have meticulous colors and details.

Clarete walks over to a small, oak table, where she sees a thick, leather-bound notebook. She opens it and finds that it's a diverse collection of Leonardo's drawings with colored washes made on parchment sheets. They are a reflection of his personal style and experiences and an unparalleled range of subject matter. She carefully pages through them and finds that many are finished, highly imaginative works. She's amazed at the in-depth understanding his drawings reveal of a woman's torso, a growing embryo in the womb of a pregnant woman, the heart, and the internal organs of the human body and their workings. Being a vampire, she intimately understands the complete workings of the human body. As she flips through the pages, she sees many untitled drawings of inventions, animals, and portraits of individuals, along with a sketch of a statue of a bronze horse, a self-portrait, and others. Others have titles: *A Giant Crossbow, St. Jerome, Vitruvian Man, Storm over a Landscape, Grotesque Head, Flower Studies, Head of a Girl, A Spring Device*. Many are completed, while others appear to be in various stages of planning and completion. Several pages are dedicated to Leonardo's "Ideal City," with elegant buildings, wide roads, and a network of upper and lower canals that would be used for travel and trade. There's also a mechanical lifting system that supplies special stables for horses. It's designed to move the animals' feed to the different locations in predetermined quantities and remove all wastes, including sewage. Also, it would carry water from a complex network of canals that run through the Ideal City and distribute it to various watering stations in the stables. Horses are one of Leonardo's great loves. He considers them magnificent, noble creatures, especially ones that are quick, versatile, and powerful.

Toward the end of the book, Clarete encounters pictures of various flying machines and drawings of wings. The wings appear to be curved on top, which makes the air lighter because it moves faster over the top of the wings. The air moves more slowly underneath the wings, which makes the air heavier and causes it to push up from below while the faster air pushes down from the top. This forces the wings to lift into the air. She finds the drawings interesting because no one understands the dynamics of flying better than a vampire bat.

On the last two pages of the notebook, Clarete finds two drawings that are even more intriguing. The first is of something called a flying disk, which seems to be traveling through a violet-shaded, starlight-speckled sky. It's painted silver, with several flashing white lights and a mixture of the visible spectrum—indigo, violet, blue, green, yellow, orange, and red—pulsating between them. She flips to the last page of the notebook, where she sees two strange-looking creatures with the phrase "extraterrestrial origin" written next to them. One appears to be female, the other male. Except for her well-contoured, firm breasts and large, dark, velvety lips, the female possesses approximately the same physical characteristics as her male counterpart. Both are tall and slim. Their skin is the color of violet and white light. Both have yellow eyes; long, slender, sculptured noses; pointed ears; and a thick, coarse tissue that forms three fleshy points that wrap up and over the front of their foreheads, accenting the heavy, thick, braided, grayish-white hair that hangs down the backs of their necks. They're magnificent creatures, displaying a certain tranquility. Written next to the drawing is the note "They search for the Ark of the Covenant."

12

EXTRATERRESTRIAL ORIGIN

Clarete is confused. Never has she heard the term "extraterrestrial origin" before, and she can speak many different languages fluently. Who are these creatures? What does all this mean, and why do they want the Ark of the Covenant? To her knowledge only Jacques de Molay knows where it's hidden, and he may not even be alive. She hears Leonardo's carriage approach the house and decides to ask him about these last two drawings when the opportunity presents itself.

"My child," Leonardo says the next evening, when they're dining together, "I have two important questions to ask you." He raises a Venetian glass, an enameled and gilded green goblet, and takes a sip of red wine. "Your eyebrows—they fascinate me. Is this something you can talk about?" He is wary lest he upset her, as he knows ladies are self-conscious about their appearance.

"Debtors' prison in France," she answers directly. As a human she might have taken offense to such a personal question. From a vampire's point of view, however, it doesn't bother her. "The guards were cruel. They told me I was ugly. They cut my hair and shaved off my eyebrows. They laughed, mocked me, and thought it great fun. I should have died in that prison, but a friend rescued me. My eyebrows never grew back."

Leonardo smiles at her reassuringly. "I don't enter into things lightly," he responds sincerely, leaning forward on the table, folding his hands. He looks directly at her. "I always give matters a great deal of thought. I've observed you these last weeks and find you...mesmerizing. Or...or possibly hypnotic.

There's something about you that draws a person in. Spellbinding? Is that the word? My proposition is this: I want to paint your portrait. I find you so unique. You have a mysterious, sensuous quality that I…I…find bewitching. Maybe it's your eyes. One day I think they're dark brown. Another day they appear light brown, with a green shade at the bottom and a darker one at the top; other days they're more of a golden brown. I just can't make up my mind, and—" he's totally engrossed in his thoughts, "your eyes shine." He takes a long sip of wine, rolls it around in his mouth, and swallows. "And your skin, your face…so soft, pale. There's a magical quality to your visage. At certain times of the day, it appears to glow, and your hands look darker than your face. If the light from a flame hits it just right, your skin glistens. Your neck, the pit of your throat—" He places a hand on his throat to show her. "The pulse seem to be beating, as if I can see it."

Leonardo tilts his head slightly toward her. "Ugly? No, not at all, my child. Quite the opposite." He picks up the goblet of red wine and then sits back in his chair, gazing questioningly at her while resting the goblet on his leg.

Clarete could tell Leonardo that her eyes frequently change color because they adjust to the slightest variations in light. She could tell him the luminescence of her skin has to do with the light being emitted from her cold body, the quality of blood she's drinking, the selection of raw meat she's eating, her overall health—all these things are reflected in the emissions of her skin and the pulse in her throat. She could explain that her hands appear darker than her facial skin because that skin is much heavier. Since all these qualities are vampire traits, however, she's at a loss for words.

"Is my proposal agreeable to you?" Leonardo leans forward, setting the goblet on the table and looking into her with those piercing, gray-blue eyes she can't resist. She will always remember the sense of security she felt when she looked into them the night he rescued her. How can she turn him down? He saved her life and continues to protect her. There's just one problem with his proposal, and she needs to buy herself some time, come up with an agreeable solution that will work for both of them. If not, she'll have to leave. Leaving—she finds that difficult to think about.

"I would like to do that," she answers softly. "When do you want to start?"

"I was thinking tomorrow." He smiles as he takes another sip of wine. "I've already worked out the painting in my mind. It will be one of my greatest pieces."

"Why so soon?" She was hoping to have more time to come up with a plan.

"One day is as good as another." He smiles again. "Why put it off?"

"And what about your other work, *The Battle of Anghiari?*" Clarete shifts nervously in her chair. "You've put so much time into it. And what about your work with Michelangelo?" Somehow she must convince him that she needs to be painted in the evening without his suspecting she's a vampire. But he's so brilliant that he'll probably see through anything she tells him.

"I'm going to set aside *The Battle of Anghiari* for now," he responds enthusiastically. "I'll return to it later."

"What if you never finish it?" she asks candidly.

Leonardo shrugs his shoulders and frowns at her as if to say, *That idea is ridiculous.*

"Tomorrow evening it is," Clarete says, "when day has passed."

"Yes, yes," he repeats enthusiastically. "Very good, my child. On the terrace. We'll be working together for a fair amount of time, so please be patient with me." He smiles broadly.

"Here, please wear this." He hands her a properly folded dress wrapped in yellow cotton cloth. "I had it made in Florence. Designed it myself, just for you. Please wear it."

Clarete breathes a sigh of relief. This was much easier than she thought it would be. She always thought paintings were worked on during the day, but Leonardo often keeps odd hours and rarely follows convention.

The next evening, when Clarete walks up the steps to the small terrace at the back of the house, everything is set up. Two large mirrors with dark-brown frames have been placed next to the house. Leonardo's oil paints and brushes are arranged on a small table, and a poplar-wood palette is positioned on an easel in the middle of the stone floor. A brown, wooden armchair sits a short distance away. Several olive-oil lanterns have been placed inside glass fishbowls that are filled with water and strategically positioned on the terrace railing. All are lit, their glow through the water providing a cool, soft light that mingles with the darkness.

Clarete is impressed; Leonardo can do so much with so little. The light is easy on her eyes, giving her a relaxed feeling, something she's never experienced as a vampire.

"You look like a rare treasure…beautiful, cherished, priceless." Leonardo steps back, placing his closed hands to his lips, gazing at her admiringly.

Clarete is wearing a deep-forest-green dress made of richly decorative shuttle-woven silk. The sleeves are a magnificent red and show through the dark-green, crocheted, lacy mantle. The neckline of her dress is embellished with delicate, interlaced embroidery, and a short, sheer lace veil adorns her hair at the edges of her face. She wears no jewelry. Leonardo has her sit in the armchair, places a dark-green blanket across her lap, and tucks it lightly around her waist.

"You've already started the painting?" Clarete says, looking at the canvas sitting on the easel. "I didn't know."

"Just the background," Leonardo answers, setting up the two mirrors. "I've traveled extensively across Italy. The background is a composite of things I've seen—my favorite parts of this country. I must create a natural order of things…create a feeling of distance between you and the landscape behind you. I hope you find it suitable."

Clarete nods. She's busy watching him as he moves the two mirrors into position. *Now what?* is all she can think.

"It's called mirror painting," he says, his back toward her. "I'll paint your reflection. It will give depth to the work." He walks over and picks up a paintbrush from the small table. He steps back, looking at the mirrors, then at Clarete, and then again at the mirrors. "So strange," he wonders out loud, while holding up his hand. "I can see my hand in the mirror, but I can't see your reflection. Very odd." He holds up his hand again and waves it around. "See? I can see my hand, but when I step back, I don't see your reflection." He shakes his head in frustration and glances around the terrace, as if looking for an answer. "Maybe it's the reflection of the light. Perhaps that's what it is." He turns back to Clarete. "We're going to start," he says, with a note of irritation. "I'll figure it out tomorrow." He walks over to the easel, takes his customary position, and evaluates Clarete's composure, sitting position, facial expression, and body language. "Relax," he says, pointing his brush at her. "The fingers, the hands—they should be limp, just touching the edge of the armrest. Don't grab. And your posture—so important—everything about it, like a wolf quietly waiting for its prey. Let your presence speak to the spectator. Display reservation and silence. He holds the end of the paint brush to his lips, focusing. When I look at you, meet my gaze as if you're drawing me in. I know that's a lot to take in all at once, but as we'll be working together for many months, it will become a habit. Last, please, my child, smile."

Clarete tries her best, but vampires can't smile.

"Surely, my child, you can do better than that."

"That's the best I can do," Clarete answers firmly. "If you expect more from me, you'll need to find another model." *It's time to call an end to this,* she decides. Tomorrow, when he's working with the mirrors, he'll find there's nothing wrong with them, and he'll figure out that she's a vampire. She'll leave tonight while Leonardo is sleeping. But first she wants to know about the drawings. "I have a question to ask you," she says. "I was looking through your notebook earlier. Quite impressive. Your brilliance blows through it like a mighty wind." She leans forward in her chair and focuses her eyes on his, confidently but not controlling. "The last two pages—the flying disk and the two creatures with 'extraterrestrial origin' written next to them and 'They search for the Ark of the Covenant.' I feel like I should know but can't remember. What does it all mean?"

Ignoring Clarete's question, Leonardo walks up and stands close to her. "Sit still, my child," he says. "I won't hurt you. I just want to see something. Is that all right?"

Clarete nods. She knows he'll never try to hurt her, and she can easily protect herself from him anyway, so she has nothing to worry about.

Leonardo bends down and lifts the left side of her upper lip with his finger. Just as he thought, there's a fang. That settles it. Clarete is a vampire, which explains her unique features—everything he finds attractive and mysterious about her. He steps back, watching her. He knows he's safe around her. If she were going to kill him, she would have done it a long time ago. "Your smile, my child," he comments reassuringly, "is perfect. I will paint you the old way—without mirrors. We shall start." He walks back to his easel. "Ah, yes." He waves his paintbrush in the air. "I almost forgot—your question. At the end of this week, it will be answered. I would like you to accompany me to Florence. I go to a graveyard on the outskirts of the city and study dead bodies before they're buried. It's how I learn."

Clarete decides she doesn't want to get close to a graveyard with Leonardo. Too often a powerful evil permeates burial grounds, overwhelming her with the urge to kill. Under no circumstances does she want to be overcome by bloodlust in front of him. Although he saved her life, an urgency is boiling inside her that needs to be quenched. *Who and what is the extraterrestrial origin?* she wonders yet again. She should remember but can't. Only Leonardo has the knowledge she craves. "I will go with you," she responds firmly, deciding she'll deal with the graveyard when they get there.

Several days later, the carriage to Florence that Leonardo hired—an exceedingly fast, light vehicle made of dark wood covered in plain leather—is pulled by two large, brown horses with white manes and tails. The carriage arrives just as the sun sets. The coachman wears a heavy, royal-blue shoulder cape that matches his uniform and overcoat. His boots are dark brown. Most coachmen wear a hat, but he's a young man and less professional, and he lets his long, blond hair blow in the wind.

Leonardo holds an umbrella over Clarete's head to block any sporadic rays of sunlight as they quickly board the coach. He's dressed for the cold ride, wearing a loose-fitting, white shirt with pleated cuffs, a velvet maroon vest, and a wool tunic that extends over his shoulders and is decorated with expensive jewels and trimmed in gold. His matching maroon leggings are tucked into white stockings that are worn underneath his black, squared-toed, leather boots. He carries a maroon-and-gold-trimmed, light-green cloak with a gold chain. Per Leonardo's instructions, the shades of the carriage have been pulled shut, and two blankets, one red and one green, have been placed on the dark, worn, leather seats for Clarete. It's the middle of October; autumn colors ornament the trees, and fallen leaves cover the road. The evenings are crisp and cool, and Leonardo wants to make sure

Clarete is comfortable. One blanket is for her to sit on, the other for her to cover her head and wrap around her shoulders if they should be stopped. Normally the road to Florence is very safe, but one never knows what's lurking around the next corner. Better to make Clarete appear as inconspicuous as possible.

Darkness shrouds the land when they reach the cemetery at the outskirts of Florence an hour later. Leonardo has been here many times. A number of stone tombs are decorated with exquisite Italian sculptures: the Virgin Mary and child, the Crucifixion, David and Goliath, Sampson—all chiseled from large marble stones. Some have a robed sculpture above and a skeleton in the grave below. There's a dampness in the air, and the smell of human blood in the silent breeze makes Clarete's fangs burn. Her throat feels parched, and her stomach churns in anticipation of blood. She's ravenously thirsty.

"There are many dead bodies here," Leonardo says, as he looks across the graveyard, where four young medical students, each wielding a shovel, have taken matters into their own hands. The oil-burning lanterns that hang from tall posts provide them with light. "The gravediggers have to dig up the old bodies to make room for the new ones, as all the graveyards are full. I call this the graveyard shift." He breaks into a hearty laugh and glances at Clarete, who doesn't smile. She has seen all this before, hundreds of times. Graveyards and tombs have been her resting places for nearly two centuries. "The bones," he continues, "they take them to the bone house where people can go and pray among the bones of their ancestors. I call them boneheads." He laughs again, but louder, while looking at Clarete, who still doesn't smile. He shakes his head while looking away. He has moments when he doesn't want to believe she's a vampire.

"They don't bury all the bodies," Leonardo continues. "Occasionally they'll slide a fresh corpse aside, pick it up later, and use in their studies. It's a prohibited practice, but it provides much better material than dogs or pigs, and it's cheaper than hiring grave robbers. There was a time when I would buy a body from them, take it back to my home in the country, and study it. I don't do that anymore. Later, when I answer your question, you'll know why."

"Why all the bells?" Clarete inquires, looking at a table with at least a dozen of them. This is something she hasn't seen before.

"They bury so many people that sometimes they bury someone who's not dead. Not intentionally, mind you," Leonardo explains. "It just happens. In the past, when they took dead bodies out of the caskets, the inside of the lid would be scratched up on some of them. Many of them broke off their fingernails trying to escape. Now they tie a leather cord around the person's wrist, run it up through a hole in the casket and out through the ground. They tie it to one of these bells that hangs next to the grave. The person in the casket awakens, moves his wrist, and rings the bell. He can be saved by the bell. I call him a dead ringer." Leonardo begins to laugh again but looks at Clarete and holds back. "Ah, yes," he mumbles. "Come. We need to go. Be quick about it. The night is seldom forgiving, and it passes quickly. I wanted to show you this so you could learn about me—who I really am—understand me. I'm more than just an artist. These things will be our secret forever." He takes a deep breath, lifts his shoulders, relaxes, and then looks at Clarete as they stand next to the carriage. "My last breath will be the second of May in the year fifteen nineteen," he says. "I'm dying." He keeps his voice down so the driver won't hear.

"I know," Clarete answers. "Death has its own particular odor. With you the scent is very weak. You still have a long time." She reaches over and places the back of her hand against his heart. "I can save you if you want… turn you."

Leonardo smiles. "To me death is only the beginning. It's why I want to show you the tiniest glimpse of a world no one else has ever seen."

As they get back into the carriage, Clarete wonders how Leonardo could possibly know the date of his death. *It's impossible*, she thinks, as they ride to the heart of Florence, where the sinkhole slums exist. The poor people who occupy this overcrowded area rely on pumps and wells that are being polluted by nearby cesspits. Men urinate on the walls of buildings. People pour buckets of bodily excretions out the windows and into the streets. Eventually the filth seeps into the water supply. The buildings are shoddily constructed and rundown, and prostitution is rampant. They pass derelict houses with broken windows patched with paper or worn, dirty cloths—anything available. Every room is home to a different family. The children learn at a young age to steal. Girls and boys, barefoot and filthy, are thieves at night and divide the spoils during the day. They hang out in gangs.

A knife in the belly or back shortens a life too young to know or too old to understand. Most children wear rags on their feet, and when they're lucky enough to have shoes, they cut off the toes to fit their feet as they grow.

The wooden carriage wheels click on the rough, gloomy, narrow street, stopping in front of a poorly constructed wooden building multiple stories tall and in an appalling state of disrepair.

After placing his long whip in its holder, the coachman steps down from the carriage and opens the door for Leonardo and Clarete. Getting out, Clarete takes the dark-green blanket and throws it over her head, wraps it around her shoulders, and pulls it tightly around her face to veil it. The rancid stink of illness and death radiates from the building, burning her nostrils, and old memories deluge her mind. She grabs Leonardo by the shoulder, digging her fingernails into his flesh, and he cringes in pain.

"What's wrong, child?" he moans. "Please, you're hurting me."

"I can't go in there," she whispers, letting go. "Bad things happen to children in these places. The evil can be so great. I may not be able to control myself. I need to leave."

"This used to be a debtors' prison," he explains. "The rich lived in apartments above the diseased, the dying, the countless dead, and the poor who dwelled below. It closed three years ago. I bought it and turned it into a home for orphans. I have wealthy benefactors who provide money for clothes, shoes, food, and caregivers. The Church collects alms, which also helps provide for the children. They're mostly babies, left by poor women who can't care for them." He leans against the side of the carriage, thinking. "Being born into these poorer families is a death sentence for many of these infants," he continues. "We have nursing mothers who come in and feed them. If I couldn't pay the mothers who help, most of the babies would die, starve to death. Leaving children at orphanages like this is usually a death sentence. But I make sure every child is baptized and has medical care. I also take in children if they're willing to work." He smiles. "One to sixteen years of age. Every day we find a newborn, left by the front door, lying on nothing more than a dirty rag. So many abandoned children. I used to buy dead bodies from the prison for my studies, but now I try to help the living. All children go up for adoption immediately. We don't have to go in. I just wanted you to see these things, to understand me as no one else does."

"Let's go in then," Clarete responds, wiping the perspiration off her forehead. "I'll be all right. To me the smell of death is still fresh in the air. I can sense—*feel* all the horrors that took place here. So many."

Leonardo takes her quickly through the orphanage so she can see the children and the less-than-desirable conditions. All the boys are wearing green shirts and dull black trousers. The girls' dresses are one-half red and one-half blue, vertically. "Most of the girls will remain here until they can work as maidservants," he says. "The boys will leave when they can become apprenticed to a tradesman. Including the babies, we have fifty-four children. If you think it looks bad now, you should have seen it a couple of years ago. It was such a smelly place. They tried to get the prisoners to eat the meat even after it spoiled. Finally the guards threw their putrid offal in the ditches and streets." He holds his nose, giving Clarete a knowing shrug. "They dug cesspits in the backyard. Dumped all their rubbish in them. Buried it up like a dog. When those got full, they dug deeper holes. The building had a thatched roof. Rain, snow, occasionally a bird or a hungry cat—anything could fall through it. I replaced it with tiles a year ago. There are three orphan rooms upstairs. One for the girls, one for the boys, and one for the babies and toddlers. Finally everyone has a cot and a blanket. There's just so much to do."

Clarete nods thoughtfully. She has seen many orphanages; this one is nicer than most. They walk out back to a large area, enclosed with a rotting, partially collapsed fence—a patch of land of mostly dirt and weeds where the children play. Four oil-burning lanterns, which provide some degree of light, hang from posts in different spots in the yard. The flickering of their flames casts imaginary shadows of the bewitched.

"I plan to make the building bigger over time and expand the orphanage." Leonardo gestures toward the property. "I'll get more help, too. What do you think?"

"How many dead are buried out here?" Clarete questions, sniffing the air.

"Dead!" Leonardo responds defensively. "There are no dead people buried here."

Her head down, Clarete walks the property as she smells the ground. "At least fifty children," she responds. "Buried in shafts in the ground. The bodies are stacked on top of one another."

"That's impossible," he says, dumbfounded. He's lived in Italy for more than fifty years and never heard such an outrageous story.

"Here." Clarete points to the ground. "And here. And over there and there."

"I don't know what to tell you," Leonardo answers sadly. "Hopefully you'll stay and help the children. One day I'll be gone." He slaps at several flies that are irritating him.

Clarete unexpectedly walks quickly to an area in the yard and slashes her wrist with one of her razor-sharp fingernails. Holding her thumb against the open wound, she sprays her bright-red blood, back and forth, over the weed-infested earth. Finished, she cups her hand around her wrist and hurries over to two other areas in the yard and sprays blood over them.

"What are you doing?" Leonardo exclaims, shocked by her actions.

"Watch!" Clarete demands, and grabs a fistful of dirt. She spits gobs of saliva into the dirt and then presses it into her open wound, holding it firmly against the bleeding artery. "Watch and learn!"

It's difficult to make out at first, with so little light, but in the area near him, which Clarete sprayed, Leonardo sees the dirt move. A little bit at first, but then more and more until—until—He can't believe his eyes. It looks like fingers and then a hand sticking out of the ground, but that's impossible!

"What's happening?" he shouts. "Clarete, look, look." He points at the ground.

"I know," she says calmly. "Watch and learn."

Leonardo can't believe she said that—"Watch and learn." He's thinking they should be running. One of the Devil's demons is crawling out of the ground right in front of them, and there will be no watching and learning about that—because it's a *fact*!

Clarete hurries over, pushes the dirt aside, and pulls the child out of the ground. The girl's stinking, dirty, bloated body is discolored and turning yellowish black from decomposition. If Clarete doesn't help her soon, the child's body will burst, and only her skeleton will remain. Her staring, lifeless eyes bulge out of their sockets as her purple, swollen tongue protrudes from her mouth, gagging her. Her long, dirty, matted hair is falling out, as are her fingernails and teeth. The skin has blistered and dried up and hangs from her body, along with the rotted remnants of clothing. She emits a gurgling noise as she drags her feet across the dirt, first one and then the other, attempting to walk with Clarete's support.

Out of the corner of his eye, Leonardo sees another one of the creatures, also a girl, stumble toward them. "I'm getting out of here, with or without Clarete," he mutters while slowly backing away. "Enough is enough."

"Help me," Clarete demands, and then, without warning, to Leonardo's incredulity, she pushes the girl into his chest. "Take her! She can't hurt you."

Confused, not knowing what to do, he manages to hold the girl in his outstretched arms. Keeping a distance, Clarete rips the dirt-covered scab off her own wrist and sprays the girl's face and body with her blood. She quickly turns and sprays the second girl, sweeping up and down, front and back, covering her entire body with blood. Instantly their hair thickens, and their eyes radiate. Their skin heals and regains a strong, fleshy, child-like appearance. Fangs protrude above their full lower lips. They run their tongues around their mouths, licking Clarete's blood off their lips and then their arms, cleaning themselves like cats.

"Go, go!" Clarete commands. "Find who did this to you and seek your vengeance! You'll know what to do!" The girls disappear into the night.

"They can't be any more than nine or ten years old," Leonardo murmurs. *Who would do something like this?* he wonders, as a third child, a boy, drags himself into view.

"I can't help you," Clarete tells the boy, her voice breaking. "I don't have enough blood left. I've given up too much already."

The boy, understanding, stares at her through his death-darkened eyes, his head bobbing up and down. His bloated body shakes uncontrollably and then bursts open before sucking back into itself.

It all happens so fast, and with the darkness and the poor lighting, Leonardo is spellbound. All that remains is the boy's skeleton on the ground. Clarete, her strength drained, collapses to her knees. She grabs Leonardo's leg. "I'm dying," she gasps. "I need blood tonight, or I will die."

He pauses, glancing up and into the dark sky. So much has happened. He considers showing Clarete his greatest discovery. He wasn't going to, but something this exciting and mysterious needs to be shared, and who's more qualified to carry this great secret than Clarete? She could be instrumental in the meeting of two different worlds, and they'll save her life, something he's unable to do.

"There's one more thing I need to show you—you and only you, the one person in this entire world who may live to see this again. If you do, remember your friend, Leonardo." He wraps his arm around Clarete to give her support; her body is so cold.

Clarete, doesn't understand what he's babbling about. She knows they don't have enough caged rabbits at his house to satisfy her blood needs, and she's too weak to run after a deer, much less take one down.

Leonardo opens the carriage door and helps her inside. As they travel toward his house in the country, she rests her head on his shoulder and relaxes into a suspended state of animation. She doesn't want to expend energy. She will die in his home, safe from grave robbers.

But before they reach his cottage, they turn off the traveled road onto a rough-cut path. The carriage twists, squeaks, and rattles as it slowly bumps along across an anemic, thorny landscape.

"Years ago I suffered from severe headaches," Leonardo explains. "I couldn't eat. I lost weight and kept to myself. My work—what work? I couldn't do any. I couldn't concentrate. My memory failed. I cut myself just to feel pain, watched the blood flow just to know I was still alive. Life was unbearable. There was no joy, no happiness. Then, on rare occasions, I saw flashing lights in the distance. Every time I saw them, my headaches lessened, and I felt much better, sometimes for days. The headaches, however, always came back, worse than before."

Leonardo places his arm around Clarete to offer some warmth, some comfort. She is so quiet; he hopes she'll be all right. "One night I walked out here," he continues. "This is what I want to show you." He reaches inside his light-green, cloak and takes out a pair of ivory eyeglasses with yellow lenses. "I made these," he says, and puts them on. Up against the hills, he sees throbbing flashes of multicolored lights. He turns to hand his glasses to Clarete, almost dropping them when the carriage hits a rough spot in the road.

"Here—quick, quick, put them on," he says enthusiastically while pointing out the carriage window. "See? See the lights?"

"Yes," she whispers, as she pushes his hand aside and refuses the glasses. "I can see them. I don't need your glasses. I've been watching them for a while now, from your home. Why are we here? I need blood."

"Trust me," Leonardo responds. "Trust me and learn."

Clarete nods in acceptance; she has no choice.

The light show that has been for their benefit, changes and blends into the darkness, and appears as nothing more than a reflection of the grayish, moonlit night. As they get closer, Clarete sees a covert craft in the sky that has what looks to be a prehistoric reptilian skin as well as the chameleon's remarkable ability to change color and shape to blend into its environment or reflect a mood. Now it vanishes into the hidden darkness of the tree-covered hills.

Leonardo bangs on the carriage for the driver to stop. "You need to leave us here," he yells. "It'll be all right." He helps Clarete get out and watches as the carriage departs. The night is dark, like an abandoned soul, with no flickering stars. "I made the eyeglasses," Leonardo tells her, "so I can see the lights. Otherwise I'd never know they were here." His voice seems loud, as the night rests on the tranquility of silence. "Years ago, when I saw them for the first time, it was because they let me. They operated on my brain. My headaches stopped. They wanted me to help them." He runs his hands through his long, thick hair, pushing it back over his shoulders.

"I shouldn't be here," Clarete murmurs. "I will die here. They will kill me. We need to leave. I need blood." She pushes herself away from Leonardo, angry at him for not helping her. She stumbles in her attempt to stand.

"No," he pleads. "I know them. They won't hurt you."

Suddenly a flash of blue light engulfs them, and when their vision clears, they're standing inside a small room that radiates white light. Except for the two of them, it's completely empty. They're disoriented, and before either of them has a chance to physically recover, the walls expand, sucking up against the ship's exterior. Long, black, spider web–stress cracks appear on the ceiling and walls.

"What is it?" Clarete asks. "Is it alive?"

"I think it's afraid of us," Leonardo responds. "I've never had that happen before. The travelers from the sky explained it to me. The walls, the floor, everything we see—it's like our skin. They call what's happening 'tissue regeneration.' If the room is damaged in any way, it heals itself before it fails. It's like us—if we cut ourselves, our skin heals itself. The bleeding stops. The room has feelings like we do. Watch." He walks to one of the walls and places his palm against it. The wall presses out and around his hand, as if holding it. "It still likes me," he says appreciatively. "I don't understand why the walls pulled away from us and all those cracks formed." A look of deep concern furrows his brow.

"It's me," Clarete answers in a dreary tone. "It knows I'm a vampire. I know where we are. I have innate experiences hidden in the folds of my mind that are revealing themselves to me. The vampire blood that flows through my veins has memory seeds planted in it. Your bringing me here… all this…" She glances around the room. "I remember it all, but I'm very weak. I need blood. I'm going to die here."

Leonardo isn't listening to her. This is the first time he's had the opportunity to explain what he's learned from the sky people. "They call this place a probe. It holds up to ten travelers," he continues, excitement in his voice. "The skin expands or contracts, depending on how many travelers are living here. With five it contracts. With six it expands. The travelers live in the room right next to us." He points at the crease in the wall. "They call it a 'habitat module.'"

"It's called a self-replicating ship or synthetic life-form," Clarete weakly interrupts. "The travelers build them with an artificial intelligence, like a brain, which allows the ships to grow and evolve into smarter machines, a form of life. They live. They have a life of their own. If the ship is damaged, it seeks out the materials it needs to repair itself—like an animal hunting for its next kill so it can eat and replenish its body. They find these materials on other planets, moons, or asteroids—wherever they are. All the stars you see in the sky, they travel even beyond them. Distances we can't imagine. These life-forms are not single ships. They're a group of life forms that have teamed together to achieve their goals, which could be conquering another race, defending themselves from invasions, or searching, exploring more of the universe. Their machines are very powerful and have their own superior intelligence."

"How do you know all this?" Leonardo asks.

"Like I said, it's in my memory, in the memories of all the vampires, going back ten thousand years. The sky people will come for me soon. For me there is no escape."

The crease in the wall opens, and one of the travelers, tall and slim, his skin the color of violet-and-white light, enters the room. He has yellow eyes, a long, slender, sculptured nose, and pointed ears. A thick, coarse tissue forms three fleshy points that wrap up and over the front of his forehead, accenting the heavy, thick, braided, gray hair that hangs down the back of his neck. He nods toward Leonardo and then turns to Clarete, mentally transmitting his thoughts to her.

So now you know your origin.

Clarete nods.

You know who we are, the traveler transmits.

Clarete nods again.

"You're dying," he says. "We can help you." The traveler reaches up, pulls down a metal strap, and attaches it to the side of Clarete's neck. She doesn't resist. "It's artificial blood but much more nourishing than real blood," he explains. "Our voices, the language we speak—they're much different from yours. The air inside the room has been seeded with an invisible mutation that allows all of us to breathe the same air and makes the sound of our voices pleasant to you. Otherwise we couldn't communicate. Our voices and speech patterns are extremely high and rapid. A chatter similar to some of your species of birds. The pitch is far outside of your hearing range and would cause you immediate, permanent deafness."

"All your faculties will be at one hundred percent in ten milliseconds," the traveler continues. "There is detestation inside you, a feeling that has manifested itself for more than ten thousand years. My kind—we come from a planet far, far away, a group of stars that resemble what you know as Orion, the hunter. We've been at war with your kind—vampires—since the beginning of time. That's why you felt so much hatred when you saw me. There are more stars than you can count in the sky, and your kind has destroyed countless numbers of them, catapulted many different life-forms to extinction. Before the Great Sphinx of Giza was built, the Vampire Empire sent Mithras, to earth to the country called Egypt, where he became one of their gods. We sent Isis, also known as the Stone Seat, there to equalize his power. She became an Egyptian goddess. Now we seek Jacques de Molay and the Ark of the Covenant. We've lost track of them. That's why we had Leonardo bring you here." He detaches the electronic IV from Clarete's neck. "You are as you were, and more."

Clarete rotates her shoulders back and forth, flexing them, feeling her newfound strength. All of her senses are heightened.

"I brought Clarete here on my own," Leonardo says abruptly. "You didn't ask me." Suddenly he jumps into the air.

"Why did you jump just now?" the traveler asks.

"Felt like it," Leonardo replies.

"No, you jumped because I planted that thought in your brain—the same reason you brought Clarete here."

Leonardo nods knowingly.

"In all the years we have fought the vampire realm," the traveler continues, "we've never known of a situation in which a vampire and a human became as one in peace." He looks at Clarete and then at Leonardo. "You accept him, and he accepts you. This gave us hope that you might be willing to help us."

"What do you want me to do?" she asks. She owes them her life.

"We must find Jacques de Molay, the one who wears the Rider of the Sun mark on his neck. He will lead us to the ark."

Clarete shrugs. "I don't know where he is. He once was in France, but that was long ago. Jacques is probably dead. I don't know." She rubs the side of her neck. "Why is the tattoo of any importance?"

A female traveler walks through the opening in the membrane and stands next to the male. Clarete notices that she has the same thick, coarse tissue that wraps up and over the front of her forehead. However, the heavy, thick, braided hair that hangs down the back of her neck shines like yellow-gold sunlight that melts into an enchanting beauty of forest-green leaves. Her sensuous lips glisten with truth. "You are safe here," she says to Clarete, and slaps her hands together. "Heal yourself," she orders, and the spider cracks in the floor, walls, and roof vanish. The room adjusts back to its original size, and everything is as it was before Clarete and Leonardo arrived. "Jacques was marked by Isis when he was in his mother's womb," she says. "His powers are greater than even he understands."

"Why do you want the Ark of the Covenant?" Clarete asks her. "The universe is yours. You have wealth greater than King Solomon's." She notices the two marks on the female traveler's neck peeking out from the collar of her garment.

"We've searched for the ark for centuries," she explains. "It possesses powers unsurpassed in the universe. Much greater than ours. Much greater than all the universes the vampires control. We must find it before they do. If the vampires find it first, they will use it to destroy entire solar systems that won't join their planetary macrocosms. It's what they do. They were going to bring earth into their orbit or destroy it, but Mithras, convinced them not to attack. The ark has been lost to the vampires and to us. We must find Jacques de Molay. Isis believes he knows where the Ark of the Covenant is. Once, you, Thomas, Jude the Great, and Jacques de Molay were friends. Will you help us?"

"I don't know where Jacques is or if he's alive," Clarete says as she takes a couple of steps toward the female traveler. Standing in front of her, Clarete closes her two middle fingers against her palm, reaching up and placing the other two fingers on the two jagged discolorations on side of the woman's neck. *Bite marks. Exactly the same size and distance between the fangs as hers. Vampire Jacques.* Clarete tips her head knowingly at the woman, who in turn blinks her eyes in acknowledgment. They both know that they are members of the same pack and will be sisters until death. Clarete wishes she could've smiled at her. *How—where, when did she ever meet Jacques?* she wonders.

"I'll help you if I ever see him again," Clarete answers, shrugging. "How do I find you?"

The female traveler grabs Clarete's hand and, lifting it, slides a kaleidoscopic ring of crushed stones over her finger. "These are precious gems from all corners of the known universe. If you request our presence, take off the ring, turn it around, and slide it back on your finger—an innocent, nervous response that no one will take seriously. If anyone takes the ring off your finger, we'll also come. Your sittings with Leonardo…quite interesting." She tries to smile, but finds it strange that she can't.

"We'll always be close. Give us a ring." She tries to smile again, straining while opening her mouth, her gold teeth flashing.

"Someday you'll understand what that means."

The two travelers step back and walk into the opening in the wall, which closes behind them.

A flash of white light envelops Clarete and Leonardo, and they're transported back to his home in the Italian countryside.

—✺—

Leonardo finishes painting the *Mona Lisa* in 1507 and considers it one of his greatest achievements. Over the next centuries, individuals from all walks of life will wonder about her smile. Who is that woman? Is she or isn't she smiling? What is the background? What story is she telling?

The nighttime setting and the fluctuating vivacity of the light from the olive-oil lamps inspired Leonardo to create darkening effects in the painting, intentionally leaving in the shadows around the outer points of Clarete's eyes and lips. Her breasts, neck, face, and skin possess a certain luminescence—a flawless, pale, soft, metallic, vampire complexion. Everything surrounding her face is dark, leaving a feeling of distance between her and the observer. As Leonardo once stated, "I have always believed that the most praiseworthy form of painting is the one that most resembles what it imitates."

Leonardo eventually moves to France, where he is supported in his old age by King Francis I. He dies on May 2, 1519, of natural causes. With his head cradled in the arms of the king, his close friend in his last days, Leonardo sent for a priest to make his confession and receive the Holy Sacrament. On the day of his funeral, sixty beggars follow his casket to his final resting place in the Chapel of Saint-Hubert in the Castle of Amboise, in France. That night, vampire bat Clarete morphs into her human form inside the chapel and walks over to the tomb of Leonardo da Vinci. His portrait and name, chiseled into a stone slab, mark his grave. Standing next to the altar, beneath the stained-glass windows, she pays her respects. She lived with Leonardo until he left for France three years ago. Theirs was a relationship of mutual respect and trust. He protected her, and she, in his old age, took care of him.

For the last three years, Clarete has lived in Florence, in a snuggery beneath a vacant, dilapidated building one block from the orphanage. At night she keeps her promise to Leonardo and guards the children. If one of orphanage workers abuses a child, she has a midnight talk with him or her. If the person abuses a child again, he or she is never heard from again. If the mothers who come to nurse the babies leave at night—which most do—she follows to make sure they arrive home safely. Everyone in the orphanage knows she's out there somewhere, watching. The children leave their dark guardian angel crumbs of food during the day. To their great surprise and delight, it's always gone the next morning.

In her life she has had three friends, three members of the pack: Jacques de Molay, Thomas the squire, and Leonardo da Vinci. She often thinks about Jacques and wonders whether he's still in France. Is he even still alive? Clarete has come to realize she has been in love with Jacques ever since childhood. He was always her defender, her white knight. Leonardo awakened these feelings, long buried inside her. He saved her life, showed her kindness, protected her from the vampire hunters, and made her feel safe again. He was so strong mentally and emotionally, and with all he did for her, there were never any strings attached, no expectations of payback. His greatest gift of all, however, was painting her portrait, the *Mona Lisa*, which restored her sense of self-worth as well as her pride, allowing her to let go of her anger, hate, and violent urges.

Clarete always believed she could walk through the darkest places with Jacques and never fear; Leonardo made her feel the same way. "Where are you, Jacques de Molay?" she whispers. "Where are you?" When the vampire hourglass of time empties, she will find out.

In France, Claude de Lavoe and his demons still rule the night, so Clarete returns to Italy immediately. There she helps the children—the forgotten ones, the orphans, the victims, those sold into slavery, lost to the evils of human trafficking or the sex trade. Being a vampire she can move through all the dark places, mingling with Satan's disciples, hunting them down, bringing the horror of night to them.

13

BENG, THE DEVIL

Belarus, the Russian Empire; 1812

*G*ypsies are an exotic, colorful people. They are fortune-tellers, acrobats, musicians, animal tamers, horse traders, and dancers. They seldom stay in one place for more than thirty days; they always travel, as if cursed. They move from grassy field to grassy field and town to town with their wagons, their tents, their backs bent low from the seemingly never-ending work.

It's an easy night, with just enough breeze to keep the bugs, especially the mosquitoes, down in the tall, yellow-green grass, yet the scent of the wildflowers teases the air. The clearing, partially open on one side, is sheltered by ageless pine trees on the other sides. A narrow stream escapes from the depths of the forest, edging along the clearing before wandering into the distance.

A small band of Gypsies with their freak show of human and animal oddities has set up their covered wagons for the night. The workhorses and their foals graze on the tall grass. The Gypsies, using rawhide straps, have wrapped the horses' front legs so they can take only small steps and graze but can't wander away.

They have two supply wagons with everyday living provisions and two heavily loaded wagons that haul the hand-stitched tents and rigging for their freak show. The other six wagons are covered living quarters. The sides of the wagons, depending on the family represented, are decorated in various hand-carved designs in an array of colors, including the universal and mystical spirit colors of gray, white, and black, as well as reds, yellows, and purples. The interior walls are wrapped in lovely, colorful, hand-stitched fabrics.

Brushed and groomed with affection, the horses are fine looking and well- muscled, with cropped tails, long manes, and stocking-marked legs. A four-horned goat and a small, two-headed deer, feeling safe next to the horses, brush close to one of the big pinto stallions. The horse, observant and alert to its surroundings, lays its head over the deer, sheltering it under its neck. Sensing that danger is approaching, the animals stomp their feet and switch their tails uneasily.

The Gypsy women know the figure is a vampire when they see him approach their camp. The fingers of the night fire reach high as a passing cloud shadows the full moon. Stories of vampire killings have preceded him, reaching like the tentacles of an octopus into even the remotest of places.

Several of the women are either standing barefoot by the bank or on rocks, washing clothes in the stream. The fast-moving water tugs at the bottoms of their long brown-and-white wool dresses. After all their years of living difficult, dangerous lives—of being targets of hatred for many people, of traveling from village to village—they're always on alert for the slightest change in the landscape. They see Jacques before the men do. Their quiet, worried voices slip away with the undertow of the swirling current as they wonder whether he's the leader of the night creatures they've heard so much about. All the birds, even the owls, have vanished into the darkness, leaving behind a bottomless quiet that settles into the clearing when a vampire is near.

Over the generations they've heard the tales of powerful, evil creatures from the night with yellow eyes and fangs that suck the lifeblood from people; these demons are the followers of Beng, the Devil.

All the women are terrified. They think of their children sleeping in the wagons, their men sitting by the fire. They are helpless, yet they continue their work, hoping Del—God—will protect them.

The Gypsy king, supporting a black top hat and with curly white hair rolling up around his ears, puffs on a pipe, blowing the smoke toward the fire. Several other men of various ages, comfortable in old worn clothes, are singing or keeping time, while another plays a violin, someone else a cimbalom, and a third the bagpipes. The music is a misty, deep, melancholy tune breathing sagacity into the forest of pine trees that safeguards the wanderers.

Among the Gypsies is a young, strikingly beautiful woman with satiny brown skin. Her name is Violca because of her mysterious, deep-violet eyes. Only she, of all the women in her clan, while washing clothes would have the confidence, the self-awareness, to wear a witchy-looking, blue cotton blouse with ragged sleeves and a knee-length skirt with alternating jewel-tone panels of blue, green, and purple. Little bells that make beautiful noises are hanging from her waist. The bottom of her blouse is tied in front, around her thin, attractive waist, just below her breasts.

She twists the fabric of her dress between her hands, wrings out the water, and pulls back her mane of cascading black hair. The other Gypsies watch in trepidation as she strides out of the stream toward Jacques. She is the fortune-teller in this small Roma tribe. She possesses the gift of prophecy along with other supernatural powers she inherited from her grandmother, Luludja, which means "flower of life." There is none like her in all the Gypsy tribes. Violca is surprised by the uncommonly handsome appearance of the evil beast. He is tall and slender, with extremely long, thick, brown, wavy hair that fans out over his ankles.

It's impossible for Violca to count the number of red eyes staring at her from the forest behind Jacques. This will be her greatest challenge—her dreams have foreshadowed this night. She remembers the first time she saw the vampire inside the glass; there has been no rest from the crystal ball's unbending resolve. Jacques is their only hope. She prays she has understood the omens swirling inside the glass sphere, or all that she holds dear will perish in the nightfall of perdition.

Violca stands in front of Jacques's magnificent form. She's prepared for the unexpected as she gazes into his startling blue eyes. What can she say? *I bid thee welcome. I greet thee. Good day to you. I know not thy name. Perhaps my good man, I could fetch thee some ale.* Gawking at the impressive creature that she has seen in her crystal ball again and again, she realizes that some things can be so bewitching that words are better left unspoken. And so, taking a deep breath of encouragement, she grasps one of his hands and leads him toward her living wagon. She'll deal with the other members of her tribe tomorrow. She'll spend tonight forming a relationship with him. During the day he will rest in a compartment under the floor in one of the load wagons, hidden in a false bottom. The false bottoms were constructed years ago to hide valuables and other items of importance to the Gypsies. Both wagons are skirted and decorated with hand-carved animals in the colors of lavender, green, gold, and red. No one will ever know he's there.

Violca's wagon has four wooden wheels. On each wheel the twelve signs of the zodiac have been painstakingly painted in various shades of brown, yellow, orange, gray, and white. The areas around the zodiac wheels are decorated with a midnight-blue heaven and a yellow sun dusted with reddish rays and countless silver stars.

She opens the creaking door, and she and Jacques step inside. Box-shaped wooden benches run down each side of the wagon, with colorful, padded, embroidered wool covers. The storage areas inside the benches are accessible by lifting the lids. A table with leather hinges lifts up against the wall. A bed with a wool coverlet stitched with yellow-and-green wildflowers, with a waterfall cascading down to a blue mountain stream, is set against the back wall. Shutters on each side of the wagon afford ventilation in temperate weather. Violca's most prized possession stands on a shelf. Handed down from her grandmother, it is taken out only when the Gypsies stop to stay in one place for a time. It's a polished black-marble-and-gold statue of a winged Isis, the Black Virgin, ancient goddess of Egypt, holding the sacred flame. The statue has been passed down through the women of her family since the Crusades. Their history says Isis fell in love with a Gypsy king, Loizi, which means "famous warrior." He lost his life saving her from the followers of Mithras. Violca's grandmother told her the statue is the source of their supernatural powers. Like her, Violca has the blood of Isis flowing through her veins—a gift of everlasting courage and truth.

Violca turns and looks at Jacques, the darkness hiding his expression. His presence intimidates her, but still she lifts his ragged, bloodstained shirt over his head and drops it to the floor. Gently she encourages him to lie on the bed and stretch his arms out. Each breath he takes is a heavy longing for France, his ancestral home and a life he once knew.

As she cleans Jacques's body with a wet cloth, she's unable to take her eyes off the birthmark on the back of his neck. In her world, the sun stands for the source of life, power, leadership, healing, truth, and immortality. She wipes down Jacques's long limbs and the thick muscles along his back and shoulders. She leans over and whispers softly, her warm breath licking the inside of his ear. Her hand rests on the back of his neck. The birthmark is tantalizing, warm. She is seduced by the soft touches, candlelight, and intimate thoughts of lasting friendship. "My clan will sacrifice their lives to try to protect you," she says. "You must promise the same in return."

Masterfully Violca pours the brown, rawhide-smelling, viscid, birch-tar oil from a small, tall-handled, silver pitcher. She pushes the liquid across Jacques's back and gently rubs it into the crevices of his sculptured body. Carefully, when he isn't looking, she pulls from beneath her bed a small, fossilized, red blood, bone-handled knife with magical qualities. The wound never scars and the wounded never feels pain. It was given to her by her grandmother. She deftly cuts a small gash in each of her wrists with the double-edged blade that's sharpened to perfection.

Slowly she moves her hands in a circular pattern and drips tiny drops of her blood onto his flesh forming a magic circle. The strong smell of the birch-tar oil masks the sweet fragrance of her blood from Jacques's acute senses.

She continues, pressing into his thick neck, powerful shoulders, ripped arms, granite-like back, and narrow waist. With each movement of her hands, she feels the power in his body. Her breathing becomes heavy as she presses her weight into him before carelessly removing her cotton dress and dropping it to the floor.

Humming, she begins singing incantations as she lays her naked body across Jacques's back and presses her breasts into the heavy oil, pushing circular lines across his skin and in the directions of north, east, south and west. As the energy inside the circle builds, her passion rises, burning like wood in a fiery furnace. To open the circle, the cone of power, to release its energy into Jacques, she cuts into his flesh a small door in the circle's blood line. Instantly, she feels the slightest transformation in his flesh, a tiny spark of humanity taking root in the depths of his cold body. The energy spent, using drops of her blood, she closes the opening by reconnecting the lines of the circle.

Jacques isn't sure why he's here. Something drew him to this place, a voice from an invisible past. It's been five hundred years since he felt warmth, the touch of a woman. Five hundred years since he left France. Three hundred since he left Transylvania. Her emotional fever spent, Violca unrolls a paper-thin piece of tanned leather and wipes it across Jacques's back, scrubbing it clean. After putting her dress back on, she lightly taps his shoulder. He rolls over, exposing his mighty chest and staring up into the most beautiful face he's ever seen—those violet eyes, the long black hair, the small jaw and plump, sensual lips.

Violca straddles his body, resting on her knees on the bed, using the strength of her hands to work the soothing blood ointment deep into Jacques's flesh. He struggles against the unfamiliar tenderness his body feels, the long-suppressed memories of Margaret. To a human, these feelings would pass like a fleeing deer. To a vampire, they last an eternity.

Outside, why weren't you afraid of me?" he finally asks in a calm, searching voice while effortlessly pulling her back towards him.

She turns into his gaze. "I'm the spiritual leader of our Roma clan," she answers, leaning down and lightly pressing her hands against the sides of his face. "I inherited this honor from my grandmother. With this honor I decided I had one of two choices to make. I could have faith in our heritage—who we are as a people. With that choice I would be expected to conform to our way of life, our customs." She takes a breath, blinking her violet-colored eyes, collecting her thoughts. "It's what our clan borrowed from the people who went before us, and our children will borrow it from us. My other choice would be to have faith in my convictions, my purpose, and the guiding rod that reaches into my soul. The life inside me is my own. I chose the latter as it allows me to do what's right and good for my people, regardless of the risk. My fears and conformities will not deter me. My grandmother lived to be one hundred twenty-seven years old. They say it was her violet eyes." She looks knowingly at Jacques while placing her hand tenderly on his shoulder. "And so shall I. I always ask myself, what is my mission?" She reaches down and takes his incredibly long, thick hair in her hands and begins to run her fingers through it, combing it across his godlike shoulders and muscle-ripped chest. "I have a covenant with my people that I can never violate. Every covenant is celebrated by family and friends together. I take responsibility when we violate our covenant. I will commit to you, no matter what, you are now part of our covenant." She leans down and softly whispers into his ear. "You are our promise."

"I will stay," he vows. "I will protect you and yours with my life for as long as I live. Can you make me strong? Strong enough to defeat Claude de Lavoe?"

Violca knows Claude. She has seen him many times in her crystal ball. "With me all is possible…if you believe, Jacques de Molay. Only if you believe." She quickly stands and pushes aside a blue shelf curtain that shields a violin case. A large green leaf covered with black horse salve lies on a strip of cloth on the shelf, next to the violin case. Using the cloth, she wipes her hands and wrists clean of the blood and birch-tar oil and smears horse salve over the cuts on her wrists. The ointment immediately helps form protective scabs over the wounds. "I want you to play this for me," she says, handing the violin case to Jacques.

Violca tells him that her grandmother, while reading tarot cards for the captain of an Italian sailing ship, predicted his death and all those who sailed with him on the day he planned to lift anchor. The captain kept his crew in port that day. All others who hoisted sail perished in the violent storms. He gave the violin to Violca's grandmother as a gift for her everlasting courage and truth. He said it was made by Antonio Stradivari, the most skilled violin craftsman in history.

"My grandmother told me I would meet a great person who would play this for me someday. See!" She holds the open violin case and points to the top of the lid. "The captain even signed it. The letters are all in silver: FOR EVERLASTING COURAGE AND TRUTH. CAPITANO VINCENTI DI CURRADO, 1737. I think you'll find it much better than the vielle."

"I've never played the violin," Jacques confesses while sitting up. He turns the instrument over in his hands. The quality of wood, its shape, the type of varnish—he's never seen such exquisite workmanship. The instrument has four gutstrings instead of five like the vielle.

Violca glances around searchingly. "I can explain the difference to you only like this: the vielle is like a dull, unemotional person, while this violin, in the right hands, is like a rainbow at the end of a hard rain, the sound of a raging waterfall, a shooting star that lights up the night sky, the full moon in all its wonder." She hesitates, takes a breath. "A lovely Gypsy woman whose voice takes your breath away, the light touch of her finger against your cheek, a thunderstorm at night…and…and…" She smiles and shrugs.

After lifting the instrument to his shoulder, Jacques tunes it, strikes it with the bow, and then plays. The violin responds with rich, powerful tones to the flawless movement of his fingertips. The sounds resonate through the wagon's walls and dance with the crystal light of the moon.

Outside the Gypsies hear the melodious music but don't sense any emotion in its tone. The sounds are magnificent but lack depth, feeling. It's as if the maestro has no passion for his art.

Over the last few months, Violca has told them about the visions in her crystal ball and in her dreams and warned them this night would come. She advised them not to panic, show fear, or try to flee. She told them not to do anything unwise. Each time she spread the tarot cards on the table, the answers to her questions were always the same. A great evil master of the night, yoked to nothing, not even time, would enter their lives. Only Violca can tame him. Only she has the powers—the gifts of knowledge and nature—to influence him.

The music fades into the vastness of the forest as the old Gypsy king, Mihai, which means "who is like God," gathers the council elders to discuss the coming day and any problems they might encounter in their travels to the next village. A couple of the men attempt to interrupt and ask questions about Jacques and his followers, but the Gypsy king silences them.

The women quickly hang their wet clothes on rawhide cords tied between the wagons so they'll dry during the night. Those with children hurry to their wagons, bedding them down in hopes of keeping them safe.

Violca has warned the old Gypsy king that they must accept Jacques into their small clan or they all will die. He glances over his shoulder. All the red eyes in the forest have disappeared, swallowed up by the emptiness of the Russian wilds. He nods knowingly. A hidden smile breaks his lips, and he claps his hands briskly for everyone to disperse. Violca has done well! Anyone who can play a violin like that deserves a chance. Hopefully, through her teachings, his music will develop feeling, perhaps even passion.

—◆—

The Gypsies move out as soon as the morning sun provides enough light to travel by. Earlier, before sunrise, Violca let down the side of one of the load wagons so Jacques could crawl inside the hidden compartment beneath the floor. The dirt road is roughly cut, with deep wagon-wheel ruts from the heavy rains a few days earlier, making the ride extremely bumpy. At first Jacques finds himself jostled around the inside of the compartment. If it weren't for the strength of his vampire body, he would be seriously injured. Using his powerful arms, he places his hands against the underside of the floor and pushes against it, pinning his shoulders to the bottom of the compartment and stabilizing his body. It's still a long, dusty, choppy, creaking ride, but he'll survive.

Three naked children, one boy and two girls, pointing and shouting excitedly, run beside the wagons. They see the grayish smoke from Navlya as the distant village's chimneys dissipate into a massive blue sky with angel-brushed white clouds.

The day is beginning to slip into evening by the time they reach the outskirts of the hamlet, which is snuggled tightly around the tiny bay of a large lake. Tall, blackish, scarred, birch trees line its endless banks and walk up into the surrounding and distant hills. The shadows of the trees form graceful reflections in the water. Several single-mast, birch boats have been pulled out of the water and rest on the grassy shore. Others are still out, their white sails dotting the emerald-green lake.

The Gypsies will burn the rest of the daylight and the night setting up their tents and preparing for the opening of their freak show. Navlya is one of their favorite stops; the villagers always have games planned and offer an array of breads, savory pastries, and desserts to the Gypsies and their children. They all look forward to the fresh fish—smallmouth bass, carp, and catfish—and the elk meat they'll cook over a birch fire. Deer jerky is by far their favorite. The village hunters kill extra deer when they know the Gypsies' traveling show is going to arrive. They cut the meat against the grain and into fine pieces so it's easy to chew, and then they mix their age-old secret ingredients in a bowl and pour it over the thin slices of meat, letting it soak all night. At first morning light, they'll cook it on a low flame of red-hot coals until it's dry. The extra—and there always is some—will be wrapped in tanned deer hide and given to the wanderers when they leave. It provides them a delicious food to munch on during the next leg of their journey. Each time the Gypsy children leave the village, they can't wait to come back.

When evening falls, Jacques wakes from his rest, unlatches the side panel of the load wagon, and steps into moonlit darkness. A short distance away, the Gypsies are rolling out tents, pounding in wooden stakes, raising the center poles, and attaching the canvas sidewalls. Oil-burning lanterns hanging from tall poles light the area. Two sledgehammers lean against one of the load wagons. Grabbing them, Jacques points at a young, shirtless, Gypsy boy whose long, curly, blond hair hangs in ringlets down his back. "Hold the stake there," he growls. He points at one of the Gypsy men who's watching him. "You pick up the other stake," Jacques commands, and points to another corner of the tent. "Hold it there, on the other side of the boy."

While the boy and man hold the stakes in place, Jacques drops his shirt to his waist and grabs the weathered handles of two heavy, cast-iron, double-faced sledgehammers. He holds one in each of his massive hands. Positioning himself in front of the two stakes, he swings his right arm around first, banging the stake at that corner of the tent and driving it halfway into the hard ground. Then, like a windmill turning the shaft on a waterwheel, he swings his left arm around and pounds the other stake halfway into the ground. Then his right arm swings around to the first stake and hammers it solidly into the ground. Immediately his left arm swings around, slamming the second stake into place. Disgruntled that it took him two blows each, he lifts one of the mallets and inspects its workmanship. "Hmmph," he mumbles. He'll find a blacksmith's shop and have heavier mallets made.

Jacques signals to his two helpers to gather the rest of the wooden stakes and to come with him. By this time Violca and others are following them. Never have they seen such an astounding display of strength.

After all the tents are raised and the wagons are positioned for tomorrow's show, Violca asks Jacques to follow her to the banya, a small hut of white birch covered with felt that sits in a hollow close to the lake. Inside are two wooden benches attached to the walls and a fire pit of red-hot stones.

Ground portions of dried animal essence—from caribou, wolves, moose, elk, bighorn sheep, mountain lions, and brown bears—have been blended with the digestive juices of venomous viper snakes, scorpions, and lizards. This mixture is piled up in a corner of the room. Bundles of leafy birch twigs soak in a large, riveted, copper kettle filled with water.

Jacques glances around the strange room. In his travels with the Knights Templar, he saw the world's greatest saunas in cities such as Rome and Jerusalem—and now this. Bathing isn't something vampires find necessary, yet the heat from the hot stones immediately soothes his skin.

"We take off our clothes now." Violca lifts her dress over her head and hangs it on a wooden post. Her brown skin is like rare silk, soft and delicate, and her body glistens in the warm room. The sight of her nakedness, however, doesn't arouse Jacques. His lust is for blood, a craving that overwhelms all other feelings and emotions. Violca knows this and, after their last encounter, doesn't feel uncomfortable in his presence. She helps Jacques take off his unkempt clothes and hangs them up.

"Kneel." She grabs his shoulder and pushes against his back. "Kneel by the stones. The heat will bring mother earth closer to us."

Reluctantly Jacques drops to his knees, wondering what will happen next.

"You will become a great power," Violca says. "All will fear you. Your body will change over time, becoming one with the dark soul of mother earth. Your name will make daylight tremble, night darken." She rests a hand on his shoulder. "Trust me. Do as I say."

She begins to chant as she dances slowly, lifting her legs high, raising her voice, twirling in circles while sprinkling the powdered animal essence on the red-hot stones. "Breathe deeply," she wails. "The essence, the life-force of the great animals…take them into your body. Let their power become one with your spirit."

As instructed, Jacques breathes deeply, sucking the smoke-filled air into his lungs. Sweat soaks his skin. His muscles quiver from being infused with higher sources of energy; his increased physical strength struggles within his flesh, screaming to break out.

Violca's chanting and dancing reach a whirlwind tempo. "Breathe, Jacques de Molay. Breathe it all in. Breathe."

She continues to sprinkle the ground animal essence over the red-hot stones. The interior of the banya is clouded in smoke, and her incantations reach a fever pitch. After grabbing a handful of the leafy birch twigs from the copper kettle, she forcefully lashes Jacques's body, striking him again and again, thrashing the sweat out of him. Each time she hits him, the minutest feeling of emotion sends shock waves through his body. Over time this emerging sensitivity will make him wonder whether it is possible for him to become human again, to experience the warmth of a woman's body against his, to love once more.

—ⅶ—

Over the next several months, Violca repeats this ritual again and again. Jacques's neck, chest, back, arms, and legs become heavily muscled, like gigantic hams. Bulging, purple blood vessels push to the surface of his skin, wrapping around the swollen layers of powerful muscles, crisscrossing his body. His hair grows thicker, heavier, wolflike. Dark creases line his face. His nose and lips thicken; the changes in his features are induced by the animal essence. Like ice cracking across a pond in spring, a spark of human emotion spreads through Jacques's body and soul and, with it, the urge to love a woman.

Jacques continues to play the violin for Violca. Whenever the traveling freak show stops to set up camp, he and Violca steal away at night to a quiet place to live in their dreams. His vampire gifts enhance his genius for song. These are the times Violca enjoys the most: their escapes to the world of enchantment amid Jacques's spellbinding music, surrounded by the night's stars, his entire body moving to the sounds of his dancing fingers. The seed of human emotion planted by Violca reveals itself in his music.

When the sun reaches its apex, the freak show begins. The Gypsies, dressed in costumes of enthusiastic colors, dance around in one of the tents as a strange tune from a snake charmer's flute enchants a cobra. A dwarf dressed as a clown entertains children and adults. The dwarf has a realistically designed cloth puppet of a silver fox that extends from his hand to his elbow. On the other hand, he wears a ridiculous-looking, hand-stitched puppet of a yellow chicken with a big beak, dumb-looking eyes, huge floppy feet, and tiny wings. By moving his fingers back and forth, he can open and close the mouths and roll the eyes of both puppets, making them interact with each other. He runs in front of and into the audience as if the fox is chasing the chicken but can't ever catch it. Finally the chicken manages to turn the tables on the fox and begins to chase it, to the delighted screams and laughter of the audience.

Everyone knows the bearded lady isn't really bearded. It's horsehair that's been woven and then attached to her waist-length brown hair. The beard does, however, cause great fun. The children call her "poop butt" because the hair has been pulled from the horse's tail.

The conjoined twins attract gawkers from far and wide. One appears normal in everyway except for the other twin that hangs motionlessly from his waist. There are none like them in all of Russia. The dominant twin has wavy, long, brown hair and a stocky build; one might consider him handsome. The two stubby legs from the nonresponsive twin stick out of his back. To the great enjoyment of the crowd, the passive twin opens his eyes, smiles, and then raises one of his deformed arms and makes a gesture to the crowd.

As times passes, stories of Jacques's Sampson-like, long hair and incredible feats of strength grow, spreading from hamlet to hamlet. The tales of his great power are even more mysterious, as his shows are held inside the tent when the moon shines full. Whale-oil lanterns hang from tall, wooden stakes, their light shrouded by finely crafted cloth cutouts. The Gypsy women have created intricate images—witches, skeletons, haunted castles, and demons—on cloth attached to sticks. Flowers, leaves, dried twigs, animal hair, and the like have been painstakingly sewn to the cloth to create a realistic effect. Gypsy women dressed in dark-spirit costumes expertly move the sticks back and forth, casting shadows of frightening scenes on the tent's walls, manipulating the movements of the cutouts in rhythm amid the darkness of night.

One violinist, two flute players, and four gusli musicians—who hold the multistringed instruments on their knees—provide accompaniment to the dramatic, frightening, dark creatures' evil deeds or the victims' sad, moody good-byes.

Adults and children from the village, sitting on makeshift wooden stands, their eyes wide with fright, holler and scream. When the time is right, Violca, dressed as a witch in a long, purple dress, black boots, and a tall, pointed, black hat, runs into the center of the tent, waving her hands and shouting incantations in Russian until the cutout creatures fade away, one by one, and the music ends.

Jacques, followed by a team of four horses and their trainer, enters the tent next. He's wearing a leather face mask with eyeholes, and his long hair sweeps down to his ankles in one long braid to which crotal bells are attached.

The trainer and two of his helpers harness Jacques to four black Russian, heavy wagon horses that face one direction while Jacques faces the other. Their muscles flex as they paw the dirt. They've done this before and have yet to win. This time, the trainer believes, will be different.

The onlookers are speechless. The children point at Jacques and ask their parents questions. None of them believes that Jacques, even with his incredible strength, can outpull a team of powerful, heavy wagon horses.

The trainer cracks the whip, snapping the air. "Pull!" he commands. All four horses—seventy-two hundred pounds of raw muscle—lean into the leather harnesses. The two assistants, one on each side of the horses, grip a long set of reins so they can control the animals' movements.

Jacques, offsetting the strength and weight of the heavy draft horses, pushes into his harness, his massive body resisting the horses' efforts to pull him backward. The trainer cracks his whip several more times in the air while commanding, "Pull! Pull!" but the four horses aren't able to break Jacques down.

Jacques shakes his head like an angry bull; the crotal bells ring; and he manages one grueling step, his thigh muscles bulging, his enormous back straining and quivering under the tremendous pressure.

The horses lean forward, throwing all their weight and strength into the contest, jacking their legs in an attempt to gain traction, snapping their leather harness tight, their heavy shoulder and leg muscles flexing.

Hesitating for a breath, Jacques takes another unsteady step and then, after spitting into the air, indomitably shakes his head and takes yet another step, slowly dragging the horses backward, their hooves digging into the ground, rolling the dirt up behind them. The trainer continues to snap the whip in the air while shouting, "Pull! Pull! Pull!" The audience is amazed; Jacques is the strongest man they've ever seen. He takes a firm step and continues to pull the four heavy draft horses backward.

The trainer steps in and stops the contest, relaxing the horses—Jacques has won. The audience is beside themselves, clapping and shouting, "Da! Da! Da!" They wave madly. "Da! Da! Da!" The assistants unbuckle the harness, and with Jacques following, they lead the team of horses out of the tent. The entire audience is on their feet; many hold their small children on their shoulders or above their heads to allow them a better view. Some spectators wave their shirts in the air. None will forget this night.

The Gypsy women who were managing the cutouts earlier hang cloth covers in yellow and blue, yellow and red, and yellow and green over the lanterns. Soon the inside of the tent is cast in a soothing light. It's time not only to step into the past but also to learn about their future. The audience sits back down, and a sheltered quiet settles in.

Wearing a bold, brightly colored blouse with puffed sleeves in different shades of yellow and blue and a matching, long, pleated skirt, Violca serenely walks up and stands in front of the villagers. A gold necklace dangles against her bosom, and gold coins are woven into her long black hair. Her immeasurable beauty is accentuated by the serious mood that has settled over the audience. All year they've waited with guarded anticipation for the moment when they finally will hear her words. Her reputation for truth and goodness lives throughout all the local villages.

Calmly she circulates from individual to individual, placing her hands on the heads of those who want to be connected to the afterworld and to speak to loved ones who have died. People reach up just to have their hands touched by hers. She never misses anyone; all are important. "*Spah-see-boh, spah-see-boh, spah-see-boh.* Thank you, thank you, thank you," they cry, as tears of gratitude stream down their faces.

Violca eventually moves to a lone table in the middle of the tent and delicately lifts the bright scarlet cloth from her crystal ball. The village leaders will ask her to predict the weather for the coming year, the caribou movement for their hunters, the fish catches. Will their harvest be bountiful, or will it be another dry year? Does good or evil walk in their future?

On this night, as she peers into the shadowy haze swirling inside her crystal ball, all changes for Violca and her small Gypsy tribe—for all the villages, the Russian people, Jacques de Molay, and the realm of vampires. All she sees is death and destruction; waves of billowing black smoke darken the countryside. Entire villages are laid to waste, burned to the ground. From the mouth of destruction, the tongues of flames greedily lick the inside of the crystal ball. Entire herds of animals are slaughtered. Violca sees great famine, mass starvation, suffering, disease. Children, too weak to stand, huddle together, their limbs shriveled to the bone, their skeletons chiseled by the deft hands of hunger. Old men and women with sunken eyes are left to die, defeated by starvation.

Violca recognizes the invaders of her country—the French, the Imperial Guard, Napoleon wearing a hat and sitting astride his white Arabian horse. He has a pale face and cold features and wears a dark-blue uniform with white lapels. The year is 1812, and the French already have crossed the Nieman River and are swarming across the motherland like locusts. It's the greatest army ever formed. What can she say to these people?

Violca's silence alarms the villagers. Even the children control their breathing. "Something is wrong with Violca," the people murmur. They sense this; she hasn't moved or spoken for what seems forever. "What does she see?" they whisper among themselves. "Will a great evil befall us?"

Violca composes herself and rises while holding up her arms. She presses a finger to her lips for everyone to shush. "My fellow children…" she begins softly. All are straining to hear. "A great storm descends on Mother Russia. Napoleon Bonaparte and his Grande Armée have invaded our country. Your village, like many others, lies in their path. They are destroying everything, leaving nothing alive. In ten days, with the setting of the sun, their soldiers will be here. One of the great battles of the war will take place in Saltanovka, just a half-day's journey away. Take only what you need to live. The cold heart of winter will beat early this year. Go now. May God walk with you."

She watches them leave with fear in their eyes. What can they do? Where can they go? An army of six hundred thousand men—there's no place to hide. The Gypsies are already breaking camp. They, like most of the villagers, will travel south, away from Moscow. Violca puts her crystal ball into its worn, tan leather carrying case, feeling Jacques's presence behind her.

"What do you want me to do?" he asks.

She's surprised. It's been such a long, lonely time since she's heard the sound of his voice. She finds it pleasing. It warms her heart, and she feels safe. "You must leave us." She runs her hand softly across the side of his face. "You and the other vampires must overtake Napoleon's army. You must destroy them—*all* of them. Save Mother Russia. Only you can do this great thing. Let none of them set foot on French soil again." She stares at him, locking her deep-violet eyes with his. "This is your road back to Margaret. After all these years, she still longs for you."

Understanding, Jacques nods. "Can I defeat Claude de Lavoe?" he asks.

"You and I haven't had much time together to increase your strength," she replies, her eyes still meeting his. "Be careful. He's very strong."

"I want to be human again, to experience the softness of a woman, her tenderness, love. Being a vampire is such a wretched life." Jacques looks off into the distance. "Is such a thing possible?" He looks back at Violca searchingly.

"True love. Find true love, and all is possible, Jacques de Molay. Follow the sails of the wind to the world across the sea. From this day forward, to become human you must never drink of their blood. If you do, a creature of both night and day you will become. Accepted by neither world; an animal of your own kind. A soldier of God, a Templar Knight, will be lost to you forever. The measured changes in your body will cease. Your vampire self and your human self are like two great armies, their cavalries of heavily armored knights charging down on each other. If you don't stand firm in the face of this terrible onslaught, the pain and confusion caused by the impact of these two immense forces will destroy you. Jacques de Molay will be forgotten in the coils of time. Always remember who you are. Be strong."

Realizing this is the last time they ever will see each other, Jacques looks at Violca as never before. She planted life inside him, the seed of emotion. He thinks of her nakedness, the heat from the banya, and he hungers to hold her breasts, to press his face between their softness, to listen to the beating of her heart. He breathes deeply, inhaling the delicious scent of her skin. He grabs her, pulling her body hard against his, kissing her, licking her neck and the softness of her face. He lifts her off her feet and muscles her to the ground. Like an animal he rips off her clothes and discards them to the wind. Smothering her naked body with his massive frame, he forces his powerful legs between hers, spreading them apart, and pins her hands to the ground. He pushes his face into her neck and opens his mouth. As he growls, his lips roll back, and he drags his fangs across her skin, scratching it. His eyes burn red, and his icy blood thaws and smolders with his hunger. He's going to take her. He slides his tongue across her flesh while ripping off his brown breeches.

"No, Jacques," Violca shouts, pushing against him. "Don't do this. Not here. Not now." She grabs his face between her hands and stares into his eyes. They frighten her; she's never seen them this color before. They look like the eyes of a wild animal. "All will come to you in time. This is not the way. Trust me. Please, Jacques, remember who you are," she cries. "Look at me. Look at me…Don't hurt me."

Jacques shakes his head, clearing his thoughts. He doesn't understand what he's feeling. It's been five hundred years; so much has changed. He drops his head slightly. He would rather die than hurt Violca. She lifts her face to his, wraps her arms around his neck, and kisses him tenderly. Her fingers brush across his birthmark, which somehow comforts her. Jacques stands and effortlessly lifts her from the ground. She holds him for a moment, and then she reaches over and touches the ruby-and-diamond-encrusted pendant that always hangs from a gold chain around his neck. "I want you to separate this," she says softly while caressing his face with her fingers. "It's all I'll ever have to remember you by." She hesitates, reflecting back to their times together. "With what we've shared, it's all I'll ever need."

"In one piece it opens the keystone, the great door to the Templar treasure and the Ark of the Covenant," he explains. "In two pieces it's worthless."

"Someday," Violca says with a smile, "it will come back to you. Have faith, Jacques de Molay."

Jacques unsnaps the pendant and places one half in her outstretched hand.

"Remember to play the violin for her," she says. "You play divinely, like no other. Don't forget. Now go! Go!" She gently pushes him away and sadly watches as he rushes out of the tent and into the night. "I gave you my heart, Jacques de Molay," she whispers to the fleeting shadows of darkness. She holds a hand over her chest. "Now I must struggle with the loss."

Following the light of the full moon to the top of a distant hill, Jacques hesitates while looking over his shoulder at the traveling freak show. The tents are down and being loaded into the wagons. He wishes for fate to smile on them. *How could Violca have known about Margaret?* he asks himself. The crystal ball must reveal more to her than he'll ever know. When he finds Margaret, he hopes they both can become human again somehow; it will be his quest.

Raising his arms wide, lifting his face toward the heavens, peering into the hidden corners of his mind, he summons hordes of vampire bats. They awaken, deep in their dark caverns and other clandestine places. In every cemetery, mausoleum, burial ground—anywhere the walking dead rest—they are summoned. Breaking wing by the thousands, they answer Jacques's call. Soon he hears their cries for blood spilling across the night air. These are his vampires, the adherents he converted after the One Hundred Twenty banished him more than three hundred years ago.

Over the next several months, under Jacques's command, the vampires devastate Napoleon's Grande Armée. Their numbers have grown so large that they can surround an entire encampment of soldiers. When night is at its darkest, the vampires emerge, attacking the stragglers, the deserters, the scavengers searching for food. They drag the sleeping from their rest. The soldiers who survive huddle around their campfires in frenzied terror.

So many men die that their screams smother all sounds of the night. Their quivering bodies are sucked dry of blood. The vampires tear off the soldiers' heads and run ahead of the retreating French army. They impale the heads on tall sticks or hang them by the hair from the barren limbs of frozen trees, forming a horror-show corridor that the French army follows during their arduous journey back to France. The shriveled skin of the dead, their lifeless, dry-socket eyes, and their ghastly smiles are endless omens of the evil stalking the soldiers.

The soldiers the vampires don't kill are left to the Cossack raiding parties and the bitter cold, their fingers and toes eaten by frostbite. Men and horses struggle through the blinding, blowing snow, which is three to four feet deep. Death, by freezing or starvation, is their unfailing companion. Days and nights quake with the screams of dying men—few will live through this nightmare.

When it invaded Russia in June 1812, Napoleon's Grande Armée consisted of more than six hundred thousand men. He reached Moscow with a mere one hundred thirty thousand. With the early and unusually harsh winter and the forced retreat from Moscow, only ten thousand soldiers cross back over the French border. Jacques's vampires have taken down Napoleon's men by the hundreds of thousands.

Violca, sitting in her wagon and peering into her crystal ball, is delighted with the images she sees. Mother Russia owes its life to the vampires. A magnificent smile crosses her face. Since Jacques left the Gypsies, he hasn't drunk one drop of human blood. He has left the feeding to his vampire followers. She lays her hand gently between her breasts and holds her half of the ruby-and-diamond-encrusted Templar pendant. "When we meet again, Jacques de Molay…when we meet again."

She feels a jerk and hears the creaking of the wagon as it's pulled by the horses. The traveling freak show will reach the village of Borvo tonight.

14

THE SHE-WOLF'S REVENGE

France, December 1812

It's been five hundred years since Jacques de Molay set foot on French soil. On the night of his return, ghostly clouds obscure the moon as a cold, northern breeze rattles the dried tree branches. Hundreds of vampires have followed Jacques from Russia to pursue the remnants of Napoleon's Grande Armée. Approaching France, with Napoleon's army decimated, many of the vampires take wing and seek out the darkest of the deep caves, the graveyards, anywhere the living dead can safely rest. They wait for Napoleon's desperate, final defense of France in what someday will be called the Battle of the Nations. It will involve hundreds of thousands of soldiers. The vampires will descend like vultures and gorge themselves on the dying, the wounded, the stragglers, the deserters. Jacques is keeping his promise to Violca to annihilate Napoleon's army.

When he enters France, only two hundred of his vampires remain. These are the faithful who know Jacques best, those who have been his followers since he left Transylvania. They are monsters—powerful men with broad shoulders and enormous hands, legs, and chests. Hair blankets their bodies like the fur of the great, Russian brown bear. Their exceedingly long beards and mustaches are combed back into their hair, which hangs down like Jacques's, fanning out in a triangular shape from the backs of their necks to their ankles, waxed with the sweat of wild animals. As they move en masse, their blood-red eyes glow over the snow-covered ground, the rocky soil poking through as though the landscape were an enormous polka-dot blanket.

Aside from killing the remaining French soldiers, they have one last impending battle: Claude and his Demons of Distortion. Jacques wishes his army were larger, but the cards have been dealt. He also knows the element of surprise isn't on their side. Claude, with his underground sources, will know Jacques has returned and also know their numbers. Jacques turns and looks back at his footprints in the snow. "Aaaah," he murmurs. He inhales deeply, lifting his face, as the fresh, cool, night air pumps through his lungs. The brown earth of France is under his feet again. He longs to see Margaret. The tiny seed Violca planted in him begins to sprout, and the feelings are unfamiliar.

It takes Jacques and his vampires two hundred seventy days to reach the land of his de Molay ancestral home. He spots the outline of the hills in the distance. The moonlight, scantily clad with feathery clouds, seems to tease him. There was a time when the lights from the Templar chapel would have challenged a star's brightness, but the lanterns have long since been discarded, their wicks snuffed out.

Something sinister and revolting triggers Jacques's survival instincts: Claude de Lavoe, leading his Demons of Distortion, is marching over the hills toward them. There must be hundreds of the beasts, overrunning the countryside like rodents.

Seeing their enemy, both sides bang their chests with closed fists and shout, creating a deafening clamor. The two armies race toward each other. At first the vampires are winning, pushing the demons back. The slaughter is enormous, but the demons continue to stream out of the blackness like massive schools of piranhas. The hills teem with red eyes, gnashing teeth, and fingers with long, hardened nails sharpened to razor-thin points. Voices gurgle from the gobs of blood running down their throats. Jacques and his vampires attempt to regroup, but the demons, with their superior numbers, are too great. Their hordes overtake Jacques's army, mutilating and killing the vampires who aren't able to escape.

Blood churns the white of snow to crimson. Jacques, with his new-found strength, lays waste to hundreds of demons, but he's no match for their numbers. A pack of the creatures suck him into the mass of their bodies, forming a large, horizontal funnel and pull him toward the narrow end, where Claude waits impatiently. Claude's hatred is fueled by the recent realization that Margaret saved Jacques from certain death. Jacques should have died that night five hundred years ago. His body should have burned up in the morning sun. That was why Margaret didn't follow him to the Templar's white-marble chapel, the mausoleum. Claude was wounded, and instead of helping him, she was saving Jacques. After all these years, it finally makes sense.

Jacques is weak, exhausted, his centuries of hope crushed, his army vanquished. Although he knows resistance is useless, he continues to fight.

Claude savagely and without quarter, pummels him. *After Jacques shows him where the Templar treasure is hidden, he'll kill him. Skin him alive. Butcher him like a hog.*

The demons, following their master, drag Jacques inside the Templar's chapel. Dust and windblown grime coat the floor and walls. The frescoes and other paintings are hidden beneath the filth.

Time and neglect have ravaged the estate. Buildings are in various states of decay. Stones have been hauled away by thieves; walls have collapsed; the ornamental lakes and the channel that once fed them are overgrown. The only water lies in puddles from the last rain. The once-lovely, manicured gardens are smothered of life, their former beauty deeply wrinkled with age.

"Hold him!" Claude shouts, banging open the caskets in the mausoleum. "Hold him so he can see." Five hundred years of frustration and anger drive him. He hurls one of the caskets to the floor, smashing it open, and a skeleton tumbles out. Claude stomps on it, smashing it to pieces, grinding the bones into powder beneath his feet, forcing Jacques to watch the desecration of his ancestors' remains. "It all ends tonight, Jacques de Molay," he screams. He grabs another coffin, yanks it off the stone rack, and sends it crashing it to the floor, smashing another skeleton to dust. Spitting words of venom, he repeats the process several times. "I will destroy you tonight. Any remembrance of you will be lost with the first wind, blown away with the dust of your ancestors. Tonight I will kill you, and the de Molay name will die forever. None will remember." Soon the room is covered with shattered caskets. Eight hundred years of de Molay ancestry have been erased.

Claude shakes his fist at the demons, signaling them to drag Jacques into the Room of Penitence. The life-size ivory statue of the Crucifixion still stands behind the ivory altar. Its gold plating has long since been peeled off by thieves.

The demons lift Jacques and place him on the altar, after which Claude slams long metal spikes through Jacques's palms and feet, nailing him down. The pain sears through Jacques's body; to even attempt to struggle is hopeless.

"I kept all this." Claude marches around, throwing his arms into the air like a catapult. "All that we used to believe in—soldiers of God. I didn't let anyone take any of this, just in case you returned. For some reason I always knew you would. I heard stories about this freak-show strong man, this vampire in Russia who possessed unbelievable strength. Word travels quickly in the underworld. I knew it must be you. Now I'm going to use all of this to destroy you!" He waves his hand around the room and then reaches beneath the podium and pulls out a long carving knife. "I'm going to skin you so you can die the old way—like a squealing boar on a butcher block," he bellers. "I can't wait to see your pain! He shakes his head, blowing spit out of his mouth. Through practice I've learned how to skin a vampire so the flesh won't grow back. I'll flay you like a pig!"

Claude skillfully makes two deep, palm-wide cuts across the full length of Jacques's shoulders. He then slices both sides of Jacques's neck and upper arms. Jacques cries out in agony. The demons relish the moment, slapping one another, doing squat leaps, grunting and groaning as snot and slobber splatter their monstrous faces.

After grabbing the edge of the skin on Jacques's neck, Claude peels it away, first one shoulder and then the other. Jacques screams, his body shaking in anguish from the torture. His vampire body fights back, but blood from the exposed tissue and muscle runs down his chest and back.

"Claude!" Margaret cries, rushing into the room. "Claude, what are you doing?"

Claude spins and savagely backhands her, knocking her down. He grabs her and violently yanks her up, and then smacks her again, sending her reeling across the room.

Recovering her senses, Margaret drags herself to her hands and knees.

"Stay!" Claude screams. "Stay where you are or die!"

Slowly raising her head, she cowers like a beaten dog. "Why are you doing this?" she whimpers. "Why do you always strike me?"

"Because of him!" Claude shakes his hand at Jacques. "He wouldn't be here if you didn't save him. There's no other way he could have lived."

"I didn't save him," she cries. She points at one of the demons, the one she's never forgotten. The memory of him has been trapped in her mind all these years, and now it's time for retribution. She knows she'll have to show weakness—be cowardly, be self-serving—in order to save Jacques and exact her she-wolf's revenge. "He hit me so hard that night that he knocked me down. All I remember is the sun coming up. I was starting to burn. I crawled under a wagon and hid there. I didn't want to burn," she whines. "I've always been with you, my love. Always faithful." She points to the other two demons. "They know. They know what I say is true. They were there. They saw him hit me and knock me down." The two of them cautiously nod in agreement.

Claude's rage quickly turns to the first demon, who turns and runs out the door. He knows Claude will butcher him alive.

Claude turns to the other two demons. Why does he always have to do everything himself for it to be done properly? He knows he can't send them after their friend because they'll let him escape. "Stay here and watch them," he says, against his better judgment. He points to Margaret and Jacques. "I'll be back with their friend—show you what I do to those who betray me." Claude turns abruptly and leaves.

The two demons seem more interested in discussing the fate of their friend than guarding Margaret and Jacques. They're also worried that Claude, when he returns, might kill them too for not telling him their friend hit Margaret. Maybe they should leave before Claude gets back—run for their lives.

Margaret knows she must do something if she and Jacques are going to escape—but what? As she glances around the room, her eyes fall on the statue of the Knight Templar. Dust, flies, and cobwebs snake in and around the iron, chain mail, hand coverings, leggings, shoes, and enclosed helmet. The knight's armor is rotting. The great helm sword, still in its brass scabbard, hangs at its side. The sword is so heavy that Margaret knows only someone with vampire strength can wield it. After scrambling to her feet, she reaches the statue and pulls the sword from its scabbard, challenging the two demons. Aware of her powerful strength, and no longer entirely loyal to Claude, they shake their heads and scramble out the door.

Margaret replaces the sword in its scabbard and twists and pulls the spikes out of Jacques's hands and feet. "Be strong, my love. Be strong. We have so little time." She pushes the concealed release on the statue, which causes it to slide across the floor, revealing the priest hole. The last time it was opened was when she was with Jacques five hundred years ago. She has never told Claude of its existence.

Dragging and half-carrying Jacques, Margaret pulls him down the spider web–infested stone stairway to the hidden chamber of ice-blue granite walls and floors. At the bottom, she pulls on the heavy iron chain that hangs from the ceiling and watches as the statue slides back into place, closing them inside. She locks the chain in place so the priest hole can't be opened from above. It's unbelievable that they've managed to get this far. Claude will tear the room upstairs apart in his attempt to find them—and he'll never rest until he does.

Holding Jacques's arm around her shoulder, Margaret stumbles over to the blue-granite wall and pushes on the slab. It doesn't open. Frustrated, she pushes again, but it still won't budge. "Please, Jacques," she whispers. "Please help me."

Slowly, painfully, he lifts his arm and pushes the upper corner of the stone. It quietly swings open to reveal the hidden passageway to the castle. Once they're inside, Margaret holds his head to her neck and lets him drink her blood for a few moments. He'll need his strength. Later she'll allow him more nourishment. Even if Claude catches them, the risks will have been worth it.

It's a struggle through the long, narrow passageway before they finally reach the end. Margaret hears the sounds of demons entering a tunnel from inside the castle. They'll be on her and Jacques in a matter of minutes. Her acute hearing tells her Claude isn't with them, and she wonders why.

Jacques pushes open a cornerstone that pivots on two elephant tusks, one on each end, and steps into the labyrinth of tunnels that runs beneath the castle. His strength is increasing, and he's walking on his own now, but the pain in his slowly regenerating shoulders is excruciating.

Margaret spits into her palm several times and wipes his open wounds, which quickly heal. "Where are we going?" she asks.

"I want to check the hidden door and see if Claude ever gained access." He flexes his neck and shoulder muscles and gives Margaret a nod of approval.

She pulls him back, stopping him in his tracks. "Claude didn't enter the tunnel. He didn't follow us. I would have heard him; I know his sound. He must be waiting for us at the hidden door. He thinks it's the first place you'll go. Let's leave while we still have a chance." She puts her arms around him, holding him. "I've waited for you forever, Jacques. I don't want to lose you now."

He turns his head and looks into her deep-brown eyes. "Has Claude ever taken you down there?"

Margaret shakes her head. "Never. Only he and his followers go there. He hasn't been able to find the treasure. The place where he thought it was hidden was empty. He was so angry, I thought he would kill all of us." She takes Jacques's head in her hands and presses her forehead against his. "Please, my love, let the past go. Let's go to the New World, leave this place. André and Pierre-Louis are at the harbor. They have a ship. Let's sail to the New World—the part Napoleon sold. They speak French there. Claude will never be able to find us. We'll start a new life. Please—don't look back. He'll kill us both."

Jacques nods, and the two of them hurry down a passageway. "The New World," he murmurs, glancing about. Thoughts of his life and ancestry run through his mind. "I've heard about it."

Margaret brushes a hand across his shoulder, stopping him momentarily. "I'll go to the Cemetery of the Mount. My vampire clan is there. They're still loyal to me. They want to go with us." She wraps her arms around him and moans gently like a she-wolf, pushing her body so close that she can feel his body heat. *Oooooh, if it could always be like this.* "Go to the harbor and wait for me," she breaths into his ear. "If I hurry I can meet you there before sunup."

Margaret and Jacques transform into bats and fly through the underground passageways. Margaret breaks off in one direction; Jacques heads in another. As soon as she's out of contact, he turns and flies through the secret tunnels, the underworld, until he reaches the passageway that leads to the hidden door. Huge mounds of stone have been torn from the walls, dirt dug up from the ground; hundreds of years of toil and frustration are piled against the chamber walls, hiding the Egyptian symbols, the artwork, the murals. Other subsurface tunnels are completely filled with rubble.

Jacques, still in bat form, obscured by a large outcropping of stones, sees that the hidden door has been penetrated, which he finds very interesting. Claude believes the Templar treasure is still hidden in one of the subterranean chambers. He's been searching for it for five hundred years. Jacques carefully surveys the area but doesn't see Claude. Suddenly he worries about Margaret. Has Claude fooled both of them? Is he waiting for Margaret at the Cemetery of the Mount? Just as he's ready to leave, several demons rush into the chamber.

Upon seeing his followers, Claude leaps out of his hiding place behind a pile of debris near the hidden door, his anger seething. With the realization that Jacques and Margaret didn't fall into his trap and may have gotten away, his body shakes like an earthquake. "Find them!" he shouts. "Find them or die!"

Unnoticed, Jacques leaves and flies to the harbor, where drunken French sailors stagger down narrow, dark streets of seawater-stained, wooden buildings. Whale-oil lamps cast an eerie glow outside. Seagulls perch on wooden dock railings, while sailing ships lie anchored in the bay.

African slaves are being marched from one of Napoleon's slave ships. The stench of the diseased and deprived hangs in the air. Tribal and clan tattoos—marks of witchcraft, superstitious beliefs, or symbols of fertility—cover their bodies. Many have been marked by the slavers to identify them should they escape. Others have marked themselves or were marked by their parents or prophets to ward off evil spirits. The slaves are starved, sick, and dying, yet they sing.

The head slaver, wearing leather boots and tattered, baggy, brown, knee pants, shouts orders to his men and whips anything that moves. He unhooks the fallen and rolls their lifeless bodies off the dock.

Jacques quickly finds André and Pierre-Louis. André, standing directly in the line of the approach of the head slaver, is taking a leak. The slaver uncoils his whip. "Move, dog! Make way or you'll die here."

André turns to face the slaver, pissing on the man's boots in the process. "Would you shake it for me, *mon ami*? It's been a rough night."

The man, his face contorted, shakes his head in disgust and raises his whip to strike. Jacques lands on the dock and materializes into a vampire. He reaches forward and rips out the slaver's throat. Several other slavers, their courage reinforced by the rum they've been drinking, attack André and Jacques, who are now joined by Pierre-Louis. The slaves, lost in the confusion, struggle back up the gangplank.

Pierre-Louis disembowels one slaver while sucking the blood from the neck of another. He immediately spits it out. "Rum! Ugh. I hate rum! Such a woody taste." He tosses the body aside.

Huddled together, the slaves eye Jacques as he walks up the gangplank toward them. Some try to hide their fear, while others begin to hum their death songs. They know who he is. From witch doctor to witch doctor, campfire to campfire, they've heard all the stories, listened to the tales of the walking dead, their blood-curdling screams haunting the night.

Jacques grabs the chain that holds them together and easily snaps it. The slaves are uncertain at first. Is he going to kill them? Then, realizing they're free, they break into cheers.

Jacques turns to leave for the Cemetery of the Mount. Margaret and the other vampires should have arrived by now. He looks down to see Pierre-Louis and André at the end of the dock, killing the last remaining slavers. Finished, André strides toward a wooden crate. Painted on the side is the de Molay coat of arms: a gold shield with a blue background, gold stars, and gold leaves, with a knight's helmet in the center. Two swords form an X behind the shield. André opens the crate, and Bisu the dwarf emerges.

"Jacques…Jacques de Molay…"

Jacques stops and listens. It's a woman's voice. He follows it to a cabin off the main deck of the ship. The heavy oak door is locked, but he easily tears it from its heavy iron hinges. "Who knows my name?" he shouts. He tosses the door aside and steps into the room.

Shackled to a large, carved, wooden chair of royalty, and adorned in lavender silk roses, is Isis. She is a black-skinned woman of unearthly beauty, with eyes of the deepest blue equaled only by the oceans of the world. She wears a sky-blue dress and an Egyptian headdress shaped like a throne.

Jacques breaks her shackles and respectfully kneels before her. "Goddess Isis, Stone Seat, power of the universe, ignorant of nothing in heaven and earth, sworn enemy of Mithras. How did Napoleon's men capture an Egyptian goddess?"

Isis rests her hand on his head. "Dark am I yet lovely, Jacques de Molay. Dark like the tents of Kedar, like the tent curtains of Solomon. Jacques de Molay, the vampire who wants to be human again. You sold your soul to Mithras, to cheat death. He released your soul, so now you defy him. All of the dark world talks of you, Jacques de Molay. With me in captivity and the guardians of Mithras, controlling the Templar treasure, the vampiric race would blend into all walks of life: kings, queens, bankers, generals. Nothing would be beyond their reach." She points at her necklace of interwoven gold rope inlaid with strips of turquoise, lapis lazuli, and other gemstones. Attached to the necklace by cobra fangs are red carnelian stones, which are meant to satisfy Isis's need for blood. "The necklace of fangs holds my powers captive. Only a vampire can remove it." She leans forward, and Jacques snaps it from her neck. Breathing a deep sigh of relief, Isis rises and glides through the door to a cell below the deck. Jacques follows her. "Release my handmaidens," she commands.

Jacques yanks on the cell door, breaking its lock and freeing the women. They're all wearing black, cobra-skin capes with full hoods. Pale yellow bands run down the length, and the scales are smooth. The front or belly is a matching pale yellow. Green eyes, divided in half vertically—with sapphire on one side and emerald on the other—peer out from beneath the hoods.

The slaves bow as Isis and Jacques make their way to the front of the ship. By an invisible summons, Bisu follows.

"Isis, you come from the mountain at midday in summer, the dusty maiden," Jacques says. "Your eyes are full of tears, and your heart is full of sighs. You who creates all things out of yourself—you have heard my cries. I swear to you that I will not go back to my old ways. I swear to be a new man. I can do it. I can change. Can you help me? Is it possible?" he asks. "Can I be human again?"

Isis points at Bisu and then raises her hands toward the starlit sky. Jacques quickly drops to his knees, displaying his respect for her. Her journey began thousands of years before the construction of the Great Sphinx of Giza, when the gods ruled Egypt.

Bisu leans forward on his hands, rocking back and forth, humming. On his right shoulder is a black-inked tattoo, a dark and damp jungle where everything struggles for light. It begins to pulsate. A white Bengal tiger with black stripes, its blue eyes peering out from behind green leaves, hungrily watches a tasty black-and-tan monkey eating a root. Bisu's shoulder rips open, and blood splatters his skin and the ship's worn deck. The tiger tears away from its jungle nesting place and transforms into a five-hundred-pound beast that leaps to the deck and walks over to sit calmly next to Isis.

"We'll sail this ship to the New World," the goddess says, casually petting the tiger's majestic white head, "away from Napoleon's armies. To become human, Jacques de Molay, you too must sail to the New World. There you will find your true love, drink her pure blood." Isis sways back and forth, humming the "Harper's Song," a poem inscribed in Egyptian tombs alongside the image of a blind man playing a harp. "I allowed the guardians of the god, Mithras, to capture me. It's been written that our paths—yours and mine—must cross. And so they have. I am the healer." She turns to the slaves who have boarded the ship and holds out her hands. "Kneel, my children," she calls out to them, and they obey. Torn and crippled bodies, with open wounds from whippings, heal under the spell of her gaze.

"Margaret is my true love. I drank her blood, and I'm still a vampire." Jacques feels the ship sway beneath his feet. The sails are flapping in the wind.

"Obsession is not love. You must learn to know true love before you can experience it. Your journey is just beginning." Isis lifts the pendant from around Jacques's neck and squeezes it in her palm. "You'll recognize her when the other half comes back to you. Remember, Jacques de Molay, what we wish for isn't always what the gods grant us. We will depart soon." She motions to her handmaidens, who transform into snakes and crawl up her arms, wrapping around her body. She leans over and kisses the tiger's face. Two mighty feathered wings sprout from Isis's back and lift her into the air.

Bisu, who's still kneeling and rocking back and forth, allows the tiger to return to its nesting place in the tattoo jungle. The torn skin on the dwarf god's shoulder pulls back into place and immediately heals.

Jacques watches until Isis disappears into the night sky. Then he runs down the gangplank to where Pierre-Louis and André are standing. "I have to get Margaret," he tells them. "She should have been here by now."

"Go! Go!" Pierre-Louis shouts. "We's got everything—food, everything."

"Go get Margaret," André shouts. "Go! Go!"

Jacques morphs into a bat and flies toward the Cemetery of the Mount, while Pierre-Louis, André, and the other vampires load the ship. The poop deck is where poultry, sheep, and cows are kept. The wooden crates are layered with shelves jammed full with live rats that the vampires will feed on during their three-month journey across the Atlantic.

In the distance Jacques sees the Cemetery of the Mount. Normally the cemetery is a forgotten place, lost in the French countryside. A great old tomb stands amid the ruins, its fine marble and granite decaying. The gravestones, wall vaults, and family tombs lie like sunken boats in the tangled sea of weeds, of the once carefully groomed landscape. The wooden crosses lie like rotting masts.

Jacques circles high overhead; tonight, however, the cemetery is a burning inferno. Priests in their long, dark robes stand under burning torches, reading from scrolls and praying. Fires are staggered throughout the cemetery, and between them move the men. They are carrying the wooden caskets from the crypts and setting them on the ground, checking the lids, making sure they are nailed shut, stacking them. Men pour brownish whale oil from large barrels over the caskets while other men light them with torches. Most of the vampires break from their fiery beds only to find themselves on fire. Their screams are like knives to Jacques's ears, and he sees their cold skin crack and split as it burns. The men, carrying oil-filled, wooden buckets, their filthy bodies drenched in sweat, blood, and the stink of it all, douse the wretched vampires, feeding the flames. They watch, crosses held high as vampires frantically run wild, throwing themselves on the ground, rolling in the dirt, trying to extinguish the fire, leaving a trail of burned-off skin behind them.

As a bat, Jacques slides under a fallen headstone, unobserved, and sees Claude directing the vampire killers. Claude has long been allied with the Gypsy trackers and gave them precise drawings of where the vampires were sleeping so they could go in during the daytime and nail their wooden coffins shut. They have enough men so they can deal with the vampires that are sleeping in the stone vaults.

Since the beginning of the Crusades, the Gypsy clans have been sworn enemies of Mithras, and his followers. Over the centuries Claude has used the Gypsies to kill the vampires in Margaret's clan.

The trackers are emboldened by the violence, the terrified cries of the vampires, and the stench of burning flesh. They pry open the lids on caskets, holding crosses as shields so that escaping vampires hesitate. It's all the time the Gypsies need to drive a stake into their chests, soak them with oil, and light them afire. The screams, like those of the damned locked in the pits of hell, blow across the forsaken land.

After transforming back into a vampire, Jacques quietly moves from crypt to crypt and casket to casket, releasing several of the remaining vampires. He crawls over to the great old tomb and pushes aside a large stone. It opens to an underground passageway, where he slips inside.

A young Gypsy king frantically waves a torch in the air and screams orders to his people. "Hurry! Hurry! We need to kill them all! None can live!" His clothes, long brown hair, and beard are smeared with blood.

The noise echoes across the countryside as the trackers batter the door to the old tomb with their heavy sledgehammers.

Claude rages, "Not this one! You promised you would leave this crypt alone. You said you would leave Margaret for me. We made a bargain!"

Inside the tomb Jacques quickly finds where Margaret and several other vampires are hiding. He takes her hand. "Come," he tells her. "It's time to leave. You've been found out. They're killing all of our kind."

The door to the old tomb is smashed, and several Gypsies push their way inside. The Gypsy king turns and shakes his cross at Claude, screaming, "I don't make bargains with the Devil!" He lunges at Claude with the pointed end of the cross, but Claude quickly transforms into a bat and flies away.

Jacques and Margaret and the other vampires run through the underground passageway with the trackers in pursuit.

Jacques stops and turns, grabbing Margaret. "Fly, my love. Fly to the harbor. André and Pierre-Louis are waiting there. I'll catch up."

Margaret pleads to stay with Jacques, but he orders her to escape.

"No, my beauty," he tells her. "Go. Take the others. I'll meet you at the ship. I need to slow them down."

"No," she says. "We won't make it. There are too many of them. I'm going to go back and wait for Claude. I'll stall him so you can escape."

"Noooo!" Jacques screams as she turns and runs back down through the tunnel.

"Go with Jacques!" she shouts at her vampire clan. "Follow him! Sail to the New World with him! Don't let him follow me! Don't let him follow me!"

Jacques immediately changes into a bat and attempts to fly after her, but her followers block the tunnel so he can't get by. Changing into a vampire, he attempts to fight and push his way through. He screams at them to move, but it's useless. There's just too many of them. They begin to shove him in the other direction, away from Margaret.

The sounds of the trackers echo through the tunnel. Several of them have circled around to get in front of the escaping vampires, attempting to cut them off before they can escape. Jacques attacks the first group of men, knocking their torches away, tearing out their throats, slowing their progress. Margaret's vampire followers join him in the fight, killing the rest of the trackers.

Jacques realizes that he will never get Margaret back now. It's too late. He may never see her again, but he also knows he'll never have a chance of seeing her again if he doesn't live. She sacrificed herself for him. Now, he needs to save himself, to make sure her commitment isn't wasted. He and her followers morph into bats and fly back to the harbor. The white moon is partially hidden by brushstrokes of dark, bluish clouds. Birds fly across the sky, their black bodies trimmed in moonlit shadows.

The three masts on the French frigate are fully rigged, and the anchor has been lifted. Beautiful, ornate, leaded stained-glass windows with scenes of the Seine River hang over the stern of the ship.

André and Pierre-Louis run up to him as he and the other bats land on the ship and change into a vampires. "Where's Margaret," they ask, while quickly glancing at the other vampires and not seeing her.

"She went back to Claude so we all could escape," he answers, dispirited. "It all happened so fast. One moment she was by my side—the next, she was gone."

The harbor breaks into bedlam as French soldiers fire their cannons at the vampire ship. The main battery of twelve-pound guns on the ship's upper deck is manned by the members of the vampire clan that Jacques has converted. The vampires instinctively know what to do and immediately take their positions. The knowledge from centuries of doing battle—planet to planet, galaxy to galaxy—was planted in the blood that Jacques pumped into their veins.

Standing tall on the ship's deck so everybody can see, he's directing Pierre-Louis and André, who are running from gun battery to gun battery, giving commands for the gunners to return fire and clear the recoil area after shooting. The smoothbore, muzzle-loading Napoleon M1857 cannon will blast a twelve-pound ball several thousand yards; it's a devastatingly effective weapon. The vampires, even without training, are deadly gunners. Their hearing and sight are so sensitive that they can hear and see a target from up to ten miles away. They send out ultrasonic sounds that bounce off the intended target, producing echoes so they can detect, localize, and identify its distance. Watching the cannonball's trajectory while listening to the velocity of the steel ball flying through the night air, they calculate the weight of the ball, its speed and distance, and the conditions of the atmosphere to determine whether the shot will be successful. If the heavy projectile doesn't sound like it's going to hit the target, they recalculate their data and, if necessary, elevate or lower the cannon's barrel a couple of clicks, add the correct amount of charge, and shoot again.

The vampires continue to return fire, hitting a powder room on one of the French ships, and the harbor erupts in flames. The wind fills the vampire ship's sails, pushing the vessel out to sea; it sways with the rhythmic rising and falling of the waves. The vampires will sail at night; Isis and the slaves she has freed will take watch during the day while the vampires rest in their coffins on the lower deck.

Jacques stands next to the captain's quarters, where he watches the harbor burn. The frigate is built for speed. The wind fills its sails as its distance from the shores of France grows greater. Jacques places his hands on the deck railing and shakes his head. "Pierre-Louis and André…" he murmurs. "Their preparations have been superb." He guesses they did a bit more than just chase the sauce for five hundred years. Taking the helmsman's position and looking out across the darkness, he thinks of Margaret. Grasping the ship's mahogany wheel, he digs his fingers into the wood. *Why, why, why, didn't she stay with him?* he ponders with a twinge of human emotion. Wolves mate for life. He thought they would be together forever. Life or death—regardless—he would've died for her. Shaking his head like a great alpha wolf, taking a deep breath, blinking his eyes. *What is my destiny?* he asks the nighttime horizon of the star-studded night sky.

André and Pierre-Louis join Jacques and watch as the anchored ships near the shoreline fade away and the distant, flickering flames evaporate. They wonder out loud whether they'll ever see their beloved France again. So many years have passed. They, along with their families and friends, have taken so many different paths. It's not a sentimental journey but more of a precept of remembrance. It's the pack mentality—complex dynamics that form more of a clique than a group of wild killers. It's an order. They do miss and always will remember their families and friends and their old homes; the hunting territories of France, Transylvania, and Russia are embedded in their minds. This night they fast for their members who have died. None are ever forgotten.

Even though they've often gotten into vicious fights with one another over food that they've stalked—such as humans, deer, or rabbits—it's still a sophisticated group hierarchy. Jacques is the alpha male. They're a family of hunters, related and unrelated, joined by their vampiric blood.

It's then that André smells a scent—so faint yet so telltale. He knows it's not the slaves who are with Isis, but it's the smell of a live human. Yet he knows there are no other living people on this ship. *What could it be?* He wonders. *Strange. So strange.*

Unexpectedly, Jacques slowly turns the wheel of the ship.

"Why's we starting to head north?" Pierre-Louis asks. "I thought we's going to this, this New World."

André nods his head in agreement.

"We are going to the New World," Jacques responds. "Just taking a little detour."

"My good sniffer," André says while grabbing his nose. "It's smelled rabbits, deer, birds, and it thinks it smells a human. Anybody else smelling a human?"

"Why don't the two of you fly up to the crow's nest?" Jacques asks, switching the subject.

"Can we pretend we're crows?" André asks excitedly, flapping his folded arms against his sides. "*Quack, quack*! It be so much fun. It be our secret. Nobody know! They think it just us crows."

"Of course," Jacques responds while glancing at Pierre-Louis. "Keep your heads up."

Pierre-Louis rolls his eyes while thinking, *tis five hundred the years, André still no understand. Vampires never the court jester, never poke the funny, never the giggles, never the fool.*

—⟋⟍—

Claude, with Margaret standing next to him, having learned of Jacque's escape, already has commandeered a ship to pursue him to the New World. In his enraged haste to catch the vampire ship, he rushes his demons in their preparations for the journey. The demons have never been on an ocean voyage and therefore don't know how to calculate the necessary supplies. On their voyage, the resulting food shortage leads to fights, starvation, and cannibalism, relieved only by the burning sun during the long days.

As days become weeks, the sails of Claude's ship turn into shreds on the masts. Discarded, rotting body parts litter the bloodstained deck. However, he makes sure that he and Margaret have plenty to eat. When they are in sight of the New World, gulls rush the sailing coffin of dead and rotting corpses to feed on the carnage. The thick mat of white-bodied birds crowding the deck gives the ship the appearance of a flying carpet. Moving at night, the few remaining demons lie in wait for one of the seagulls to land next to them. It's all that remains to supply their starving bodies with nourishment.

Claude and Margaret, determining that the shoreline is close enough, transform into bats and fly away from the ship, leaving the handful of surviving demons to their own devices. Many, unable to fly or to navigate without their leader, perish at sea.

—⋙—

The following year, in 1813, from October 16 to 19, France goes to war against the coalition armies of Russia, Prussia, Sweden, and Austria. The battle involves more than six hundred thousand soldiers. Defeated, Napoleon eventually is forced to abdicate the throne of France in April 1814 and is exiled to the Mediterranean island of Elba. In March 1815, he escapes from Elba, returns to France, and reassumes power. Three months later he's defeated at the Battle of Waterloo and subsequently exiled to the remote island of Saint Helena, twelve hundred miles west of the coast of southwestern Africa, where he eventually dies in 1821.

Between Napoleon's two campaigns—his invasion of Russia and the Battle of Nations—Jacques's vampire clan slaughtered more than three hundred thousand French soldiers, resulting in the defeat of the Grand Armée and the end of Napoleon's rule as emperor of France. Fear breeds disobedience. The number of men Napoleon's armies lost due to the lack of morale and desertions from their dread of the terror-filled nights can't be calculated.

—⋙—

Violca, naked, sits on the bed in her living wagon and holds her crystal ball between her legs. She sees it all. An alluring smile crosses her face. Memories of her fingers massaging the muscled contours of Jacques's sculptured physique heat her body, and beads of sweat form on her forehead. She reaches up and tenderly touches the half of the Templar pendant that hangs from her neck and dangles between her breasts. She remembers back to when she watched Jacques disappear into the night, and she knows she is deeply in love with him. A heaviness weighs on her chest. They went through so much together...and now the parting. Tears fill her violet eyes and trail down her cheeks. She tenderly presses the pendant against her lips, kissing it, remembering the banya, their nakedness, their openness, and their wild, uninhibited, honest, and complete acceptance of each other. "When we meet again, Jacques de Molay," Violca whispers, "when we meet again. Remember to play the violin for her."

References

1. The Knights Templar, Knightly Combat (www.theknightstemplar.org/statutes-of-the-order/) xi
2. Jacques de Molay's dying words, 1314.[src]. (Assassinscreed.wikia.com/wiki/Jacques_de_Molay), xi
3. The Knights Templar, Brotherhood (www.theknightstemplar.org/statutes-of-the-order/) 3
4. The Right Stuff, 1983 (www.great-quotes.com) 118